Cursed

Gowns & Crowns, Book 5

Jennifer Chance

Copyright © 2017 by Jennifer Chance

All rights reserved.

ISBN-13: 978-1-943768-23-3

Cover design by Liz Bemis, Bemis Promotions

This book is a work of fiction. References to real people, events, establishments, organizations, or locations are intended only to provide a sense of authenticity, and are used fictitiously. All other characters, and all incidents and dialogue, are drawn from the author's imagination, and are not to be construed as real.

All rights reserved.

No part of this book may be reproduced, scanned, or distributed in any printed or electronic form without permission. Please do not participate in encouraging piracy of copyrighted materials in violation of the author's rights. Purchase/Download only authorized editions.

Also by Jennifer Chance in the Gowns & Crowns series

~ The First Family ~

Courted

Captured

Claimed

Crowned

~ Carolina Royals ~

Cursed

Charmed

Chosen

~ Royally Wed ~

Wedded

For Ann

The best sister a girl could have.

Chapter One

Someday… my prince will come…

But he could stow it for the moment.

Countess Edeena Saleri strode along the bright, cheerful corridors of the Charleston International Airport, slightly behind her sisters Caroline and Marguerite, half-disbelieving they'd finally made it. The six-thousand-mile flight from Garronia had taken nearly two months to arrange, every day fraught with anxiety that her father would realize that Edeena and her sisters weren't merely heading off for a vacation, but attempting to create a beachhead from which at least two of them could start a whole new life.

A life that had nothing to do with the kingdom of Garronia—or any of its princely curses.

Now Edeena focused on her sisters as they chattered excitedly. They'd all agreed to only speak English from the moment they got on the plane for the final leg of their journey, headed for the United States. It wasn't much of a hardship; the trio could speak Garronois, Greek, and English proficiently, and Caroline spoke a little French as well, mainly because there were so many French visitors to their little seaside kingdom.

Marguerite had started and stopped a dozen different languages in college, as the mood struck her. Like most things for Marguerite, she could never settle specifically on one language that made her happy, so she simply chose not to choose.

But neither of her sisters would have to make any choices for a while, Edeena resolved. This journey would take them to their mother's vacation home of Heron's Point, one of the largest houses on Sea Haven Island, South Carolina, perfect for a getaway. In fact, they were just coming to the secured exit of the airport now, where waiting for them should be...

Edeena's stride faltered, her heart jolting as her gaze connected with a pair of intense, laser-beam eyes from across the corridor. She recovered as smoothly as she could while her sisters exclaimed in delighted recognition of their family name, featured on the tablet held aloft by Laser-Beam's partner.

The two men stood slightly apart from the others car service representatives. Though they were dressed in subdued dark suits, they seemed far more restless, more competent than their peers—they should, of course. They were more than limo drivers.

The shorter man smiled broadly at Edeena as she caught his eye, his dark bald head gleaming in the harsh fluorescent lights. Then his gaze locked on her sisters as if he was memorizing their stride, their faces, the very distance between them as they walked. Edeena forced herself to study him as well, though it had been the taller man who'd nearly bowled her over.

Was he Greek? He had to be Greek. But in South

CURSED
Carolina?

Regardless of his nationality, he *looked* Greek—as in Greek god, to be more specific. Tall, dark and ridiculously good looking, with all the confidence and charisma to go with it, the man was easily over six feet tall, with cropped tawny brown hair and bronzed skin, his muscular physique filling out his suit with impressive solidity. Dismay skated through Edeena as she took in his no-nonsense expression. She'd long prided herself on being able to overwhelm her staff, friends and colleagues by the sheer force of her personality. Frankly, she'd expected to be able to do the same with anyone sent by the security firm she'd hired to protect herself and her sisters while they vacationed in America. This man didn't look easy to overwhelm, however. He looked like...

She stared at him a little longer.

Hot, she decided. He looked hot.

Focus, Edeena chided herself as they cleared the security gate. This man was her employee, even if he did manage to make his polite smile look more like a concerned scowl. More unsettling, his gaze remained focused on her—it hadn't shifted away since the moment he'd seen her. She'd never been studied so closely, at least not when she was aware of it, and she'd been living in the public eye for most of her life.

With her habitual concern for her sisters' safety, Edeena scanned the baggage claim area, then herded Caro and Marguerite forward, uncomfortably conscious of the man's narrowing eyes. This wasn't any low-level bodyguard, she suddenly knew. This was the firm's owner.

Edeena tightened her lips. She hadn't been a hundred percent honest with Mr. Vincent Rallis of Rallis Security in their numerous phone conversations, and it seemed like he realized that, somehow. But how could he tell such a thing at a glance? Or had he known from the start?

The man nodded as they reached him, holding out his hand. "Miss Saleri," he said. It wasn't a question, and Edeena grasped his hand firmly, her chin coming up as her pulse jumped. Rallis's hand was rough, calloused and warm, and her mind instantly leapt to what he did to keep his skin so hardened, his grip so strong.

"You must be Mr. Rallis," she said, her tone perhaps a bit harsher than she wanted. She removed her hand a little too quickly from his. "I didn't expect to meet you here."

"I thought it wise. This is Rob Marks," he said, turning and introducing his partner, who also held out his hand first to Edeena, then to Caroline and Marguerite. Edeena started as she realized that Vincent Rallis's voice had a distinctive slow drawl to it, despite his formal manner. Rich and full, it sounded like warm caramel drizzled over a cold scoop of—

Stop it.

"Once we collect our bags, Rob will escort you both in his limo, then we'll follow behind," Rallis continued, addressing her sisters. Edeena's gaze jumped to his face as he slid his glance back to her. "That will allow us to go over the particulars of the work without taking up any more of your time, Miss Saleri."

No doubt about it, he *had* somehow ascertained that

she hadn't given him the whole story. That was only fair, she supposed. Probably a good thing, in fact. She didn't want a security firm staffed by fools.

Still, what had tipped him off? She hadn't said a word beyond his name, hadn't done anything, in fact, but approach him.

She puzzled over the issue as they collected their bags. In short order, they'd left the baggage area and were whisked into their respective cars, Edeena hesitating as Rallis held the back door open for her. She didn't want him stealing searching glances at her via the rearview mirror the entire way to Sea Haven.

"It would be best if we kept up appearances of me as your driver, Miss Saleri," Rallis said quietly. "Especially if the people who you believe are following you are, in fact, here."

She blinked in surprise. "Excuse me?"

"Yo, Prince!"

Edeena's heart almost stopped as Marks came trotting around the SUV, his face instantly abashed as he realized she was still standing beside the vehicle and not inside. "Oh, pardon me, Mr. Rallis."

His grin was infectious but Edeena couldn't get past the address.

"Prince?" she nearly choked out, looking between them, trying desperately not to sound unhinged. "You're a prince?" The curse of the Saleris clanged loudly in her head, but surely this man — surely it wasn't possible —

"And a gentleman and a scholar," Marks assured her, then addressed Rallis, speaking quickly as he glanced to his own car and back again. "Marguerite is already asking about arrangements with the security team, how long they'll be assigned, scope of the operation. Seems there's a resort she's eager to visit. How much information should I provide?"

Rallis turned to her and Edeena sighed. Marguerite far more than Caroline had chafed under the need for security, especially since she'd managed to pull several strings in advance of their departure from Garronia to ensure she wouldn't be "wasting her time" while on vacation. Through an intercession by Count Matretti, Garronia's ambassador to the US, she'd finagled some internship for the remainder of the summer at a vacation resort near their residence on the island—the perfect capstone to her hospitality management degree, she'd insisted. And she wanted to visit that resort *immediately*.

"Tell her that security will accompany her everywhere," Edeena said tersely, and Marks's brows lifted at her tone. "*Everywhere*. She won't like it, but at least for the first several days, I don't want to take chances."

"I've assigned Rob here and his wife, Cindy, as their detail," Rallis told her. "They're the best I have. Your sisters will be safe."

"You got my word on it." Marks grinned. He nodded again to Rallis, then turned on his heel.

"We should get going," Rallis said before she could ask him about the husband-wife security duo. Instead he ushered her into the SUV with an almost stern formality. Sighing with frustration, Edeena slipped into the back seat, then watched him stride around the front of the vehicle. His gaze never stopped moving, and he

CURSED

waved Marks's town car forward as he slid into the front seat.

Then he stared at her in the rear-view mirror with exactly the kind of searching intensity she'd been hoping to avoid.

Edeena cut off whatever he was going to say. First things first, and her heart was already in her throat. There simply was no way this drop dead gorgeous Greek-American could be a prince...especially when a prince—a real prince—could potentially solve all Edeena's problems. Her life simply didn't work that way.

But she had to know for sure.

"Before we discuss anything, Mr. Rallis," she said in her sternest voice. "You mind explaining why your associate called you Prince?"

Vincent "Prince" Rallis had seen his share of beautiful, tightly-wound women, but the gaggle of females that had bustled off the airplane in the Charleston International Airport had taken him by surprise, even though he'd been emailed their photo IDs in advance. On screen, they'd been pretty enough, but in person they'd turned out to be vibrant balls of energy, each more vivacious than the last.

Except for the most senior of the Saleri women, anyway, who now glared at him in the mirror, her rigid demeanor and frankly bizarre question at odds with her lush Mediterranean beauty. But she seriously needed to chill out—at least until he figured out why she was such a bag of nerves. He knew she hadn't told him everything up front—clients frequently didn't—but that didn't account for the tension that'd practically radiated off her from the moment he'd locked eyes on her. A tension that hadn't abated despite his and Marks's presence. And *nobody* stayed tense around Marks very long.

Edeena Saleri continued staring at him stonily, however, so he needed to clear up her strange confusion first. "It's a nickname," he said, keeping his voice as patient as he could manage. "My first name, as you know, is Vince. I'm the oldest son of a very proud Greek family who are first generation Greek immigrants, and our home looks ever so slightly like a temple. Since we live in South Carolina and not, say, *Greece*, the building didn't so much say 'temple' to our friends and neighbors as it did 'castle.' You see where I'm going with this? I'm not a prince, Miss Saleri. It's simply an old name that stuck, and Marks and I go back far enough that he uses it all the time. Fair enough?"

"Fair enough," Edeena said, her cheeks flaring with embarrassment. "It's just—I thought…" she sighed. "I don't know what I thought. The word caught me off guard. I apologize."

"I'll instruct the team not to use it," he said mildly. "No apologies necessary." Apologies, no. Information, yes.

"Thank you." Edeena slid her gaze away to look out the window, and as he idled at a light Vince was able to examine her more closely. No question about it, she was a stunner—a pile of dark curls framed her face, which

Cursed

was dominated by large, flashing eyes, a heart-breaker of a mouth, and smooth olive-toned skin. She was the same medium build as her sisters, but her coloring was decidedly darker than theirs, her features more delicate. Yet she nevertheless gave an impression of overall strength, carrying an air of somberness far weightier than her siblings' playful demeanors.

What had happened to her to make her so serious? He wondered. Her face looked like it had been fashioned for laughter, not frowns, but she wasn't laughing now — and hadn't for a while, he suspected.

Then again, Edeena Saleri's penchant for worry was why he was there. According to her cousin Prudence, a friend of his mother's and the woman who'd first contacted him about the Saleri job, the young countess 'could fret an ocean into a thimbleful of salt.' He'd done some research of his own, of course, but the Saleris seemed fairly run of the mill, for all that they were nobility. There was nothing about the sisters, their long-deceased mother, their newly-remarried father, or his somewhat younger and by all accounts heavily pregnant wife that bespoke more than the usual amount of family drama. Yet Edeena was acting like she carried the weight of the world on her shoulders and had a knot of enemies on her tail.

And he needed to know why.

"Miss Saleri," he began, but Edeena held up her hand, the faint blush remaining on her face.

"Please, call me Edeena," she said. She glanced to meet his gaze then stared resolutely away, as if preparing to give a speech that pained her. "And allow me to forestall your questions. I haven't been entirely forthcoming with you about the nature of our stay in Sea Haven. I owe you that full explanation."

Well, that was certainly easier than he'd expected it to be. Easier and ever so slightly disappointing. If Vince was honest with himself, he'd been secretly looking forward to interrogating the woman, getting her alone like this, forcing her to focus on him—

*Annnnd…*boom. With that one highly inappropriate, totally unprofessional thought, his entire body had gone hard, alert and ready for action.

Vince grimaced. *Great.* This was going to be one hell of a job.

Fortunately, Edeena was far too caught up in her own confession to notice how tightly he was gripping the steering wheel.

"The Saleri name is a very old one, stretching back to the founding of the country of Garronia and even earlier," she said, and Vince gratefully refocused his attention. "Unfortunately, we've suffered a fair amount of adversity over the years and made our share of poor choices, and our continued misfortune became so famous that it was formally calcified in the mid-tenth century as a curse."

"A curse." Vince was proud of himself for keeping his voice steady, because of all the things he'd expected, this wasn't one of them. "What kind of curse?"

Edeena sighed again as they approached the bridge that would lead them to Sea Haven Island. Her tense frown lightened somewhat at the sight of water, and despite himself, Vince felt a pang of pity for the woman. Whatever she was facing, she believed it was real. He

Cursed

needed to respect that until he knew the whole story.

"The kind of curse that presaged that doom, gloom, and dire happenings would continue to beset our family, unless a set of highly specialized demands were met. The oldest records of the curse maintain that a child from a special generation is destined to marry a prince — or princess, presumably. If the child succeeds in fulfilling that destiny, the curse will be broken."

"And you're a member of an, um, special generation?" he hazarded. She glanced at him with a rueful smile.

"A generation of only daughters qualifies, yes," she said. Her lips twisted, as if she fully understood how ridiculous this all sounded. "So too does a generation of only boys, or of twins, or of a single child. As you might imagine, the Saleris have had many opportunities to marry into royalty over the intervening centuries since the curse first came into play, but no one's been able to pull it off."

Vince frowned. "But your father has remarried, and they're expecting. What if the baby — "

"It's a girl," Edeena said flatly. "He recently had the appropriate tests run."

Vince didn't bother hiding the expression of distaste that curled his lip, and Edeena seemed to relax further in the face of his disdain.

"I know, I know," she said grimly. "But the fact remains my father is quite serious about the curse being broken in our generation, not for the least reason that he retains all of the familial outrage that we ourselves are not royal, that instead our distant cousins by marriage, the Andris family, rose to the throne when Garronia was first formed. The Saleris have nurtured their indignation over this slight for centuries, and Silas—my father—is its champion. He's determined that the curse will end in this generation."

Vince couldn't believe he was actually following the logic Edeena was laying out. "Which means you need to marry a prince."

"Exactly. I do or one of my sisters does, in any event. A matter complicated by the fact that the two eligible princes in the realm are otherwise spoken for."

Vince narrowed his gaze on her. "You were involved with one of them?" He couldn't imagine anyone turning down this woman for any reason, other than the fact that she apparently believed in ancient curses.

"In a manner of speaking, yes. Everyone expected I'd marry the Crown Prince of Garronia, and to keep my father occupied, I encouraged that rumor, though Ari and I never seriously dated."

"Ari." Vince kept his voice level, but there was no denying the quick stab of irritation at the smile now on Edeena's face as she thought about this other man.

"Aristotle Andris," she said. "But he's very much beside the point. He's engaged, his brother is engaged, and that means I'm fresh out of princes." She gave a small, scoffing laugh. "Present company excluded."

Vince found himself suddenly annoyed that he wasn't a real prince, despite the absurdity of Edeena's story. He pushed that thought away.

"And you came to Sea Haven...why?"

Edeena's gaze had returned to the view from her

Cursed

window, taking in the enormous, Spanish moss-laden trees stretching over the two-lane road they were taking out to Heron's Point.

"I will find a way to beat the curse, Mr. Rallis, but I need time. More importantly, I need to ensure that my sisters have the space to start a life of their own choosing regardless of what I do. I don't want the weight of the family baggage to fall on their shoulders. It's not fair."

"But it's fair to you?"

"I've been brought up with it, they haven't." She shrugged. "Caro and Marguerite should be able to choose their own paths freely. And that means I have to act first, before my father does." At Vince's confused glance she tightened her lips.

"Garronia has many charming characteristics. Our ancient code of law isn't one of them, particularly when it comes to the marital rights of noble children," she explained. "If I don't choose who to marry by the time I'm twenty-seven years old, my father can choose for me—or he can marry off one of my sisters in my place if I refuse. It's his paternal right."

Vince could only stare. "And you turn twenty-seven . . ."

"In three weeks." Edeena managed a wan smile. "As you can see, I don't have a lot of time to find a prince of my own choosing—and why I was so concerned when I thought you were, in fact, a prince. Fortunately, you're not."

Vince found himself compelled to argue that point, but at that moment a pair of large, modern pillars flanking an ornamental gate rose up ahead, set off to the left of the main road.

"Oh! Is that Heron's Point?" Edeena asked, clearly happy to talk about anything else.

"No—though Heron's Point is the next turn." He nodded as they passed the gates. "That's the entry for the Cypress Resort." A sudden, not particularly happy thought struck him. "That's not the resort your sister is interested in, is it?"

"Cypress...hmm." Edeena turned to peer in the rear window. "There were several resorts she investigated. I'm not sure which one came through. Either way, I didn't realize we were so close to a resort. The Google Earth images I saw of Heron's Point certainly didn't show that."

"Even Google takes time to update," Vince said, taking note of Edeena's flash of annoyance. The woman apparently didn't like to be caught off guard. Something they had in common. "Cypress opened nine months ago, and has been building out continually since then. Rental villas, restaurants, spa, golf, horseback riding, shopping—all the trendiest amenities for tourists. It's proven to be very profitable."

"I see. What sort of tourists, do you know?"

Vince didn't see any reason to sugar coat it. Edeena needed to understand her neighbors. "Singles, mostly, I guess you would call them. It's already becoming popular as a vacation destination."

"Singles?" She immediately caught his emphasis on the term. "What do you mean?"

"I mean it's targeted to men and women who are unattached, or couples without children. It's not designed to be a family-friendly resort so much as an

CURSED

adult getaway."

"An *adult* getaway." Edeena sank back in her seat. "Why do I suspect this is exactly the resort that Marguerite targeted?"

Despite himself, Vince chuckled, earning him an irritated scowl from the back seat. "It's not all that bad," he assured her. "And you'll be right next door if that's any consolation."

On cue, he turned into the graceful entryway of the estate, following Marks's limo down a long dreamy-looking track cut into the foliage, the narrow lane once again overhung with Spanish moss that fairly dripped from enormous trees. After a few minutes, they exited the trees and approached the main house through an open park.

Vince had seen Heron's Point many times, but it still impressed him—a three-story mansion that fanned out to either side with smaller two-story wings, as if it was embracing visitors. The place was a Southern showpiece, all yellow-painted brick and white trim, fronted by an imposing white staircase that swept up to the second floor. The ground floor was walled in stone, probably once used as stables.

"Good heavens," Edeena said quietly, her worries apparently assuaged for the moment. "I'd say this is some consolation, you're right. No wonder Mother loved this place."

Vince didn't see any reason to answer that, and he scanned the building as they neared. "That's your cousin, standing at the top of the stairs. Have you two met?"

"We haven't," Edeena said. She leaned forward, her

slender hand gripping his seat beside his shoulder. The scent of her perfume wafted over him, honeysuckle and lavender, and Vince grimaced as his body reacted once again. This was seriously going to become a problem.

"She's my second cousin, twice removed, by the way," Edeena corrected him as she took in the trim, elderly woman in the flowery pink dress, standing like a sentinel before the enormous front doors of the house. "She's related to my mother—who usually referred to her as an aunt, instead of cousin, given their age differences—but though Mother visited here often, we never came. Father wouldn't allow it."

Vince digested that additional detail, lining it up with the rest. Silas Saleri seemed to rule his children with an iron fist, none of them more so than Edeena.

"Well," she said briskly, cutting across his thoughts. "Let's get this adventure started. If I know my sisters, they'll be keeping you quite busy."

Vince pulled the car behind Marks's limo, and glanced at her. "Your sisters, but not you?" he asked, trying for levity.

Edeena's return smile was rueful. "Oh, I won't be here long enough to cause you any trouble."

Chapter Two

Morning dawned bright and cheerful the next day, so Edeena and her sisters celebrated the balmy August sunshine with an impromptu breakfast on the back porch. They'd spent most of the previous evening catching Prudence up on fifteen years' worth of Garronia gossip, and their cousin had told them all she could about the lovely little island they'd be calling home for as long as Edeena could manage. Already, Edeena felt like it was a second home. A small inlet was barely visible through the marsh grass if they looked in one direction, and rolling dunes rose toward the beach in the other direction. It was quite possibly the prettiest setting Edeena had ever seen—in a completely different way than the sand, surf and cliffs of her own kingdom.

"I think shopping is a must-do," Marguerite announced, looking up from her dish of pineapple and oranges.

Caro nodded, her eyes bright. "Yes! Shopping. Not solely the trinket shops, though we have to hit those as well. But I want to see what sort of local stores there are for things like fruits and vegetables. Prudence said she tries to buy local whenever she can, but she does most of her bulk purchasing on the mainland. There must be another option."

"That sounds perfect," Edeena said, mustering up a smile. "I need to go over some paperwork with Prudence this morning, but you both should go."

As expected, her sisters' expressions dimmed.

"Oh, Edeena, really?" Marguerite said. "It's your very first day here."

"It's *never* as much fun without you," Caro put in, though Edeena knew this wasn't at all the case. If anything, her overprotective streak tended to put a damper on her sisters' wilder schemes. Part of her—a very small part—wanted to be more carefree, but the much larger part of her wanted *them* to be carefree. And to ensure that, she needed to focus.

"Well, I'm being quite selfish in fact," she said, holding up a hand at their protest. "If I can get through all the paperwork and find out why in the world no one has put a bid in on this beautiful house despite Father listing it ages ago, I can spend the entire rest of the week doing nothing but buying seashell-encrusted mirrors and trying out local restaurants with you. Assuming you haven't bankrupted the family by then."

Her sisters laughed as she'd hoped they would, and talk moved on to the long weeks and even, perhaps, months ahead of them. Caroline had studied anthropology in college, so she was all about the things they would learn on the island—its history and its people—while Marguerite gushed over all the places they would go and the trips they would take during their stay in America. Edeena agreed with all of it, though her heart grew heavier with each new adventure Marguerite dreamed up, each holiday Caro described enjoying with a "low-country" flair. If she did all she needed to do, she'd be gone long before the first harvest festival.

"Ah! There you are." Lugging a heavy tote bag, Cousin Prudence sailed in as Marguerite finished her pitch for a trip to New York City. "Your bodyguards have arrived, it appears. They're young enough and dressed suitably enough to pass as college friends, though rather a bit bulky I should say."

Marguerite groaned. "We don't really need bodyguards, do we, Edeena?" she complained, rolling her eyes. "It's not like we're ten."

Edeena smiled firmly. "Humor me okay? It won't be for long. We'll scale back soon, I promise."

"For you, anything," Caro said, instantly defusing Marguerite's complaint as she stood. Caro's worried eyes betrayed her, however, and Edeena stifled a grimace. If Caroline had any idea what Edeena was planning, she'd find some way to circumvent it. As the middle sister, Caroline seemed to have taken on the job of balancing Edeena's worries with Marguerite's impulsiveness, and all too often that meant she compromised her own simple joy. Caro had turned down all too many social engagements to keep Edeena company when their father went on a rampage, and she'd chaperoned Marguerite on countless adventures she would have rather skipped when Edeena's presence would have stifled their youngest sister too obviously.

But at least now they could enjoy themselves

equally. As Prudence herded her sisters on their way, Edeena turned her attention to the gorgeous views outside the screened back porch and finally, happily relaxed.

By the time she heard her cousin's voice again, the sun had warmed the veranda to a balmy heat, the day promising to be steamy. Lulled by the heavy scent of magnolias and rose bushes, Edeena didn't at first register the import of her cousin's drawling chatter and soft, murmuring laughter.

Chatter meant conversation. Conversation meant another person, despite the fact that her sisters had clearly left.

Edeena turned in time to see her cousin enter the back porch with Vince Rallis on her arm. As it had the first time, seeing the man gave her a jolt. He was simply too big, too unnervingly good-looking, and his ready smile and golden-brown eyes unnerved her. She schooled her expression into one of polite civility, but her keen-eyed cousin outed her immediately.

"No scowling, dear," Prudence said primly. "Vince is your head of security here, and he needs to keep informed of what we discuss today. If your father accosts us in the dead of night, you'll thank me."

"He's not going to accost us in the dead of night." Edeena sighed as Vince's brows shot up. Did he have to be so attractive? Seriously? Or staring at her with such obvious concern that had nothing to do with her as a woman, and everything to do with her as a client?

Of course he did. Because she was cursed.

She waved them both to sit, then eyed her cousin,

CURSED

whom she'd commandeered weeks ago to assist in her research. "Okay, let's get this over with, then. Where do we stand with the royal rolls? And before you even suggest it, Prince Henry is not an option. I know him far too well. But Luxembourg and Lichtenstein remain available, right? And Greece if we don't put too fine a point on it. At least the list has some possibilities." She picked up a file folder and flipped it open, then grimaced, setting it down again. "If only Prince Albert could forgive me for that gas tank prank. I was just a kid."

Prudence cleared her throat delicately. "Well, ah, now that we've come to it, it's . . . not that clear cut, I'm afraid," she said, and an uncharacteristic stiffness strained her voice.

Edeena looked up from the second folder she'd selected. "What do you mean? Are those princes *all* out of the running already?"

"Not exactly," Prudence said. She glanced from Edeena to Vince, then fluttered her hands. "This isn't the first time I've heard of the Saleri curse, dear. Your mother knew about it, though I know she didn't speak of it much to you. Still, she and I discussed the matter when you were young. It . . . I should say it doesn't go exactly the way you've recounted it to me."

Edeena stiffened. "What do you mean? I don't have to marry a prince?"

"Well . . . yes, though 'prince' is a bit open to interpretation. You need to marry a man of nobility, whose bearing is princely, to be exact, but it goes beyond him being of suitable rank. He must have the ability to draw your house together. That's the true root of the Saleri curse. That you all fell apart, and you can never be successful until you come back together."

Edeena's brow furrowed. "Come back together . . . like in a group hug?" She shrugged. "If the man has enough money and a royal pedigree, Silas will greet him with open arms."

"No, dear," Prudence said quietly. "I mean your entire family—the *extended* family, including those branches that don't even recognize themselves as Saleris anymore—they must agree to come together, in peace and joy. In one place. That's what your prince must accomplish."

Edeena stared at her a long moment. "Oh," she said. "So we're doomed."

Vince barked out a sharp laugh, shattering the heavy silence, but Edeena didn't object to his response. He didn't understand—couldn't understand. Not only was he American, he appeared to be someone from a normal family, who lived and made friendships on his own terms. He could have no idea what life was like for her and her sisters.

Even *that* sounded ridiculous, she knew. Curse or no curse, Edeena and her sisters were rich, pampered, fêted members of the Garronois aristocracy. She was not about to complain about her lot in life. She was blessed beyond all conceivable measure. It wasn't lost on her, of course, that all of those blessings had come in large part from the sacrifices and compromises made by generations before her. Life hadn't always been easy for the Saleri family, but they'd done what was necessary to ensure a better life for their children, and for their children's children. Surely, she could do no less.

Still, what Prudence was saying now was inconceivable—and in the pursuit of it, her father would most assuredly marry her and her sisters off in rapid succession, chasing after a goal they could never reach. "Where are you getting this information, anyway?" she demanded. "Is there some sort of record of the curse? Because going from prince to princely is a bit of a jump, and nowhere close to the jump of someone who can pull us all together again."

"It's been officially recorded, yes, including what qualifies as a special generation—such as one with all girls," Prudence said. "It's in the Saleri family illuminated bible, from the tenth century."

Edeena frowned at her. "I've never seen that bible."

"Few people have." Prudence's gaze shifted to Vince again as Edeena's phone pinged. Edeena could sense a long-winded explanation coming on, so she grabbed the device, flipping it over, and smiled as Prudence wound through the family history. Though the phone hadn't rung for some reason, she'd received a voicemail. Probably from Caro, letting her know they were having a good time. Caro was thorough that way.

Vince's voice jerked her from her thoughts. "Enough is enough, though," he said, addressing her. "You can't really be planning to live your life according to the rules of some old book, right?"

Prudence gave a little bleat of distress and Edeena blinked at him. His American shock was becoming a touch less charming now. "It's a little more complicated than that," she said.

"No, it's not," Vince cut her off. Definitely less

charming. "You're simply *making* it more complicated."

"I—" Edeena's sharp reply was cut short by another trill of her phone. That was a new sound. They'd gotten the devices right before arriving in the US, and she hadn't had time to learn every feature. She picked up the phone again, frowning at it. Truth was, Vince was probably right, but she wasn't about to give him the satisfaction of saying so.

"What does that sound mean?" she asked instead. "There doesn't seem to be another missed call."

"Text, most likely," Vince said gruffly. His own phone buzzed in his pocket, but he reached over to Edeena's first and swiped a couple of screens over. "There." He pointed to an icon, and sure enough, another ping sounded and the number surmounting the little green square turned from 1 to 2. She tapped the icon as he pulled out his own phone.

There were two messages, from numbers she recognized as belonging to her plan. They didn't have names attached to them, but undoubtedly they were Caro and Marguerite.

You have to come! was all that was visible on Caro's text, while Marguerite's had a series of smiley faces with hearts for eyes.

"What in the world?" she murmured.

Vince's sudden sharp curse brought her head up, simultaneous with Prudence's gasp of alarm.

"What?" Edeena demanded, but he was already standing.

"We didn't provide clear enough instructions," he said. "Your sisters have free rein to go anywhere they want on the island. That was a mistake."

"A mistake?" Edeena asked, also standing. "How can that possibly be a problem? The island isn't dangerous."

Vince looked at her sharply. "You don't have a problem with them visiting the Cypress Resort? On a Tuesday?"

"What are you talking about? We were planning on going later today anyway."

She glanced back at her phone and clicked on Caro's message, scrolling quickly. "What in the world is 'Bachelorette Party at the Cypress?'" she asked, dumbfounded.

Vince groaned. "I'll explain in the car."

Vince grimaced as Edeena slammed the door behind her a few minutes later, sliding into the passenger seat. Apparently, he no longer was to be playing the chauffeur's role.

Worked for him. At this point he was beginning to wonder if he should simply drive off the island as fast as he could. The Saleri sisters were setting up to be a colossal nuisance.

"What is going on?" the eldest sister asked now. Her tone was no longer alarmed, merely curious. "What can possibly be wrong with the Cypress Resort? Marguerite confirmed that's where she'd gotten an in to do her internship, at least once the paperwork clears. She said it was a nice place!"

"It is a nice place," Vince said, putting the car into gear. "But it is a multi-functional place." He winced, not knowing how else to describe it. "I told you it was a resort for adults. Well, in some sections, it's more like a resort for *consenting* adults."

"Consenting..." Edeena turned to him sharply as she made the connection. "It's some sort of sex club?" she asked. Once again, she didn't sound aghast, more simply startled. "In South Carolina?"

"We do more than drink sweet tea here, you know." Then he jabbed a finger at her phone, which she still clutched in her hand. "What'd they say, specifically?"

Edeena fumbled with the device, eventually calling up the text screen again. "Caroline says they met some sort of social ambassador for the club wherever they were shopping, and the woman encouraged her to attend a bachelorette party of some kind. Which, apparently, is going on now. And *apparently*, your people are taking them there." She tapped another message, but shook her head. "This one's all smiley faces. Marguerite appears to be on board with the program."

Vince nodded. "That tails to the text I received. Right now, Marguerite and Caroline's personal guards are already in place with them, dressed casually, with backup hitting the club in twenty minutes." He slanted her a glance. "How, um . . . sophisticated are your sisters?"

Edeena winced. "Do I even want to know what you mean?"

When he didn't respond right away she groaned.

"Well, they're not idiots, if that's what you're worried about. They have . . . dated. They've had sex. They've seen naked men. Ugh!" She threw up her hands. "Just what sort of place are we talking about here, Vince? And how can there be some sort of weird sex club for 'consenting adults' on one of the most exclusive islands in South Carolina?"

Vince snorted as he turned out onto the main road, heading for the new resort. "The Cypress *not* a sex club," he said, shaking his head. "It's a resort, a resort that caters to the young and unattached, or the coupled-up but childless. As a result, about eighty percent of it is pure up and up — villas, restaurants, gift shops, spas, you name it. High-end, plush, as classy as you'd expect. But there's also a couple of private pool areas and some nightclub venues that are tailor-made for a slightly edgier clientele. And they've taken off like a shot, so the club is trying to promote them while staying within the bounds of decency."

"Well, that all sounds fairly reasonable. And this, ah, bachelorette party? What's that about?" He could sense her eyes narrowing as she glanced at him. "How do you know about it, exactly?"

Dangerous waters here, but he waded in anyway. "I make it my business to know everything that happens on the island."

"Which means you've been there when it was going on. How bad is it?"

"It's . . . harmless," he said finally. "Basically, a parade of women wearing bathing suits and sashes that say 'new bride' and . . . well, a collection of men who buy them drinks and chat them up."

"A collection. Fabulous," Edeena snorted, rubbing a hand over her face. "Caro will be puking her guts out within a half-hour. Marguerite . . ." She looked at him. "Is there an actual drinking competition? Because Marguerite will drink the locals under the table, I'm telling you right now."

"It's not going to get to that," Vince said firmly. "Though you're probably wrong, if it makes you feel any better. In the South, we pride ourselves on a lot of things. Holding our liquor is one of them."

"In the South, you don't have *tsipouro*," Edeena retorted. Before he could respond to that, she shifted in her seat. "That's it?" she asked, peering ahead. "It doesn't look that bad."

"It's *not* that bad." They were approaching the main clubhouse of the resort, and it appeared every inch the gracious southern beach residence, with dove grey ramparts trimmed in bright white, white decking, stairs and ramps at all levels, and gorgeous container gardens spilling over with softly swaying flowers in rich hues of purple, red, and violet to complement the seagrass that was carefully planted all around the building. Every hurricane that passed over the island carried with it the potential to destroy all of this landscaping, but so far, the new resort had been lucky. And judging from the stream of cars pulling through valet parking, they were accruing more than enough cushion for future landscaping modifications.

Edeena barely waited for him to reach the front of the queue at the valet station before she was out the door, hastening up the front steps.

CURSED

"Not that way," Vince said, and she halted, her expression questioning as she turned back to him. He gestured to a side pathway. "That's the main area of the resort, truly impressive, but not what we want."

She strode forward quickly, but when she reached him, he extended a hand and grasped her shoulder. She stiffened at the unexpected touch, but she didn't pull away. Her cheeks were tinged pink, however, as he focused on her.

"I'd rather not cause a scene here," he said quietly. "The resort is new and it's state of the art. They've got security cameras everywhere and they take notice of anyone acting out of the ordinary. If you want to keep a low profile, I suggest you follow my lead."

Edeena sighed, then nodded. "I'm sure they'll be fine, it's just . . . well they haven't had a lot of freedoms. You'd expect they would, but my father kept us in line pretty heavily. And we don't have many clubs with sections for, um, consenting adults in Garronia." She winced. "With my luck, Marguerite will decide that's what she wants to focus her internship on."

Vince elected to refrain from commenting as he steered Edeena to the side entrance into the Cypress Resort. The adults-only section was in the midst of an expansion, with more villas cropping up along the left edge of the building, but the large gated entrance remained subdued, very much in keeping with the design of the main resort. It was only after you got inside that you noticed things were . . . slightly different.

"Please let me be clear," he said as they continued along the manicured path, "it's not an adult club in the way you might be thinking. There aren't wild orgies on the front lawn. It's simply more permissible for open displays of affection, edgier clothing choices, and—"

"And bachelorette parties in broad daylight. On a Tuesday," Edeena said. Instantly she glanced up at him. "I'm sorry, I know you must think I'm a prude, but these are my sisters. I've always managed to handle them carefully enough that they have fun while still staying safe, but this . . ." she gave a small laugh. "This is a little out of my purview."

Handle, he mused. Edeena pulled out her passport for identification, and he fished for his wallet. What would it be like to think that you had to 'handle' your younger sisters to make sure no harm befell them, and how long had Edeena been doing it? More intriguingly, who'd been assigned as *her* handler all these years?

They flashed their IDs to the concierge, and the shrewd older woman's eyes lit up as she surveyed Edeena appraisingly. Beautiful women were the life's blood of these kind of establishments, Vince knew. Something else he should have warned Edeena about before they arrived. Too late now.

They swept into the open courtyard of the complex, and Edeena's gaze went immediately to the high walls that provided a distinct visual barrier between the "consenting adults" section of the Cypress and the main resort. The management's attempts at discretion were notable and immediately obvious, which contributed to the gentility of the place, despite the three large nightclubs that bordered the half-dozen pools clustered in the center of the courtyard.

"No one here is swimming laps, I take it," Edeena

commented drily. The largest pool was a circle, and about half the length of a regulation swimming pool. It was surrounded by a kaleidoscope of other, smaller pools—some apparently heated to hot-tub temperatures, some with waterfalls, all of them boasting men and women in various stages of undress. Not even this section of the Cypress allowed full nudity, but as long as there was a thread of cloth covering the essentials, you qualified.

Edeena's gaze had already moved to the center pool, and she drew nearer to Vince, as if taking comfort from his presence.

He liked that, he decided. He liked that a lot.

"Oh, dear God," Edeena choked back a laugh. "They seriously are wearing sashes. I thought that was a joke!"

"Vince! Well, bless my soul. I haven't seen you here in an age!"

The woman's sultry voice cut across Vince's focus, and he turned abruptly to see Janet Mulready, guest experience manager of the Cypress Resort, strolling up to him, her impressively-toned body encased in a swimsuit and sari bottom that left very little to the imagination. Edeena turned as well, and he practically hear her aristocratic eyebrows arching in surprise.

Janet had been the manager assigned to Vince when he'd toured the facility after it had first opened, and she'd offered him far more than a survey of the buildings and grounds. He'd been momentarily tempted, but also late for an appointment on the other side of the island, so he'd managed to keep a hold on his professionalism. The woman was knockout gorgeous, like most of the Cypress's management. No matter their shape or size, they were all beautiful people, and Janet was more buff than most of them.

"Miss Mulready," he said, offering her a polite smile—a smile that wavered as she held out long, glistening arms toward him, her fingers fluttering. He caught both of her hands and she pulled him close, bussing him on the cheek while managing not to press her body against his.

"That's the closest I can get to a kiss, covered as I am in sunscreen," she cooed. "But perhaps we can work around that later?"

He blinked as she backed up again, her gaze turning to Edeena. "And who is this?" she asked brightly. "Your sister?"

Chapter Three

Edeena had been justifiably startled when the barely-dressed woman had sailed toward them, comfortable and confident despite the fact that she wore little more than a kitchen towel. But when the statuesque blonde had grasped Vince's hands and embraced him so familiarly, her surprise had quickly turned to annoyance.

And now with the question. Vince's sister. Not his girlfriend, his client, or his bestie, but his *sister*. Instantly relegated to the sidelines while Tall, Blonde and Glistening muscled in, smelling of coconut butter and salt.

Before she could respond to the woman's question, however, Vince spoke in his cool southern drawl. "Miss Mulready, I'd like to introduce you to Countess Edeena Saleri, newly arrived from the kingdom of Garronia. She and her sisters are pleased to be exploring the Cypress Resort today."

Edeena blinked at the fawning introduction, but the woman's demeanor instantly changed. "Countess," she breathed, her avaricious eyes glinting with new and patent interest. "Here with your sisters?"

Edeena had been about to announce that she was Vince's fiancée, if merely to wipe the smug condescension from the woman's face, but she'd forgotten the power of a title in America. Garronia's entire noble class was made up of counts and countesses, the only other titles in the country being those assigned to the royal family. You couldn't turn around without tripping over a count back home. But she wasn't in Garronia, she was in Sea Haven, South Carolina. She needed to remember that.

"I trust you'll find our resort meets all your European tastes and preferences," the woman continued, then she peered more curiously at Edeena. "How *did* you two meet?"

Once again, Vince interjected himself smoothly to deflect the question with the simple truth. It was tidy and easy, and he did it with such calm assurance that he left no room for the oiled-up Miss Mulready to maneuver. "Countess Saleri hired my firm to provide them with security on the island."

"Oh! Well, of course. You'll be pleased to know that the Cypress Resort takes our commitment to security very seriously," Mulready said, her honeyed voice modulating now to one of hushed confidence. "Here in this section most of all. We draw quite an exclusive clientele, you understand."

"Oh?" Edeena's gaze swiveled once more to the bachelorette party in the pool. She'd spotted her sisters immediately—well, one of them. Marguerite had found a one-piece swimsuit somewhere, its bright red color and spare cut making up for the fact that it wasn't a bikini like most of the other girls wore. Caroline wasn't in the line-up of brides-to-be, however.

"Oh, yes, indeed," Mulready said. "We don't have any royalty here at present, but we have several international travelers, most of them business professionals looking to unwind after work on the mainland. Then there are several prominent individuals from Washington D.C. and, of course, Atlanta, who've found our resort to be exactly the kind of respite they need."

Edeena gestured more expansively to the pool area. "What's the, um, competition that's going on?"

Mulready beamed. "Just a little fun and games we put together to get everyone chatting. Would you like to join in? We can easily find you a suit."

Edeena was spared from responding as a young man in a skin-tight muscle shirt and loose shorts approached, flagging down Mulready. The man gave Edeena a warm grin before turning away. "Sorry to interrupt, Janet, but suite forty-seven has arrived and you asked to be informed. You want me to entertain them?"

"You're not the kind of entertainment they're looking for, I'm afraid," Mulready said with a leer of her own, and it was all Edeena could do not to wince. Everywhere she looked there were nearly naked bodies, and the sheer volume of undressed people in the small space made her head spin.

Mulready pivoted back to them. "If you'll excuse me? I can have Josh show you—"

"We're good, thanks," Vince said summarily as the

young man fixed his attention on Edeena. He really was good-looking in a blond surfer way, and she smiled back at him as Vince steered her off, leaving Mulready and the beefcake to chat.

"Caroline is out of the pool already at the bar," Vince informed her, and Edeena quickly picked her sister out of the crowd. "Her assigned guard, Cindy Marks, is behind her to the left. You see her?"

"I do." The woman wore a workout top that complemented her extremely buff physique, and loose trousers that had a beachy flair to them. "She's a good choice for Caro, not too intrusive."

"I switched out their assignments after meeting your sisters," Vince said, and she nodded. She'd thought that's what had happened. She remembered Caro having a male guard and Marguerite a female when they'd first discussed arrangements. But now . . .

Her gaze swiveled back to the pool. "I don't see Rob, though. Who's on Marguerite?" she asked. "And despite what's happening in that bachelorette pool, I don't mean that literally."

Vince chuckled. "Your sister may not be safe from Southern Comfort, but she's well protected otherwise. Rob's right there, wearing the red skull cap."

Edeena peered more intently. "Oh!" she said, when she recognized the bodyguard. "I can't believe he's in the pool with her. That's outstanding."

"Rob was the one who texted first when Marguerite got targeted by the rep from the Cypress. We've thought for a while that the Cypress sends out runners to draw in the new arrivals, so it's something we'll need to add to our briefings for new clients."

"They would have found their way to the resort sooner or later." Edeena shrugged. Then she glanced his way. "But who's my bodyguard? Or did you decide I won't need one after all?"

Not likely. Vince kept his gaze on Marguerite, now clambering out of the pool, apparently having lost her bid to be Bachelorette-Most-Likely. On the other side of the pool, Rob hauled his body out of the water as well. Good.

"You're with me for the time being," Vince said, not looking at Edeena as he made a quick scan of the pool area, noting anyone paying particular attention to the youngest Saleri sister, though she was merely one of many options for roving eyes. Nevertheless, he noticed a familiar face eyeing Marguerite with interest. Figured. Vince had been in the Charleston area security business long enough that he'd brushed up against Wyndham Masters more than a few times. The guy was a billionaire hotelier and all around pain in the ass, though he was rumored to be engaged, if Vince's mother's sources held any water.

Then again, Vince expected those "sources" were quite probably *Us Magazine* and *TMZ*, so he wasn't holding his breath on that.

He realized Edeena hadn't said anything for a while, and he looked her way. She was staring at him, irritation writ large on her face. He tried to remember what he'd said to piss her off, but couldn't. "What?"

"I thought I was assigned a *female* guard," she said, her cheeks once again tinged pink. "Meredith or something."

"Yeah, well, I unassigned her. This business with your father changes things."

"Then give me Caro's guard," Edeena suggested, a touch too quickly. "You guard her."

"Caroline looks like she's smart enough to stay out of trouble," Vince said, realizing that it wasn't his imagination—he was making Edeena uncomfortable. That didn't bode well for their business relationship, but he hadn't been kidding before. Now that he understood a little bit more of the unfortunate relationship the Saleri children had with their father, he didn't think any of his basic security measures were going to be enough. If this Silas character decided to swoop in and gather up Edeena after she turned twenty-seven to be auctioned off to the highest royal bidder . . .

He focused on her more intently. "Look, I'll change the rotation after a couple of days, but until I get a full handle on the threat you all are facing, I'd feel more comfortable being on site and in the loop. Rob is the best I have, and Caroline is safe with Cindy, so that leaves you. I figure if I'm assigned to you directly, I keep you secure *and* stay informed. It simply makes sense."

He could tell Edeena was thinking about it, despite whatever misgivings she had, and he gave her a winning grin. "C'mon. Janet Mulready already has no idea whether or not we're a couple or you're my client, but either way she's taken note. If you show up with

CURSED

another tagalong, she'll know for sure you've got increased protection. From there, it won't be a leap to figure out the tails on your sisters, and the woman's an incurable gossip."

"Said incurable gossip is coming our way again," Edeena said. "So what are we, client and strong man, couple of the year, or what?"

"Whatever you prefer, as long as we stick to it." He glanced up and confirmed that Edeena was right. Janet Mulready was heading back toward them, her smile wide and calculating, a cell phone to her ear. There was no question she'd informed management that the Cypress Resort could now add a legitimately royal connection to its clientele. "What's better for you?"

"Would you mind…couple of the year?"

The question was so soft that Vince though he'd misheard it, but there was no questioning the hard thump of his heart against his ribcage or the immediate intensity of his body as every one of his nerve endings flared with interest.

"Not at all," he drawled, equally quietly.

"Oh, thank heavens," Edeena said, sounding genuinely relieved. "That woman is truly insufferable, and I've known her all of three minutes." She paused another beat, then her words tumbled out in a rushed, nervous heap. "Please act like you like me, okay? I'm not very good at this."

Before Vince could process that comment, Edeena turned to him excitedly, her eyes wide and dancing, her grin huge.

"Vince!" she exclaimed, as with one elegant hand she reached for him and encircled his neck, pulling him toward her. "That sounds absolutely perfect!"

And then she kissed him soundly on the lips.

This wasn't the first time Vince had been kissed out of the blue by a woman, but it was the first time he remembered liking it so much. He pulled back enough for Edeena to murmur urgently against his mouth. "Has she stopped? I think she's stopped."

Vince didn't care what Janet Mulready was doing. He was too busy following Edeena's lead, wrapping his arms around her then sliding his hands down her back. She pressed up against his body willingly, and whether it was for Janet's or his benefit, he still came out ahead in this game.

He deepened the kiss as Edeena sighed beneath him. She was sweet and soft and tasted like honey, he thought distantly, and he'd never more intensely enjoyed his job more than he did right now.

He should probably give himself a raise.

"Vince," Edeena murmured urgently against his lips. "Is she gone?"

Pulling back, he glanced across the commons area, then met Edeena's gaze.

"She got distracted, but she's coming again. You going to take the lead here?"

The word that Edeena breathed was definitely not English, but had the peculiar salty intonation of a curse. She edged back a little further as well, then beamed up at him, leaning up to brush his lips once more before favoring him with a dazzling smile. "You think she bought the girlfriend schtick?"

Vince didn't have to glance over Edeena's shoulder

to confirm that. He could feel the steadiness of Janet's glare at twenty paces. "Yep."

"Good," Edeena said summarily. Then she turned in his arms to regard the woman bearing down on them.

Vince had to hand it to Janet; she didn't miss a beat. Instead, she waved two envelopes at them. "I'm *so* glad you're both still here. It seems our Southern hospitality has rubbed off already on you, Countess," she said breezily. "Here, you simply must come to the party we're hosting in the Sea Witch Club tonight." She gestured to one of the looming nightclubs surrounding the pool area. "It's going to be one of the highlights of the season, and you *don't* want to miss it."

"Oh, . . . well, thank you," Edeena said, automatically taking the envelopes. "I'm sure it will be quite enjoyable."

"Don't worry, I've invited your sisters as well," Janet said, and Vince could track the triumph in her expression as Edeena turned quickly. Sure enough, the over-pumped pretty boy was even now bearing down on Marguerite as she tossed back what looked like a margarita, Marks hovering close, while Caroline looked on pensively as her bodyguard intercepted another Cypress staffer bearing a similar envelope. "You'll be our honored guests tonight! You have to come."

"Thank you so much," Edeena said again, and Vince suspected her good manners prevented her from saying anything further. He watched as Marguerite opened the envelope and squealed in delight, immediately looking around for Caroline. Instead she spotted Edeena, and her entire face brightened.

Vince glanced back and saw the truth in Edeena's

eyes. They'd be coming to the party tonight, because Marguerite wanted it. If Caroline wanted to go harvest organic mushrooms the following morning, he suspected Edeena would do that, too.

He kept his arm around her, surprising himself with how natural it felt. "Miss Mulready," he said, nodding to Janet, whose gaze had turned shrewd as she took in his proprietary hold on Edeena. "We'll see you tonight, it would seem."

"Oh, I'm planning on it," she said, her own southern drawl firmly back in place, as she lifted her gaze to him. "If everything goes the way it should, it'll be a night to remember."

Chapter Four

Edeena stood in front of the gracious, free-standing mirror in her bedroom, scowling at herself. She looked ridiculous.

"This is such a bad idea," she muttered.

"It's not a bad idea, it's an amazing idea, and I don't feel even the slightest bit badly that I badgered you into it." Marguerite sailed into the room, looking effortlessly perfect in a skin hugging black mini-dress and sky high platform heels. Silver hoops hung in her ears and jangled on her wrist, and she looked far more suited to a big-city nightclub than a low-country resort buried in the middle of nowhere.

Caroline followed behind her, and Edeena's brows lifted. Caro was dressed with an equal flare, but in a flaming pink dress that set off her beautiful coloring and her softer-toned, honey-brown hair. But she was smiling, even laughing, as she fixed a glittering rhinestone earring to her ear, and Edeena couldn't help but stare.

"You're good with going tonight, Caro?" she asked, wishing despite herself that at least one of her sisters would say no.

"Are you kidding? It couldn't be better," Caro said with a happy smile. "We'll be as safe as can be with our bodyguards there, and they get a night out, away from the kids."

Edeena frowned at her. "Away from the . . .?"

"They have kids!" Marguerite said triumphantly, as if Edeena was the last to know—which she was. "Rob told me all about it. He and Cindy have been friends with Vince since they were all grade schoolers, and after the two of them grew up, got buff, and got hitched they both worked on Vince to hire them until they wore him down. And they are the *cutest*, don't you think?"

"They are, and you both you look great," Edeena said, trying to shake away her negative thoughts. Why was she so nervous? Tonight wasn't an actual date with an actual man. Vince was her security detail, the height of professionalism. He hadn't even referenced her impromptu embrace in the middle of the Cypress pool area in broad daylight again after they'd left the resort. He'd taken it solely for a ruse to distract Janet—not as Edeena simply angling for a way to kiss him.

And thank heavens for that. She needed to stay professional with him from now on. This wasn't *her* vacation, after all—she was here for her sisters. Not to ogle the security guy, no matter how ogle-worthy he was.

"I'm so glad you think so, because you need some work, girl." Marguerite interrupted her reverie, and Edeena blinked as her younger sister called to someone standing outside the door. Then a member of

Prudence's housekeeping staff entered, carrying a half-dozen outfits.

"What's this?" Edeena asked.

"An intervention," Marguerite said succinctly. "You look like you're our mom, not our not-so-older sister, and you need to relax."

"I *am* relaxed." Edeena looked down at her loose, filmy shift, a knee length black chiffon overlay that drifted around a tight black sheath. "What's wrong with this dress?"

"Nothing, if you were three months' pregnant. Wait, are you?" Marguerite stopped pawing through the dresses to turn and stare at her, and Caro burst into giggles as Edeena lofted a pillow at her youngest sister.

"I didn't think so," Marguerite grinned. "But seriously, that dress doesn't do anything for your figure, and you work out too much to hide it."

"I don't—"

"You do," her sisters said in tandem. They draped three other options over her—an electric blue sheath, a mini tank dress in aquamarine, and a deep crimson above-the-knee number in a fabric that seemed to cling and gather everywhere.

"That one," Marguerite said.

Edeena frowned. "I don't know. It feels like it's hugging me a little too snugly, and I haven't even put it on yet."

"Trust me, that's not going to be a problem. Nothing's going to crowd you any closer than Prince Vince."

Even hearing the nickname made Edeena stiffen, but Caro immediately jumped in.

"I think he's doing a wonderful job. Having Rob and Cindy as escorts is perfect, because they're a couple. It doesn't feel like we've got the palace guards with us, yet it's perfectly appropriate. Even Father couldn't fault us, with chaperones who know self-defense."

"I don't think Silas would be a fan of the Cypress Resort."

"I know, isn't it perfect?" Marguerite said, throwing her arms out as if she was preparing to hug the whole of Sea Haven Island to her. "Everyone was having so much fun, totally without a care in the world, because they were on vacation! Not only vacation, but vacation in an adults-only hideaway where they have absolutely no worries except what their next drink is going to be. I'm so glad I chose the Cypress, I had no idea of the special section of the resort."

She said this last so quickly that Edeena misdirected the earring she was trying to hook in place and ended up jabbing herself in the head. "Ow! So that's official then? Count Matretti's intercession was for the Cypress?"

"They were the first to respond, and I jumped on it." Marguerite said. "I'm supposed to meet with HR tomorrow, but I already told them via email that no job was beneath me, as long as it interacted directly with the public." She grinned. "Think about it. I could be a bartender!"

Caro coughed out a short laugh. "*Drinking* a wide variety of beverages doesn't exactly equip you to *make* those beverages, sweetheart," she said wryly, and Edeena blinked. Since when was Caroline so at ease ribbing her sister?

"Okay, then I could clean—"

"No," Edeena and Caro both chimed at once, Caroline bursting into a wide grin.

"You don't clean your own room, Marguerite. Do not for a second imagine you'd be willing to clean someone else's."

"Then waitress. I could be a waitress. Lord knows I've served enough dinner parties for Father when I was younger—we all did."

"You could easily be a waitress," Edeena said gently. "But honey, are you sure your internship will allow that kind of service work?"

"Not at all, but I'll cover all that with HR," Marguerite said loftily, waving her hand. "But no matter what, it's international experience, and if I want to get work in the hospitality industry, I need that. Plus I'll get to meet *so* many people. It's a total win-win."

"She does have a point," Caroline said. "The work I did for the tourist service was the absolute best way I found to meet new people and work on my languages."

"Done deal," Marguerite said. "I should be a bartender to start, I'm almost certain."

Edeena shook her head, but she couldn't come up with a good reason to say no to her baby sister. Which was Marguerite's super power.

There was a soft knock at the open door, then Prudence stepped in. "The Markses are here to drive you—oh, my," she said abruptly, taking in the three women. Surprisingly, she began blinking rapidly, and Edeena's heart twisted a little in her chest. She suspected the older woman was perhaps a bit lonelier than she let on. She lived out here at Heron's Point as caretaker, but how long had it been since she'd had any family visit?

"Prudence?" Caro said instantly, going to the older woman. "Are you okay?"

"It's. . . it's just . . . well, goodness me, I'm becoming a watering pot," Prudence said, lifting to her eyes a kerchief she'd managed to ferret out of some hidden pocket. "You're all so lovely. Your mother would have been so . . . so very proud to see you like this."

"She'd be grateful you were here to watch over us, you mean," Caro said cheerfully, hugging Prudence as Edeena shared a look with Marguerite. In truth, if their mother knew they would be heading for a nightclub in the heart of the "consenting adults" section of the Cypress Resort, she would probably faint. But what Prudence didn't know definitely would not hurt her. Not hurt them, either.

The ride to the Cypress was, of course, brief, but Edeena watched with interest as they joined a long queue line of cars. "Where are they all coming from?" she asked.

"The city, mostly," Rob said from the driver's seat. His wife sat beside him, but Edeena hadn't gotten a good look at her dress yet. She tugged her own crimson glove a little further toward her knees.

Cindy chimed in. "A lot come from the other villa estates as well. The island residents don't have much use for the Cypress, but they're heavily outnumbered by the island's guest villa vacationers. And the club draws guests from Charleston and the other islands as well. There's no hotel at the Cypress, but they have special three-day villa packages through the week, that oh-so-conveniently fall on these party days. It's proven to be a good strategy for them."

Cindy's phone crackled, and she pulled it from her purse, checking the display. "Pri—Vince is inside already, and he's secured a table for us in the Sea Witch. We can stay as long as you'd like, he said."

"How long does the party go?" Marguerite asked instantly, and Edeena did her best to hide her wince. She was nearly twenty-seven, but she suddenly felt forty, wanting nothing more than to wander the quiet halls of Heron's Point instead of drawing ever nearer to the booming music and glittering light show shooting up into the sky above the Cypress Resort.

Cindy glanced into the rearview mirror and met Edeena's gaze. "It'll be hopping until after midnight, but there's an unofficial curfew on the island at two. If you're out, you'll get hassled by local law enforcement, who'll be waiting at the end of the lane."

The woman was lying, Edeena realized, but Marguerite seemed to accept her words. Garronia was no stranger to curfews of late, and they'd all led an almost pathologically protected existence under their father's watch. They'd get home before two, she thought. How much of a nightmare could one little party be?

This place was an absolute fucking nightmare.

Vince scowled around the room, making eye contact

with two of his additional guards he'd brought in for the night, having no problem getting them entrance passes from the giddy Janet Mulready. If he didn't know the woman, he'd have pegged her for doped on drugs, but he suspected her good mood had everything to do with the resort's most popular party to date. The Cypress adults-only grounds had been closed from four p.m. to nine, and had opened up moments before he'd arrived. The place was now drenched in a million spotlights of every color of the rainbow, some pointed straight up, drawing the attention to the resort from all over the island. Hell, you could probably see it from the moon.

He'd been inside the Sea Witch, the main nightclub of this section of the resort, only once—again, when the Cypress had first opened. It had looked like standard fare, but it hadn't been in the midst of a party, either. Now the place looked exactly like the image it was trying to portray—a sex club, minus the actual sex. There were men and women dancing on multiple tiers of the club, most of them staff of the resort, but a good many tourists starting to get into the act as well. The staff members were easier to spot given their attire, or lack thereof. Alcohol flowed freely, and there were several fountains set up that he suspected burbled forth with straight vodka, given the number of frat boys surrounding them. The club's security was very much in evidence, but they didn't seem to put a damper on the crowd.

Nothing would put a damper on this crowd. What in the hell had he been thinking, letting Edeena and her sisters get caught up in this their very first day on the

CURSED

island?

His phone vibrated in his hand—the only way he'd know if the damn thing would ring given how loud the club was. He glanced at it, reading Cindy's text. They were at the front door, waiting for him.

Good. Signaling his man to hold the table, Vince stalked through the room. He was dressed more or less appropriately for the club, but he hadn't knocked himself out. No one would be looking at him.

He shouldered his way to the front of the club, his gaze scanning the room. The crowd was young and affluent, from all appearances. They had to be affluent to afford the $100 cover charge—a charge that, had been notably waived for the Saleri sisters and their guests. Royalty had its privileges, it appeared.

Vince's eyes sharpened as he neared the opening to the large foyer of the club. It didn't take but a moment to spot the Marks team and their charges, and he wasn't the only one looking. The three Saleri sisters cut an impressive swath through the crowd in their low-cut dresses and high-heeled shoes, in contrasting shades of black, pink and deepest red.

They were all runway-worthy, but his eyes were only for Edeena. He wanted to tell himself it was because she was his particular charge, but he'd never been especially good at lying, not even to himself.

She looked like something out of a magazine.

In deference to the evening, her hair was down, curled around her shoulders. Her exotic eyes and lips were touched with the barest hint of makeup—far less than Marguerite, but a bit more than Caroline, he decided, sweeping the other girls with a clinical glance.

The dress that hugged her athletic frame was made of some sort of soft knit, looking like nothing so much as something he wanted to pull off her body at the first moment.

Chill, he ordered himself, fixing a firm smile on his face as he approached the trio. The Markses watched carefully from a few yards away. They were playing this simple and open, no overt security needed.

"Vince!" Marguerite saw him first, but he didn't miss how Edeena's head came up, the relief on her face that he was there. That made him feel better than it should. He'd been in the security business for going on ten years now—it wasn't like him to care one way or another about a pretty face. Why was he so drawn to this one?

"Countesses," he nodded as he approached. He said the word quietly, and the younger Saleris beamed, while Edeena rolled her eyes. No one around them heard the term, but he needed to get them inside the main part of the club if he wanted that to last.

"The game tonight, ladies, is to avoid anyone who wants to make a spectacle of you. You're here to enjoy yourselves, mingle, dance, not to help the Cypress promote itself. If you feel pressured by any of the staff, you walk away. If someone announces your presence on the mic, you ignore it. The kind of attention they'll want to lavish on you isn't the kind you want, trust me."

Edeena stared hard at her sisters as Vince spoke, and to his surprise, neither one of them objected. Once again, he wondered how controlled their lives had been back in Garronia.

CURSED

Garronia. Even the name of the place sounded ridiculous. Who would believe that a seaside kingdom still existed in today's day and age, let alone one that was snugged up between Turkey and Greece that hadn't been blown up during the crossfire of the interminable wars in the area?

Vince shook his head as he watched Cindy and Rob take up their positions on either side of the younger Saleris. Edeena stepped naturally to his side, and he snaked his arm around her as they entered the glittering lightshow of the Sea Witch.

He heard Marguerite's laugh—barely—and smiled despite himself as they trooped all the way to the table he'd staked out beyond the dance floor. In the wild, artificial light of the club, the Saleri sisters seemed to glitter even more brightly, and they'd no sooner reached the table than purses and clutches were dropped and the two younger sisters grabbed Cindy's hand and pulled her out on the dance floor. Rob followed, but Vince's eyes were on Edeena. Instead of heading for the dance floor as well, she slipped into the banquette seat of the round table, then turned her attention to her sisters.

Vince settled in opposite her, watching her as much as the room around her. He'd expected this to be how the evening played out—the younger women dancing and drinking, and Edeena setting up court nearby, watching like a worried mama bear. Only she wasn't worried, exactly. Not here. Not with his team in place. He'd provided that moment of freedom of her, away from the father who seemed to hold them all in such an iron fist, and even more so away from the insane curse that had followed them around since they were born.

Tonight, it was as if Edeena was shrugging off a heavy coat of worry, and as she watched her sisters, a smile of genuine joy lit her face. Her entire expression seemed to swell with pride and admiration and a fierce love for Caroline and Marguerite, and Vince had the sudden sense of knowing that there was *nothing* she wouldn't do for her sisters, her family. Even if it meant confronting this so-called curse head on.

A kernel of resentment formed in Vince as he turned that truth over in his mind. It wasn't his place to make Edeena's life harder than it already was, but she was being unreasonable, flat out. It was like she was willing to throw her whole life away before she'd even lived it.

If she hadn't kissed him earlier in the day, then maybe he could believe that she was meant to be the older sister, the responsible one, willing to give up everything so that her sisters lives would be easily. But she *had* kissed him. Kissed him and turned his entire body inside out as he'd felt her body lean into his, tasted the salt and sunshine on her lips, smelled the honeysuckle and lavender in her hair. Edeena Saleri was made to *enjoy* life, not merely ensure that her sisters did.

And just like that, an idea formed in his mind.

It wasn't necessarily a good idea, but it was an excellent decision, all the same.

"Edeena!" Vince blinked as Marguerite trotted up to the table, waving a black and red keycard at them. "No more sitting off to yourself. They have *private VIP rooms* here, and we've got a free pass to go see!"

Chapter Five

Edeena snatched the card out of Marguerite's hand before her sister had even finished speaking, but in her heart of hearts she knew how this was going to end. If she didn't go with Marguerite right now, her resourceful sister would go exploring on her own. And unless Edeena wanted Marguerite dragging Rob or Cindy along as she discovered exactly what "VIP suite" meant in Sea Witch lingo, Edeena needed to go with her.

"I'll be right back," she said turning to Vince.

"We'll both go." His gaze was on the crowd again, face set. "You got that card from Janet?" At Marguerite's blank look he clarified, "Tall blonde, works for the club."

"Yes!" Marguerite brightened. "She's been so nice. She gave Caro about two dozen drink tickets at the same time."

"Yeah, she's a regular saint." He glanced to Edeena and gestured her to precede him out of the booth seat. "Now's going to be the best time. It'll only get more crowded back there later, as the alcohol starts to work on people's wallets."

Edeena grimaced at Marguerite as she pulled herself upright again. "You know that VIP suite is code for 'come have sex in the back room,' right?"

"Well, of *course*," Marguerite said, holding out her hand for Edeena. "But what better way to see how sophisticated this place is? It could be completely scary or super high end, but we won't know if we don't see."

"Fair enough." Edeena turned, reaching for Vince, but he brushed by her to take the lead position in front of Marguerite. Apparently, Vince knew where the back rooms were. Edeena wasn't sure how she felt about that, but she let his shoulders lead the way. No use trying to push through the crowd when they had a snowplow at their disposal.

They skirted the dance floor and Edeena scanned the room, relieved when she caught sight of Caroline. Her sister was chatting with a group of young women about her age, handing out tickets to their evident delight, while Cindy Marks hovered in the background. She'd be fine for the next few minutes.

The music and laser light show dimmed to a slightly less panic-inducing level as Vince flashed the card to an attendant, then led them into a darkened passageway, which was lit with an odd purple glow.

"Black light?" Marguerite murmured, peering upward into the corners. "That's still a thing?"

"Apparently." Edeena squinted, trying to get her bearings." After another dozen feet, the dark-painted walls gave way to a series of ornately trimmed doors . . . not tacky, exactly, but definitely over the top, each of them framed by faux wrought-iron flourishes—some black, some silver, some gold.

In spite of herself, Edeena couldn't help being intrigued. "What's the meaning of the different colors?" she asked.

"And which one is our keycard coded for?" Marguerite crowded close, peering at the card in Vince's hand. The black and red plastic rectangle had a distinctively gold patch emblazoned on its front.

"Gold, I'm assuming?" Edeena looked at Vince, who nodded. He gestured to the light panels above the doors. All of them glowed softly green.

"Red means occupied, green means unoccupied, if I recall there's also a yellow, which means occupied, but that additional partiers are welcome."

Marguerite snorted. "Of course."

He stopped in front of one of the doors surmounted by a green glow and framed in gold. With a swipe of the keycard, the door clicked open.

"Give me one second," he said, and Edeena stayed Marguerite's arm when she would have surged in after him.

"You've got to be kidding me with him scouting the place first," her sister said. "If Dad is in there lying in wait for us, it'd totally be worth it."

Vince's soft call cut off Edeena's need to respond, and she gestured Marguerite inside. Her sister darted in, Edeena following more slowly.

The room was dimly lit, but Edeena's eyes had already adjusted to the darkness in the club and intervening corridor, so she could see easily. She looked around with as much curiosity as Marguerite did, and her disappointment echoed her sisters, as well.

"It looks like a man cave," Marguerite said, turning to take in the whole space. "How is this a VIP room?"

She wasn't wrong. There were at least a half dozen thick leather couches—or they looked like leather, anyway—a large flat screen TV, a wet bar and fridge and what she suspected was a stocked built-in pantry, and a wall covered with a heavy drape. A sound system was set up on the low table next to the couches.

"It's . . . nice," Edeena said, not wanting to tip Vince off to what she was expecting.

"Gold is the kingman room, master of all he surveys," Vince said. He was fooling around with electronics over at the bar, and two walls of curtains parted to reveal large windows, both of which looked in to empty rooms. "You come to gold to watch and to party, you go to the others to party with or without an audience. Silver is for privacy. Black is for no privacy."

Despite herself, Edeena peered at the rooms on either side of theirs with curiosity, soft light filtering through what she assumed was a one-way mirror. They looked a lot like this one—couches, chairs, stocked bar—but there was a large armoire set against the wall.

As if tracking her gaze, Vince spoke up again. "Armoire contains a fairly vanilla assortment of sex toys, bondage stuff mostly—collars, restraints, some low-grade flogs, brushes, that sort of thing. There're hooks in the walls and beneath a couple of the couches."

Edeena blinked, both intrigued and vaguely disturbed. Collars and hooks? Was all that really necessary? Maybe she was more of a prude than she gave herself credit for.

Cursed

Even Marguerite was staring now. "That is messed up," she breathed.

"And how do you know all this, again?" Edeena asked, looking around their own room. There was no armoire, but beside the bar was a low storage bench. She had a sneaking suspicion their own room could become a mini party palace if visitors wanted it to be.

"I told you, I got the full tour when the Cypress first opened. I make it my business to know all the clubs, on the mainland and the outlying islands. This is, arguably, one of the more unique operations in the area."

"Have you ever been here when someone else was, you know, in one of those rooms? And they know they're being watched?" Marguerite sounded more amused than aghast, but Edeena's own reaction was more complicated. She felt too hot and too cold at once, imagining what it would be like to be in one of those rooms, so carefree and careless that you didn't worry about what you did with whom—or who saw you.

Who lived like that? She wondered. What could that possibly be like?

"When I was being given the tour, it was broad daylight, and the cleaning crews were in the room. The resort was still in its first weeks, and the club wasn't fully up to speed yet," Vince said. Was it her imagination or was his voice softer now, silkier. Edeena shivered despite herself. "I saw enough to know that if I were here on any other night, there wouldn't be a detail I would miss, looking into those other rooms from here. It really is a voyeur's paradise."

Edeena could almost feel the physical weight of his gaze as he turned from the windows to stare at her. She refused to look at him, but the hot wave of sensation rolled over her again, flushing her skin. She didn't know where to look or what to do, trapped by Vince's gaze like that, even though this all was perfectly safe, perfectly appropriate—her sister was in the room, for God's sake. It wasn't like Vince was going to make a move on her. Not that he would anyway.

She really needed to stop thinking altogether.

Vince sauntered over to the bar, pulled a bottle of champagne out of its bucket. Then he turned his gaze back on them. "Is there anything in particular you want to see?" he asked.

Satisfied that he'd shocked Edeena into leaving the room at the earliest possible moment, Vince shifted his glance to Marguerite. She was scowling at the empty rooms, her interest waning as they lay there empty.

Then one of the doors opened.

"Oh, my God," Marguerite breathed, slapping a hand to her mouth as a tall, willowy and very familiar figure appeared, entering the room with a broad smile.

"Is she doing a tour?" Edeena asked, her voice vacillating between fascination and dismay

Somehow, Vince didn't think so. Janet Mulready hadn't been subtle when she'd left him a voicemail earlier that day. She'd liked what she'd seen out in the pool area, and she wanted to know how long Edeena Saleri would be occupying his time. She'd clearly assumed that Edeena wouldn't be here for long, in spite

Cursed

of the fact that the countess had apparently fallen under his spell. When she left, Janet would be here, and she'd be waiting for him.

Now he grimaced as the woman's lithe form turned and a man strolled in. Two men, actually. *Oh, boy.* He recognized the slightly older man as the hotelier they'd seen at the bachelorette party earlier, Wyndham Masters. But the younger man didn't ring a bell.

They didn't have long to focus on them, though, as a bevy of additional women paraded into the room, bearing champagne flutes and martini glasses, some even toting a bottle. They burst into loud, breezy laughter as Marguerite took a step closer to the window.

"I cannot believe they know we're watching this."

"It's better than that. They know specifically *we're* watching. Or at least our good friend Janet knows."

Vince's gaze shifted abruptly to Edeena, who was also staring at the window as she spoke. "That's the third time she's glanced this way. She set this up, or at least is pretty sure she set it up." Her gaze sharpened as the women peeled off in multiple directions—some into the arms of the younger man, some to the bar. Wyndham stood by Janet, and as they watched he lifted a slow, lazy finger to trace a lock of Mulready's hair across her forehead, tucking it behind an ear. The move was nowhere near as salacious as what was going on up against the bar, but Marguerite seemed mesmerized as she stared.

"She's putting on a show," Edeena continued, her voice incredulous. "A show for us—for you," she turned to Vince, and though he half expected dismay or even outrage in her expression, what he saw wasn't that at

65

all. There was irritation, yes, but also pure feminine calculation.

Beside Edeena, Marguerite flinched. Vince's gaze went back to the window. One of the other women had now removed most of her dress, leaving behind a very artfully draped undergarment that he supposed functioned as both bra and panties.

Edeena tilted her head. "We don't have to keep watching this, you know — "

"We can go," the youngest Saleri said abruptly. She scanned the room, her eyes alighting on the wet bar, where the open bottle of champagne remained, loosely stoppered. "Could you grab that, Vince?"

Then she stalked over to the door, pulled it open, and exited the room.

The door slammed behind her, and Vince checked his phone. "Marks is waiting for her at the entrance to the VIP suite section," he said, tapping out a quick message. "I'll tell him to take her wherever she wants to go."

"Thanks," Edeena said absently. No longer apparently titillated by what she saw through the window, Edeena nevertheless frowned as she strode forward, peering at Wyndham even as he disentangled himself from an overenthusiastic blonde. "Who is that man, again? Wyndham something?"

"Masters. Hotelier. Billionaire. Engaged, as it happens," Vince said, also eyeing the window. Wyndham rebuffed another stunning brunette, turning instead to say something to the younger man. "I don't know who the younger guy is."

"Engaged," Edeena said, and once again, he got the sense that she wasn't dismayed. Merely intrigued. Challenged, even.

Vince's own attention sharpened on Wyndham. He was an attractive enough man, and richer than God. He wasn't a prince, of course—

What the hell am I even thinking?

Vince shook off the completely irrational surge of jealousy that rolled over him, then looked up to see Edeena eyeing him intently. "We can leave at will, right? You don't have to . . ." she waved her hand at the room. "Check out or anything?"

"Key is one use only. When we leave, I scan it, and it informs security and housekeeping that the room is no longer occupied. At that point, I can keep it as a souvenir, or toss it."

"Keep it, for now," Edeena said thoughtfully. Her gaze shifted to the windows again. Now Wyndham was gone, but Janet remained holding court, sashaying around in her mini-dress and—yes, Edeena was right—positioning herself to best effect for the window. Edeena snorted, then turned back to him, pointing at the champagne. "And like Marguerite said, please bring that, would you? I think it's time for a celebration."

Vince grabbed the bottle of champagne, not even trying to understand Edeena's words as he exited the room behind her. She took the bottle from him as he rescanned the keycard, but instead of hoofing it down the long passageway, she moved more slowly, peering into every alcove.

"You want to tell me what you're looking for?"

"Vantage point."

They moved out into the antechamber where the VIP suite guards were stationed, the wall of noise smiting them with a physical force. A few other partiers were now lingering in the area, And Edeena stopped abruptly as she scanned the heavily-fringed damask curtains.

"This will do nicely I think. It's been about five minutes since we left?"

"Something like that."

"Good." She turned into his body, her face tilted up with an expression of pure, doe-eyed expectation, the bottle of booze hanging limply from her hand. And instantly, Vince got it.

"I suppose you *are* paying me a full retainer," he said, taking the bottle from her. "I'll hold onto this."

"That you so much for not making me explain."

Vince chuckled as he led Edeena more deeply into the shadows—not so far that she couldn't be seen in her short minidress and dark tumble of hair, but far enough to give at least the impression of discretion. Appearances were important here, he knew. Then he wrapped both arms around her, holding up the distinctively labeled bottle of champagne, label out. No one passing by would be able to miss it.

He looked down at Edeena, glad she'd chosen a location for this tableau that was at least was partially lit. She was absolutely stunning, her expression caught in a haze of desire that might be real or fake. He didn't know, and honestly, he didn't care which it was at the moment. Her lips were slightly parted, her eyelids dropped ever so much, and her color was high. As he pressed her against him, he could feel her heart beating wildly behind the soft swell of her breasts, and the necessity of their positioning left no question as to the state of his own arousal.

He refused to apologize for it.

"Ahhh." Instead of shifting away, Edeena plunged right into the fire, pressing herself more firmly against his body, her right leg running up against his. She leaned back, and he didn't wait for permission to nuzzle his mouth against her soft skin, his lips following the trail of skin from the tip of her delicate ear down the curve of her neck, inviting him to kiss, lick, explore his way along the long, slender column and into the sensitive hollow where her pulse thumped and hammered.

Edeena drew in a harsh hiss, then she was clutching at him, her words an inarticulate question that brought his head up for only a moment before he found her mouth with his.

This was something more than the kiss they'd shared briefly in the bright sunshine of the pool area—something more and something continued, he realized in an instant. Edeena's mouth opened before his and she pressed herself against him almost hungrily, the movement threatening to make him loosen his grip on the champagne bottle and send it crashing to the floor.

Instead, he gripped it more tightly—and gripped Edeena more tightly, tasting her mouth, sliding his tongue past the barrier of his lips to explore her wet heat, his body almost rigid with urgency.

It was only the dimmest portion of his brain that registered the waft of perfume and rustle of silk that marked the passage of a second woman next to him — close but not too close — a woman who hesitated only slightly before pushing past the damask curtain. He hoped — no, prayed — that Edeena hadn't noticed, but of course she did.

She didn't stop kissing him, though. Not for another long, delicious moment anyway.

Then she pulled back, and he didn't think he'd ever seen anyone more beautiful in his life.

"Thank you," she whispered, her eyes shining.

Chapter Six

Had it really been two weeks?

Another gorgeous late summer day dawned bright and full of promise, and Edeena sat on the gracious back porch savoring the view. It was almost impossible to believe they'd been on the island for nearly fourteen days. One lazy afternoon flowed into the next, and time seemed to drift along.

After the initial party at the Sea Witch had exposed them to more sound and noise than they'd experienced in a year in Garronia—and Janet Mulready had disappeared, never to bother them again, she hoped—the lives of Edeena and her sisters had quickly settled into a more sedate pace. Caroline had made it her goal to learn everything about the local farms in the area and was already beginning to meet some of the resident homeowners, as well as members of the community works foundation. She'd dragged Cindy all over the island with her, but maybe that wasn't so much necessary anymore, Edeena mused, her eyes not quite focusing on the flowers fluttering softly in the breeze. Caroline knew the island well enough and was always home well before evening, preferring to stroll along the beachfront at Heron's Point versus the more crowded public beaches lining the seaside edge of the island up past the Cypress Resort. She, at least, Edeena could stop worrying over.

Marguerite was a different story, but in all truth, she was also proving to be less trouble than Edeena had feared she'd be. They'd even cut Rob's hours to occasional drive-bys at the Cypress—and, of course, he was there to pick her up and drop her off.

As promised by Count Matretti, Marguerite had been picked up by the Cypress Resort as an intern, working her way through the food service roles on site at the resort. She'd moved up quickly enough to a sit-down breakfast and coffee bar, then had set her cap for the lunch crowd. She'd never spoken again about Wyndham Masters, but Edeena had done the research anyway. It was too bad the man was engaged, but merely seeing Marguerite's clear interest in him had done Edeena good. The idea that her sisters could potentially fall in love with their future husband was the real stuff of fairy tales to her. Fairy tales that she could help come true.

Edeena smiled as her mind turned again to Vince Rallis. He'd shown up for duty the next day after the party, both of them acting as if they hadn't made out in public the night before, but she hadn't given him much reason to protect her from any further danger. He stopped by the house once a day to give her an update on her sisters, to ask after her, and to encourage her to do more than walk the beach at Heron's Point, but

Cursed

Edeena had more than enough work to keep her busy in the house. She'd been reviewing the family's financial statements—particularly her mother's, to which she'd gained access through a private trust that Silas could not touch. No matter what Silas did, her sisters would be well cared for, and that was the greatest gift a mother could give her daughters. The greatest gift an older sister could give, too.

Edeena had also confirmed an interesting fact about Heron's Point. Though the house had always remained in her mother's family, there had been several years where it had been occupied by the Saleris—from all accounts in the same typical high-handed way they'd been annoying their countrymen for generations. Apparently, the Saleri guests left rooms full of unwanted belongings behind with the Contoses when they'd returned to Garronia. Edeena suspected said ancient belongings remained stuffed in the attic, waiting to be reclaimed. She grimaced. She really should begin looking into listing the house, but they'd have to explore that attic, first.

"Oh! There you are." Cousin Prudence stepped out onto the porch with her own cup of tea, and Edeena looked up as she approached. Her cousin's gaze lingered on Edeena's untouched breakfast, but she said nothing as she fussed with getting herself arranged comfortably. "It'll be a warm one, today," Prudence said. "I thought the girls might enjoy going into town. Marguerite doesn't appear to be working today."

"Oh! A visit to Charleston would be lovely for them," Edeena nodded. "I've received yet another package from Garronia, and eventually, I'm going to have to look at them." She sighed. "It's the sixth one this week."

"I noticed that," Prudence lifted her brows at her. "You don't know what they are?"

"No. I spoke with Silas via email yesterday and confirmed receipt, but I put him off, saying we'd been traveling the eastern seaboard. He wrote back entirely too cheerfully, however, saying there was no rush, that my birthday was still a week off."

She made a face as Prudence set her teacup carefully down on its saucer. "That sounds like a threat," her cousin said.

Edeena nodded. "I thought so, too. A very pleasant one, admittedly, but a threat all the same. So I need to know the girls will be away long enough that . . . you know, they don't see whatever is in those packages." She tapped her chin thoughtfully. "Maybe we can tell them we're interviewing real estate agents and they should stay away all day. That will sound sufficiently boring, don't you think?"

Prudence sighed heavily. "Edeena, you know they would be more than happy to help you bear this burden. You don't have to go through it alone. It seems like you're all so much closer than that."

"Oh, I know," Edeena said. She'd worked through this all in her own mind, already, preparing for the questions when they inevitably came. She didn't expect them to come from Prudence, but now seemed as good a time as any to practice her responses. "But they were so much younger than I was when our mother passed away, and I got to enjoy her for those years when they didn't really know enough to connect with her. Then she passed away and it seemed like everything I did, they had to do, too—the lessons, the exact same schools, the endless round of events we attended as Silas's perfect children. Every memory of Mother he could, he gradually whittled away, until there was nothing in the house left of her. It was all *his* relatives, *his* family's past, *his* family's future. Even if I'd wanted to protect Caro and Marguerite from all of that, he wasn't about to spare any of us from learning about the proud heritage of the Saleris and the responsibility that came with it."

She waved toward the lush back yard. "But this, I did for them, bringing them here to get away. And whatever's in those packages, I can manage that, too. It can't be so terrible as all that. It's undoubtedly more dossiers on global royalty, probably with financial statements this time."

"Maybe . . ." Prudence said.

"Definitely."

It was the work of a few hours to get the girls on their way to Charleston, both of them so intrigued by the idea of shopping that they willingly relinquished Edeena to the task of meeting with realtors. By the time she and Prudence gathered in the front parlor, Edeena was feeling almost hopeful. There were really only a handful of royal contenders, and the Saleri name and modest fortune had to be appealing to at least a couple of them. Surely she could get one on the hook long enough for her to figure out how to beat the Saleri curse some *other* way than through marriage. There had to be an out.

Prudence handed her a large set of shears, almost

comical considering the size of the first package. They'd decided to open the boxes in the order they'd arrived — the largest and most official looking one first.

"Are you sure these enormous scissors are necessary?" laughed Edeena, but Prudence nodded.

"There's something in these boxes that has been weighing on you for days, if you haven't been willing to open them," she said. "It's good to give that discovery the respect it deserves."

"Fair enough."

Edeena set the shears to the first box, cutting through the packing tape. Inside, there were files on the royal families outside of Garronia. She already knew this information, of course. Either way, seeing them made her expel a long breath of relief. "Well, fine," she said, paging through the folders — even stopping on a candidate she hadn't considered, before.

"Who is Prince Ferdinand?" she asked, looking up at Prudence.

"I . . . well, I'm sure I don't know."

But Edeena was already paging through the file. "Ugh, he's ten. Never mind."

At the bottom of the first box was a summary sheet of the contents, and she checked the files against them. "Well, at least this one isn't a surprise but . . ." she frowned at the other half-dozen packages. They were all small, barely enough to hold more than a dozen folders each, but — why were there so many of them? And if she'd already gone through all the likely candidates after the first box, including the ten-year-old, then what could these new deliveries signify?

CURSED

She picked up the next package, this one a thickly padded envelope, and tore the flap wide. A single letter in an envelope peeked out, and she pulled it free with a frown.

"That doesn't look like Silas's crest," Prudence said, peering over.

"It's not," Edeena agreed. She frowned at the envelope. "It's from the family lawyer. I can't imagine . . ."

She took Prudence's proffered letter opener and slit the creamy envelope open, then slid out a rich sheet of stationery atop a thick sheaf of copied pages. She quickly scanned the cover letter . . . and froze.

"Oh, no," she said, lifting her gaze to Prudence's startled face. "Oh, no, no, no."

"What? What is it?"

But Edeena dropped her hands to her lap, staring out sightlessly as the magnolia trees waved. "This changes everything."

Vince barely held his temper in check as he carried the couch around another set of stairs. "Are you serious?" he growled. "A third floor walk-up and this is the couch you wanted?"

"Almost there!" His brother's voice sounded nearly desperate, and Vince put his shoulders into the couch, heaving it higher to give his brother a break in the weight. The twins had recently moved out of their parents' house into their own apartment near the university campus, and he'd agreed weeks ago to help them move. Lord knew he needed the break from thinking about Edeena.

He grimaced, lifting the sofa higher as his brother yelped and scrambled further up the stairs. The second twin was waiting for them, offering completely unhelpful moving advice.

The indomitable Countess Saleri had been driving him and his detail crazy for the past two weeks. Not because she was causing them trouble—far from it. She'd basically been wasting her money. Not leaving the house, not relaxing, flitting around that big old mansion like she was some Civil War-era ghost. She'd explained it away by saying she needed to focus on her family's financials, but there had to be more to it than that. It was like she'd given up.

"Excellent! Excellent." He heard his mother's voice announce her triumph, and he gritted his teeth further. Only a Greek mother would insist on managing her sons' exodus from the family home, thereby somehow managing to trip up their first step toward independence before they'd even taken it. But his brothers would learn eventually.

And for the moment they were getting enough food and maternal nurturing to bury them.

"Bring it here, Vincent, it will be perfect."

He moved in the direction of his mother's voice, lowering the couch carefully so his brothers could maneuver through the piles of stuff that had accumulated on the floor. Even with his mother present, there was only so much cleaning that could happen in

CURSED

the midst of moving.

Together, he and his brother dropped the couch on the floor as gently as possible, and then the boy sprawled to the side, gasping as if he'd been asked to run uphill for an hour.

"Don't plan on moving this back out, okay?" He surveyed the ugly couch one of the boys had gotten from . . . somewhere. "It'll be easier to chop it up with an axe and throw it out the window."

"Vincent, it's good exercise," tutted his mother. He didn't miss her accusing dark eyes as she scowled at him. "And good for me, too. I haven't seen you in a month. A month! How can you treat me so poorly?"

Vince grinned despite himself at her mortally wounded tone, and his mother's face broke into a wide smile. "There it is, the smile I love so much," she said. "Come here and help me pick up after your barbarian brothers, then walk me to the car so I can escape."

For as much as much as his mother worked their Greek heritage, she also was a pragmatist. She'd not complained—much—when Vince had moved out himself after launching his security business in college, and she'd tried valiantly to encourage his brothers to leave the nest. The fact that they'd shown no real interest in flying away had served both parties well enough for the past few years, but now it seemed like his mother had come to terms with the boys growing up.

Which should have made Vince nervous, but at the moment, he was merely grateful to be finished lugging the couch upstairs.

"Come, come," his mother said nearly a half hour later, the boys now deposited on the couch eating a pizza and the apartment as clean, he suspected, as they'd ever see it again. "Walk me back to civilization."

She trotted down the three floors lightly enough, and he found himself appreciating anew how healthy she and his father were. How healthy and, if he was honest, how sane. Turning Edeena's situation over in his mind had yielded only endless frustration. How could you combat a father who still believed in arranged marriage?

When they reached street level, his mother turned to him, her eyes searching and serious. He finally realized the danger he was in, but by then it was too late. He was trapped.

"So," his mother announced imperiously. "When are you bringing Countess Edeena Saleri to our home, eh? Your brothers are gone now, it will take me one, maybe two days to clean. But then, she must come."

"What?" he looked at her, stunned, then immediately put the pieces together. "Just how well *do* you know Prudence Vaughn?"

"Well enough that she was willing to tell me her young and beautiful cousin has a crush on you, and well enough that she begs me to encourage the flirtation, because this Edeena, she is so sad." His mother's Greek accent was surging to the fore again, a sure sign she was emotionally invested in the conversation. "It's not like you to not help someone in need, Vince. I didn't raise you to be so callous."

"Edeena does not have a crush on me," he protested, lifting his hands to ward off his mother's accusation. "I've seen her every day for two weeks. Trust me, I'd know." Even as he spoke the words, though, he ran his memories of Edeena through his mind. She'd been polite, cheerful, and reserved ever since the night at the club. While he hadn't imagined the attraction between them then, she'd had a highly defined purpose at the time—irritating Janet Mulready. Which she'd done, and to spare. The woman had not texted Vince once since that night, and he suspected she had quite definitely moved on.

"Ah! You are making some important connection. Tell me, I'm your mother."

"I . . ." Vince shook his head, but what would it harm, truly? "Edeena Saleri doesn't have a crush on me," he said firmly. "But since she doesn't, she . . . well, she did something that doesn't make a lot of sense."

"And that was?"

"She . . . suffice it to say she did something that seemed completely unmotivated, other than to make another woman jealous. But after that mission was accomplished, she went back to a perfectly appropriate, business-like demeanor. So maybe I imagined her interest."

"Business-like demeanor," his mother echoed. "This is the woman who is haunting Heron's Point, and you call that business-like?" She shook her head. "What kind of security service are you running, that you lack so much discernment?"

"What are you talking about?" Vince stared at her. "Edeena and her sisters are perfectly safe. We've got a full-time team with them whenever they set foot out of the house, we're tracking all incoming traffic to the house and any electronic hits—which have been nonexistent—and we're even keeping tabs on international travel manifests out of Garronia in case her father decides to take a trip. No one can be any safer than Edeena Saleri right now."

"But is she safe from herself?" protested his mother. "No. No, she is not. Prudence has not told me nearly enough, but I know that your Edeena worries all the time. That's no way for a young woman to live, I don't care who she is. *That* is what you need to save her from."

"It's her life, Mom," Vince grumbled, but that only merited him another scoff.

"It is not her life. It's the life she is choosing to live because she has no other alternative, because you are not helping her. Go!" his mother ordered. "Go and let that poor girl relax for whatever time she has left of her own. In fact, bring her to dinner tomorrow night, yes? Dinner at our house, with our whole family. She is not Greek but she is close enough. We'll take care of her."

"Just her, or do you want her sisters, too?"

"Her," his mother said emphatically, surprising him. "I'm sure her sisters, they are lovely girls. But this is about Edeena. You bring her tomorrow, and before that you take her somewhere, anywhere. Get her out of her own head."

Vince was still shaking his own head an hour later, as he found himself trotting up the wide white staircase of Heron's Point. The place was quiet, but he expected it to be quiet, the two younger sisters off for a day of shopping in Charleston.

Still, a sense of vague uneasiness slipped over him as he crossed the front porch to the door. Having arrived here every day for the past two weeks, Prudence had finally convinced him simply to enter and announce himself, so he unlocked the door and slipped inside the house, drawing breath to call out.

And then he heard a sound that nearly chilled him to the bone.

Hysterical sobbing.

Chapter Seven

"You have got to be kidding me! Boris?"

Edeena nearly doubled over in laughter, her sides hurting so much that she thought she might have burst something. Surrounding them were nearly twenty short stacks of files detailing the marital prospects of every quasi-noble family within the borders of Garronia.

And all too soon, she'd be declared open season for all of them.

The shock of her father's initial letter had taken two stiff mojitos to work through, but as the sweet, yet potent, drink seared through Edeena's system, the hilarity of her situation had quickly come to the fore.

No longer did she have to worry about catching the eye of a prince, as Prudence had suggested. She merely needed to catch one who "comported himself in a princely manner, or was known to be princely." This—*this!*—was what the letter from her father's lawyer had pointed out, recalling the same ancient language from the Saleri illuminated bible that Prudence had shared with her. Apparently, with Edeena's birthday nearing, everyone was hitting the good book.

"Boris goes into the pile of last resort," Edeena said now, wiping her hand against both cheeks. "I can't possibly be expected to entertain marrying him with a straight face."

At that moment, they heard the sound of resolutely-striding feet, and both of them turned on the ornately embroidered couches to see Vince stalk into the room. His face was set in a rictus of pain, and he looked like he hadn't breathed in three days.

Prudence rose quickly from her seat. "Prince, what is it?" she asked, clearly forgetting herself enough to use his nickname. "Is it your mother—"

"What? No!" Vince jerked to a halt, scowling first at her, then Edeena. "Who was *crying*?" he growled.

"I'm sorry. That was me," Edeena said hastily. She wiped her eyes again, more fervently this time. "I wasn't crying so much as . . . well, I probably sounded hysterical no matter what."

"Sit, dear, sit," Prudence said, pushing Vince into a wing-backed chair. "Maybe you could help us puzzle through this."

"Why are you hysterical?" He eyed the stacks of folders with a frown. "What's happened?"

Before Edeena could speak, however, Prudence gathered herself up. "To understand that, you must first understand the history of Edeena's country, or at least a small portion of it."

Edeena instantly turned to her. "Prudence, truly. He doesn't."

"He does," her cousin said dourly. "The way your father has interpreted the curse may not be what its originators intended, but it is viable nonetheless."

Prudence eyed Edeena repressively. "Even Boris is viable."

Edeena pursed her lips. Boris was *so* not viable.

Prudence turned her gaze on Vince. "What do you know of the history of Garronia?" she demanded.

"I, uh, don't," he said, and Edeena noted the flare of a blush that edged over his crew-neck technical tee. He was dressed casually, in his tee shirt and khakis, no doubt expecting her to be sitting in her house as she always was, waiting for life to catch up with her . . . so she could watch it pass her by.

Suddenly, Edeena didn't feel like laughing anymore.

"Then consider this your introduction," Prudence said. "The country of Garronia was created in the tenth century by Otto the Great, then Holy Roman Emperor, in exchange for services rendered by the warriors of the region. There were many, many small families who produced those warriors, and they existed in harmony, content to manage their own small fiefdoms without much need for centralized government. Times changed, however, and with it the needs of the people."

Edeena wanted to groan. Vince didn't need to be bored with all of this. "Prudence . . ."

"No, it's fine," Vince said, leaning forward "I want to know."

Edeena sighed, picked up another file folder. "Then cut to the chase, if you would."

Prudence merely nodded. "Eventually the age of familial wars resulted in the rise of the Andris family, Garronia's current ruling family. Second in strength was

CURSED

the Saleri family, but they'd been playing poor younger sibling for some time even before the declaration of Otto. There has been an ancient and well-sown line of jealousy in the Saleri family, and a constant push to ensure the family is put in its rightful place at long last. But that push has not always served the family well. There has been great estrangement among the more distant branches of the Saleri family—an estrangement that is, essentially, the family's curse. Along with the curse, come several ways to beat it."

"*Several* ways?" Vince's eyes widened. "There's more than one?"

"Of course. Whichever one is most expedient for the generation is the one proffered as *the* proper method to break the curse, usually conjured up by the oldest member of the previous generation. In this case, it would have been Silas's mother, a battle axe of a woman. As the story goes, Edeena's grandmother waited until her mother could or would no longer bear children, then consulted the good book to determine the fate of Edeena and her sisters, which she announced at Marguerite's christening. If the old harridan was a little bitter, she could be excused. Her fate had similarly been decided when she was born the oldest of two sisters, with no boys. Once again, a 'special generation.' She also had been challenged to secure a royal paramour in order to bring the family back together again, and failed."

"But the line didn't die out, even though she didn't marry her prince," Edeena protested, drawn into the story despite herself. "I mean, sure, there wasn't a reconciliation, but neither was there was plague, sickness, financial loss . . ."

"Oh, there were all of those things, if you looked deeply enough." Prudence waved her hand. "The Saleri family has many branches linking it to your main line. And they all hold the primary family bitterly accountable for the failure to bring those far-flung branches back together again. Which is why you don't know or speak to any of your extended cousins."

Edeena fought the urge to put her head in her hands. She knew she *had* cousins, great armfuls of them, according to her mother, yet Prudence was right. She'd never met any of them. She stared in horror at the file folders stacked around her. Surely her father knew who their extended relations were . . . right? He wouldn't make her marry some *actual* first cousin to break the curse. Surely not.

. . . right?

Prudence plunged on. "If the family had united earlier against the monarchy, it's quite possible that it would be a Saleri upon the throne now, not the Andrises. By the nineteenth century, however, overthrow was no longer on the table. Instead, marrying into the monarchy was the preferred method of regaining family honor. As you can see, however, it's never been accomplished."

"Because the Andrises don't want it."

Prudence shrugged. "In all truth, previous generations of Andrises have come close to intermarrying with the Saleris, but such is the nature of curses . . . it's never happened. The family remained at odds with itself. The curse evolved over the years, and it couldn't be broken. The Saleris have always married well, but not well enough. And certainly not well enough to bring the family together."

"Bring the family together," Vince frowned. "So that really is required?"

"So it would seem," Edeena took up the narrative from Prudence, since Vince seemed determined to hear it all. "Father has reviewed and interpreted what he's found as an edict requiring me to find a man of princely comportment who can bring together our extended familial factions. I do that, then success for the Saleri family is assured for all future generations."

"And if you don't?"

"Technically, the family dies out," Edeena said, grimacing. "More realistically, one of my sisters will be put under tremendous pressure to marry a man she doesn't love, will never respect, and will likely end up resenting all the rest of her days." She shook her head. "There's no way I can allow that to happen."

"So, what, you're just going to sacrifice yourself?"

The anger in Vince's voice made Edeena look up sharply. Over the course of the past hour she'd gone through every emotion imaginable, from manic laughter to grim acceptance. But anger was new, and anger mixed with defensiveness was both new and sharply irritating.

"Yes, I'm going to sacrifice myself, Vince. And before you express your outrage, I'd suggest that if you had a similar situation befalling your family, your first instinct would be to sacrifice yourself, too."

"You don't know that," he taunted her back. "You don't know a thing about my family. You don't have any idea what I'd do."

"Yes, I do. I'm not an idiot." Edeena's tone was sharper than she intended it to be, but she didn't care. Vince didn't—couldn't—understand what she was facing. "You don't handle your business, handle women, handle your work the way you do without a strong family bond. If your parents, your brothers and sisters were here right now, they'd tell me you'd do anything for them."

"Fine," he snapped. "We'll ask them ourselves tomorrow. But that's not what's important here. You don't even know what you're giving up."

Edeena stiffened. *'Tomorrow?'* she wondered, but Vince kept going

"You're so quick to give up your freedom because you've never had freedom. So my challenge to you is: live a little. You've got all the time in the world to cozy up to Prince Wafflecone or whoever you decide to marry. Why not enjoy yourself until you turn twenty-seven or whatever, and experience what life truly could hold for you?"

Edeena lifted a sardonic brow. "And I suppose you'll be my guide?"

He stared at her, eyes glittering. "You could do worse."

Vince gripped the sides of the ridiculous wing-backed chair and leaned forward, sure that he'd gotten Edeena's attention. "Way I look at it, you've got one week. One week to choose one of these idiots for your husband, and one week for you to realize there's more to life than doing what your daddy tells you."

As he suspected, that hit a nerve, but he didn't care.

"You don't know anything about what it's like to be me," Edeena said hotly.

"You're right, I don't. And the only way I could possibly figure that out is if you tell me. So I'll give you that option. Let yourself go for the next week, be crazy, actually take the vacation you've so carefully set up for you and your sisters. Go on a bike ride. Eat ice cream sundaes and elephant ears and walk barefoot on the beach at sunset. And if along the way you can convince me that your way is the better way, that your way makes sense, I'll personally escort you back to Garronia and serve you up to your father on a silver platter. If you don't, however, I'm going to track you down and hold you accountable for making the dumbest decision I've ever heard of in my life. I'll send Christmas cards to you and your husband until three years after you're dead. My mother has a neighbor who does that kind of thing."

Edeena stared at him. "She sends Christmas cards? That's a job?"

Vince snorted. "Not the most ridiculous job we've discussed today, I can tell you that. But every year you'll get your card, and you'll lean over and kiss—" he looked at the nearest file folder "—Frederic, and know that he may be an absolutely stand-up guy but you married him because you were in the chute and you'd *decided* to get married, not because you loved him or loved yourself. You're making a choice for your past, not your future, and that never ends well."

"Why are we even having this conversation?" Edeena retorted. "I'm paying you and your team to provide security services, not to be my therapist."

"Because somebody needs to do it." Vince had her though. He knew he did, and he suspected Edeena knew it, too. He swiveled his gaze to Prudence.

"First things first. How many of these . . ." he waved a hand at the stacks of dossiers, "guys know that Edeena is now on the menu? Is her father making a general announcement in Garronia, or will it be more circumspect than that?"

"At this point, he's in no position to act," Prudence said. "He's only recently emerged from . . . ah, convalescence after he attacked Prince Aristotle, and he's being watched very closely. I suspect that will continue until Edeena's birthday."

"So we have a week."

"I fail to see what value a week will provide one way or another," Edeena groused, but Vince ignored her complaint, instead fixing on her for a different reason.

"None of them are going to come over here, as far as you know?" She shook her head. "What about the real princes?"

Edeena made a face. "I suspect those *are* now officially off the table," she sighed. "I went through this once before, when Ari had been missing for a few months. I knew Silas would eventually come around to having an issue over my continued mourning for the Crown Prince, and force the question. But the true princes who were available were every bit as hopeless then as they are now. My father's not an idiot—he knew

Cursed

that. He's apparently spent his *convalescence* working out ways to get around the prince issue. 'Princely comportment' appears to be the ticket, currently."

"Excellent," Vince nodded. "Then there's something else I need to discuss with you. In private."

Edeena didn't move. "I'm not finished organizing the files."

Prudence spoke hurriedly. "You go on ahead, dear. I can put these documents into a possible order, and it will be much easier for you to re-sort them once I'm through. Whenever you get back."

Vince stood and held out a hand, and Edeena reluctantly took it. The touch of her fingers in his sent a jolt of fire through him, but he was done trying to resist it. He had Edeena for a week, and a week would need to be enough. As long as she was completely on board with the program, that is. He had some work to do to cover the rest of his assignments for the next several days, but he could do that later. After he made a few things clear.

"Where are we going?" Edeena asked warily as she moved with him through the house. She'd expected him to head for the front door, he knew, but he wasn't about to do that. He was the one who'd placed all the cameras in the house. He didn't want any footage of him making a pass at his own client surfacing somewhere on his servers.

"We're going for a walk," he said instead.

"I'm not dressed for—"

"A short walk."

They emerged from the screened porch moments later, and Vince dropped Edeena's hand as he trotted down the steps ahead of her. Camera 7 tracked them discreetly from above the gutter, and he pointedly did not look at it. Camera 8 would be picking up their trail at the fountain, but the magnolia tree forest became denser at that turn, and he had a good hundred feet or so of relative privacy until they reached the dock with its cameras 9, 10 and 13.

Thank God he'd not decided to use drone coverage for the Saleri house, or even this moment of privacy wouldn't be possible.

"You're being very strange," Edeena said testily as they moved beneath the canopy of the trees. He glanced back as they turned another corner, the move casual enough to pass muster, then stepped closer to her.

"Pause a moment here, if you would."

Obediently she stopped, turning to look at him, and then understanding flashed in her eyes.

Only as usual, it was the wrong understanding. "This was all a misdirection, wasn't it?" she asked, her brows lifting sharply. "You have something you need to tell me, only you didn't want Prudence suspecting. What is it?" She clenched her fists at her side. "Is it Prudence? Something you've learned about Silas?"

"No," Vince said in an effort to quell her response, but Edeena was already turning away to pace a few short steps then come back.

"The girls are in Charleston, but they're safe, they have to be safe." She looked up at him, and he nodded, willing to let her work it out. "It's not Silas, it's not Prudence—ah! It's the house."

Was it his imagination, or did she sound relieved?

Cursed

"There's something wrong with the house. The realtors said they would have to do research to ensure Mother's estate was clear, and . . ."

Vince couldn't help it, he laughed. Edeena stopped cold, her face blanking with anger. "What?" she snapped. "Explain this, because I seriously do not understand."

"Is it so hard to imagine that I simply wanted you alone, Edeena? That I couldn't bear arguing with you anymore?"

That stopped her, and she blinked at him. Vince pressed his advantage. "Have you even stopped to consider that the idea of you marrying someone else so carelessly, so casually . . . is making me a little bit crazy?"

"But, why would you care?" Edeena sounded genuinely perplexed, even as a blush darkened her cheeks.

"Because *I* want to be with you, Edeena. God help me, I want it more than anything. I swore that I wouldn't—couldn't—make a move. But now that I know this plan of yours to throw your life away . . ."

Vince edged forward, intimately close, and Edeena reflexively stepped back, her hands lifting to his chest as if to ward him away.

But she didn't push him away. Instead her hands lingered there, light and firm on his pecs, and his abs tightened in response to the touch of her fingers. He stepped closer, and Edeena's breath caught, her face lifting.

Instead of crowding her further, however, Vince lifted his own hands and covered hers. Her skin was hot, her fingers shaking, and he squeezed them gently as he met her gaze. "I need to make something very clear, Edeena. I want to spend time with you this coming week, not for any sort of professional security reasons, though I can assure you you'll be completely safe at all times while you're in my presence."

Well, not *completely* safe. He hurried to amend his words. "Completely in control." Also not quite right, but Edeena didn't seem to be paying close attention. Her eyes were thick with an emotion he couldn't quite place, her lips had parted to accommodate her rushed breathing, and her heart was beating loud enough that he could hear it in the hush of the magnolia trees.

"No?" she managed faintly.

Vince shook his head. "No. I want to do it because I haven't been able to get you out of my mind since that night at the Sea Witch. Your beautiful eyes . . ." he leaned forward and drifted his lips across her forehead, down the gentle curve of her cheek. "Your soft skin . . . your mouth." He tasted that mouth then, feeling it warm and firm beneath his. "I'm doing this because I can't imagine wasting another week, another day, thinking about you cooped up in this house, while I'm off working jobs that'll be there next week and the week after. But you won't be here, will you, Edeena?"

"No," she whispered and he nodded, then pressed his lips more firmly to hers for one, long, exquisite moment. She kissed him back, and he could taste the beginnings of her own desperation in that kiss. It was enough, he realized. It was more than enough.

Then he stepped back. "Today I have to take care of

everything to clear the decks for the coming week. I suggest you do the same," he said as she stared at him, her hands still locked in his. He quirked a grin to lessen the intensity of his words, though in truth he was ready to haul her off through the trees right then.

"But starting tomorrow, Countess Saleri . . . you're mine."

Chapter Eight

Edeena sat stiffly next to Vince the next morning, doing everything she could not to wring her hands in her lap. Why shouldn't she enjoy her last week on the island? Despite his very credible attempt at flirting, she knew in her heart that Vince was merely feeling sorry for her. She'd even entertained horrified suspicions of Cousin Prudence putting him up to be her chaperone, but she didn't care. She *did* want to get out, to be squired around by an attractive man, to enjoy herself for once. It wasn't going to last long—it certainly wouldn't matter in the long run—but she'd already made the crucial decisions and set up everything perfectly for her sisters, her family. She could enjoy this.

The top ten most likely candidates in the files her father had sent her were not bad options, she told herself for the millionth time. All of them had money, some of them even worked for it. They would likely be reasonably interesting and charming, right? Even if they weren't, she'd be fine.

They wouldn't be Vince, of course, but Vince wasn't noble. She needed to stop thinking about him altogether.

Besides, no man should look the way he did, and at the same time, look *at* her the way he did, with those dark, flashing eyes and the curious intensity of his expression, as if he were a spring about to be released. He was too alive, if there was such a thing. Too rough, too raw. Nothing at all like the men Edeena had met in Garronia.

Men who would be waiting for her when she returned in a few short days, she reminded herself again. But until she was officially summoned, she didn't have to worry about that, either.

"Do I want to know what you're thinking?" Vince asked, his voice almost gentle, despite the heat she could feel pouring off him. The moment he'd arrived that morning to collect her, she'd sensed that heat. Sensed it and matched it with her own, a curious thrill of excitement curling through her. *So this is what flirting feels like.* She wondered if she'd ever start breathing normally again.

"Where are we going?" she redirected him. "You still haven't said. Caroline is completely beside herself that you're exploring someplace with me she hasn't visited herself."

"Well, it's not on the island proper, and I'm pretty sure you haven't given approval for a boat excursion," he said. "So yeah, I doubt she's seen it."

That did catch her attention. "Not on the island proper?" They'd taken the main island road in the opposite direction of the Cypress Resort, and were now, true enough, angling down toward the beach and the public marina. "You're taking me on a cruise?"

He barked a laugh. "Not exactly. It's a short trip, actually, but a place my mother reminded me of. You can get there by ferry."

"Ferry." She fell silent as Vince pulled into a parking spot at the marina. She eyed the lone speedboat in the nearest slip. "That doesn't look like a ferry."

"I don't like to wait." They boarded the boat a few minutes later, Edeena gratefully accepting the life jacket. She could swim, and it was high summer, but that didn't mean she had any burning desire to try out the crisply-rolling South Carolina waves anytime soon.

Under Vince's capable hands, the boat eased out into the ocean and began jetting over open water, and Edeena felt another rope of tension fall off her shoulders. She'd forgotten how much she loved the water, any water, but especially the wide open possibility of the ocean. The Aegean Sea that fronted Garronia's capital city was certainly more blue than the Atlantic, but she reveled in the saltwater spray, the stiff breeze, and the bright sun overhead. Had Vince known, somehow, that she'd missed the water so much? Surely not.

Still, he seemed equally happy to be leaving Sea Haven behind them, and within only a few minutes, a new land mass emerged on the horizon, a cheerful island of lush trees and swaying grasses. "Are those wild horses, there on the beach?" she asked, her eyes going wide. Vince cut the boat's power and they approached the no-wake zone.

"Probably," he said. "Like the land opposite Heron's Point, most of Pearl Island is a nature preserve. There are only a few businesses—bed and breakfasts, some artists' shops, and a small museum—and the island caters to an exclusive clientele."

She frowned. "There seemed to be plenty of money on Sea Haven."

"Not so much money here as isolation," Vince said. "People come here to get away—truly get away—without having to travel too far."

"Like a retreat vacation? Yoga and meditation?"

Vince laughed. "Give it another five years and some favorable zoning changes, and probably. Right now, it's a little more rustic than that. But pretty."

"I like pretty," Edeena murmured, and in truth, she was already half in love with the quiet little island before even stepping foot on it. In another few minutes, Vince had docked the boat and helped her out to the tidy little pier, and she waited while he ducked into the marina's small white-washed office to pay for his water parking. The sun seemed warmer here, the breeze softer, and she looked around the cute area surrounding the pier with interest. There were a few old, large, Victorian-style houses lining the long block and curling around the road that she could see, and even a bit of a main street, with cute shops sprouting between what had to be more residences.

Vince joined her, holding out his hand. It seemed the most natural thing in the world for her to take it, to feel that zing of excitement when his fingers squeezed gently.

"I thought you said this place didn't generate traffic. How do those stores stay in business?"

He looked where she was pointing. "During

summer season, there's a tourist crowd, especially for the folks staying here longer than a few days. Most of the shop owners live in the house next door, and a lot of them are artists, writers, that sort of thing. They work right in their studios, so if someone happens to want to buy something, well, they can come on in."

"That's . . . lovely," Edeena sighed, and Vince was right. They passed two painters and a potter, the potter working in the back of the shop, while the painters' storefronts boasted small placards featuring a telephone number and a cheerful request for anyone interested in something in the shop's window to call. A cute coffee shop across the street with what looked like a large tree-shrouded back lot doubled as an internet café and reading room, and the entire place seemed to work further on Edeena's frazzled nerves, lulling her with the cadence of the quietly lapping ocean.

They stopped at the shop and ordered two lattes to go, then Vince pulled her outside again, setting off along the main road as it curved up the small rise. There was no longer a sidewalk here, but with virtually no traffic and wide, sandy berms to each side, it was no hardship taking the long, meandering walk.

"Is that another B&B?" She shielded her gaze from the sun. As the dunes gave way to slightly higher grasslands, she could see a large rambling house. It was nearly as large as Heron's Point, weathered by endless sun, salt, and wind, but majestic as it rose up around the piled dunes. It was maybe a full mile inland, the only house she could see for at least a half mile in either direction. "I'm surprised it's not on stilts."

CURSED

"Owners of that place were legendary for their stubbornness, convinced that no storm would take a house so big. They've been proven right so far. And it is a B&B technically, though no one has stayed there for years. It's more known for its private museum on island life. The current owners are in their eighties. Kind of benignly scattered, in the way some old people can get."

The words were judgmental, but Vince spoke them easily, and Edeena eyed him. "If they're 'scattered,' as you say, then how can they live all the way out here on their own? That seems dangerous."

"Grandson is staying with them now, fixing the place up—not to sell, though he'd get a hell of a price for it. He's some kind of professor, researcher, something like that. Keeps to himself, but while he's at it, he looks after his grandparents and their friends."

"Friends?"

"Old folks home on Sea Haven. The whole lot of 'em ferry back and forth several times a week to play cards, wander the grounds, paint, you name it. Today's Wednesday, so they won't be here."

"And that's because . . ."

He grinned at her. "Bingo tournament. Gotta have your priorities straight. But that works out. I wanted you to see the collection without the grandparents hovering."

Vince knew he shouldn't feel this happy simply squiring around a woman on Pearl Island, but he couldn't help himself. He hadn't taken full week of vacation since he first started the business ten years ago as an idiot college kid hustling house sitting jobs. Now the week ahead stretched out like an open promise, and he knew instinctively that bringing Edeena here had been the right decision. She fit the place the way he thought she would, at home on the beach, on the water, the sea wind lifting her hair. And she didn't even know the surprise he had in store for her, if the professor was up for visitors.

Edeena picked up on his excitement, and cocked a glance at him. "What kind of collection?"

"You'll see," he grinned. They entered the grand walk, and sure enough, there was a figure standing on the stairway leading down to the wide front yard. Pinnacle House wasn't run down by any stretch, but it still possessed the quiet sort of disrepair that had ensured it would never draw too much attention from the untutored eye.

The man who watched over it now was similar, Vince thought, staring at them as they approached. He didn't know much about Simon Blake, other than he came from a modest amount of money and an immodest amount of intellect, a muckety-muck professor already making news at the College of Charleston though he wasn't yet thirty. He researched something highly specific and not very useful, Vince remembered, but he couldn't place it exactly. Like music's effect on the nervous system or the development language in hamsters. He was a little tweedy, to Vince's eye, but he wasn't a bad sort, just a little gruff.

Cursed

Now the man was on sabbatical or on summer break, Vince wasn't sure, but as with most summers and weekends, he was out at the big house, running down the endless repairs and managing the occasional guests of his grandparents.

To Vince's surprise, Simon didn't bark at them that the museum had closed, as Vince had thought he might. He was tall, slender and built at odd angles, but Vince had seen him up on the roof of the house after a storm. The man didn't shy away from hard work. "Simon," he called out.

"Vince Rallis," Simon rumbled, his gaze swinging to Edeena. "Playing tour guide, I see."

It was quite possibly the most words he'd ever heard the man utter, and Vince eyed him strangely. "Miss Edeena Saleri," he said, and Simon's eyes lit with interest as he studied her, though Vince suspected it wasn't because of her title.

"Saleri," he said the word as if tasting it. "An usual name. You're not American, but not European exactly either. Further south, east. But not Middle East. Greek?"

Edeena laughed with delight and Simon's gaze darted back to Vince, uncertain of whether he'd guessed correctly.

In that moment, Vince remembered Simon's primary field of study—a branch of anthropology that tracked the impact of environment on mannerisms and personality. Edeena wasn't a mere stranger to South Carolina, she was an entirely new research subject, and Simon had picked her out at sixty paces.

Maybe Vince could learn something from the man for his business. Either way, he drew Edeena a little more tightly to his side. Simon was too late, Vince found himself thinking, somewhat irrationally. He'd met Edeena first.

Edeena glanced at him as well, confirming Simon was someone she could tell her story to. At Vince's nod, she turned her sunny smile on the man and spoke.

"Garronois, actually," she said, and the sound of her voice had Simon straightening, renewed interest coloring his features. Not the kind of interest a man normally had for a woman, though — it was intense but impersonal, almost clinical.

Vince suppressed a chuckle. He suspected he would not have much to worry about from the professor after all.

"Parents both from the country, yes? And you've not been here long. Your consonants are only now beginning to soften, vowels to lengthen." Simon lifted a finger. "Be careful, it will become a habit quickly enough, and one you'll need to unlearn when you return. The Garronois appreciate tourists, but they're quite proud."

"Quite." Edeena bowed. She turned again to Vince, her eyes remaining merry. "I didn't know you had an anthropologist hidden away here."

Despite his certainty of the nature of Simon's interest, Vince wasn't keen on pushing his luck. "I thought Edeena would enjoy the museum, if you're accepting visitors today?"

"Of course, of course," Simon waved them vaguely inside, but he still watched Edeena keenly. "You've not left your homeland before, have you?" he asked as she

CURSED

passed him.

Edeena shot Vince a startled look. "I... well, no. Not in any real sense. A few vacations in foreign countries, but we remained cloistered in private villas or on vacation compounds." She waved at the house. "Not unlike this, I suspect. Set apart from everything."

"Excellent," Simon muttered, and Vince cleared his throat.

"I was hoping you knew enough about the collection here to explain it all?" Vince interjected. "I know your grandparents are in town."

"Wednesday," Simon nodded, as if that explained everything. Which it did. "But I know a little about it, yes." He glanced quizzically at Vince. "Island royalty," he said succinctly.

"What's that?" Edeena asked as Vince nodded.

"Why your . . ." Simon hesitated only slightly, blinked, and Vince colored. "Why Mr. Rallis thought you might be interested. The museum here isn't so much a true museum as a collection of castoffs from Sea Haven's most prominent residents, past and present. The house at Heron's Point has been in the family of a Garronois for three, maybe four generations now?" He narrowed his eyes. "Not Saleri, though."

"It was my mother's family, Contos," Edeena supplied. "A century ago, the Saleris and the Contoses were very close—a contingent of them stayed with the Contoses in the...thirties, I think? But they didn't intermarry until my mother and father." Simon nodded, satisfied.

"Yes, yes, that makes sense." He led them through the house to a wide back hallway, the house neatly bisected by the pale, polished hardwood floor. "To the right is the living space of the Pearl. We have twelve bedrooms, if you can believe that, and breakfast is served here and in the dining area—or out on the deck, weather permitting." He allowed himself a small grin. "When we have guests, which isn't often any more. My grandparents can only get around so well, and prefer to entertain their friends instead of strangers." He stopped, shook his head slightly as if he'd said too much, and turned to left. "The museum is this way."

He opened a heavy door and Vince kept his gaze on Edeena, taking in her reaction. As he'd hoped, she exclaimed in instant delight. "Oh, this is so charming!"

She took several steps into the wide space, turning around. "How in the world did you gather so many items?"

Vince moved in behind her, and Simon pulled the door shut. The place had a sense of not being disturbed for weeks—maybe months—but Simon gave no indication of irritation at their intrusion. Maybe he, too, was going a little stir crazy on the island. "We've had a lot of time to do it," he said now, gesturing to the shelves lining the wall, the large white tables boasting all manner of items—some open to the air, some under glass. "Pinnacle House was built at the turn of the nineteenth century, by a woman who loved collecting things more than she loved breathing, I suspect. She was willing to pay to host collections, too, and at the time, money was tight for more than a few of the wealthy landowners of the area. In some cases, she paid more to keep the collections permanently, and one by one the

Cursed

items took up residence here. Now, there are records that would release the items back to their original owners, but most of the families recognize that the collections have little more than sentimental value. They prefer to think of them here, out on the Pearl, where they'll be preserved and viewed on occasion instead of boxed up and shoved into an attic."

"How could you ever box these up!" Edeena said, staring at an entire menagerie of animals created out of sea shells.

"An eccentric widow provided those, in 1930," Simon explained. "She was too old to manage pets herself, but her mind was nimble, and so were her fingers." He continued to supply Edeena with information while she drifted around the room, offering tidbits and anecdotes as she lost herself in the collection. There were dresses and hats and parasols, beach toys and a matched set of tea spoons, books and baubles and beads. But it wasn't until she'd nearly circled the entire room that she reached the true treasure of the collection, as far as Vince was concerned. He wondered if she'd recognize it.

She stopped, her head tilting as she paused in front of the glass case. "What in the world . . ." she murmured, leaning close. Then she flinched back, her startled gaze flying to Vince's.

"Those . . . that jewelry belonged to my family," she spoke, the words all coming out in a rush. "They bear the Saleri seal!"

Chapter Nine

"Well, that's intriguing." Simon's words sounded overloud in the hushed room, but Edeena could barely focus on him with the way her head was suddenly pounding. What . . . how . . .?

The jewelry in the case wasn't expensive, she could tell at a glance. The stones were all semi-precious, and not high grade at that, no matter how attractively they were set into the bands of gold or draped on long gold chains. They were large—large enough for the seal to be obviously stamped into each, a crown beneath an arc of three stars. It was a simple enough seal, and easily copied, but she didn't think these were copies.

She looked up at Simon. "Where did you get these?" she asked, only barely keeping the accusation out of her voice.

He didn't seem to mind the baldness of the question. "I didn't know they were Saleri jewels," he said thoughtfully. "All this time we've referred to them as the Contos Collection. They were given to my . . . let's see, great grandfather, in the mid 1930s," he said. "The Contoses owned Heron's Point then as well as now, though they didn't live there full time. Instead they paid a caretaker to keep up the grounds, and housed immigrant families there on occasion as I recall. That all changed in 1919 when an entire contingent from Garronia moved to Sea Haven for an extended visit.

"The war," Edeena said, turning back to the case. "They were fleeing World War I."

"Most likely, yes," Simon nodded. He was watching her closely, but Edeena didn't mind. She was used to being stared at, whether by the press, the public, even her own family. She'd avoided a lot of that scrutiny by coming to Sea Haven, but even that respite wouldn't last long. The shock of seeing the Saleri seal in a public case of trinkets and relics from this island's history sent a wave of obligation surging through her. She was the head of her family in this generation. She had obligations to fulfill.

She glanced back to Simon. "But how did these . . . how did Saleri jewels get all the way to Pearl Island?" Even as she asked the question, she remembered the financial records citing the endless luggage and bric-a-brac the Saleris had left behind. Could the Contos descendants have pawned off the jewelry out of spite when they found it, rather than returning it to Garronia? She probably would have.

"It's an interesting question." There was a wisp of good humor on Simon's face, but the man sobered as he realized she wasn't in a joking mood. "There's some doubt as to where the jewels originated, but the prevailing theory is that they'd been stored at the house since the Contoses had first bought the property in the late 1800s. I see now we were a bit mistaken on that point. No one knew where they came from, however, and even at the time, they were considered little more than costume jewelry. With the Depression still hitting the area hard, my own great grandfather's museum was failing, and the Contos family offered up the jewels on permanent loan, as a way of drumming up business for us." Simon gave her a grave nod. "It worked. Despite the war hitting a few years later, tourism kept trickling into the low country, and the jewels were quite a draw. There were any number of stories that sprang up around them. If my grandparents were here, they'd be the first to tell you all about them."

"I'm sure," Edeena said. She could sense the question coming next, and held up her hand to forestall it. "You can keep the jewels, Mr. Blake. You've cared for them better than we would have at Heron's Point, I suspect, and if they bring attention to your lovely little museum, then so much the better."

She managed a smile for both men, but her heart churned at the reminder that even on this tiny, remote island, she couldn't escape her responsibility to her family. "What's next to see?"

It took another half hour to finish the viewing of the museum, then to take a tour of the beautiful old house on the dunes, Simon remaining courteous but distant throughout, apparently a loner who'd been well-trained in the art of managing surprise visitors with a maximum level of efficiency. They returned to the front of the house as the sun went behind a thin brace of clouds, and the immediate change to the heat level was a welcome relief.

CURSED

"Thank you so much for your time," Edeena said, turning once more to Simon. "I'm sorry we missed your grandparents."

"I probably won't tell them you were here, to be totally honest," Simon said with a rueful grimace. "They'll be devastated to know they missed you, and if you're not careful, they'll hijack the bus from the Grove Senior Citizen's Center and take a road trip to Heron's Point."

"Oh!" Edeena laughed, but the sudden image was a welcome diversion. "Well, you'll be glad to know my younger sister is our family's unofficial ambassador, and she's loved nothing more than exploring bits and pieces of island lore since she arrived at Sea Haven. I'll tell her she simply must visit—just not on a Wednesday."

Simon's return smile looked almost strange on his taciturn face, but it was authentic. "They'd like that very much," he nodded. "They have all sorts of tales attached to the items in this old museum, and they'll take great pride in telling her every single one."

"Then we'll have to ensure they get the chance." She shook Simon's hand and turned again to Vince, allowing him to lead her back down the steps toward town. It was a beautiful day, and she couldn't remember enjoying herself quite so much, even with the unpleasant reminder the jewels had afforded her.

"Did you recognize those pieces specifically?" Vince asked. His steps had also seemed to slow as they strolled back toward the little town.

"I didn't," Edeena shook her head. "Not that I would, necessarily. They were pretty pieces, but they weren't valuable." She shrugged. "I'm sure my predecessors wouldn't have left them behind, otherwise. It's one thing to be forgetful; it's another to cut into your own family fortune because of it."

"They seemed to have been valuable enough, though, if they saved the museum." Vince gave a short laugh. "Hard to believe that's been operational since the thirties. The house doesn't even have adequate parking. No way would it pass business inspection today." He rubbed his hand over his chin. "Maybe they don't charge anymore."

"Or maybe it's been grandfathered in? Or in this case, great-grandfathered?" She smiled as he grinned back at her, and her heart gave another hard twist. She had serious responsibilities, but the day was so warm, the breeze fragrant with sea grass and wildflowers, and they were separated from the world by a band of glittering water. She sighed, and Vince's grin faltered.

"What's wrong?" he asked, searching her face. "What is it you're worried about? Something to do with that jewelry?"

"Oh, not specifically that, no," she said. He'd stopped now and was peering down at her, so she managed an offhand smile. "Could we have another coffee, or an iced tea perhaps? Something at that one shop?"

"Of course," he said, and he reached for her hand again, resuming their walk. He didn't speak though, and after another minute, Edeena continued. There was no real reason not to confide in Vince, after all, and he was so attentive, in his way. Granted, she was paying him to be attentive, but at least she knew without question that he had her safety and security as his top priorities.

"The seal of the Saleri family is what did it, I think," she said. "Seeing that mark made me realize that the future of my family isn't merely an inconvenience for me. It's something I must take seriously. If I don't, it will fall to Caroline or Marguerite, and neither of them are as familiar with the politics and personalities of the Garronia nobility as I am."

"Because you've been protecting them from it."

"It hasn't been that much of a hardship," she laughed. "The extended Saleri family hasn't come together in generations, so there were only a few hard-nosed curmudgeons to endure. But yes, better me than them, especially after my mother died." She sighed, finally willing to acknowledge the truth. "Even before my mother died, if I'm honest. She traveled as much as she could, especially toward the end. I don't think she and my father much cared for each other, though she would never admit it. Of course, I was only ten years old. I'm sure there's a lot she didn't wish to tell me when I was so young."

Vince said nothing at first, merely squeezed her hand. They'd reached the coffee shop, and within a few minutes were sitting on the quaint screened porch, overlooking a shady back space. They were the only customers there, and she realized how grateful she was for that. This time on the island had been an unexpected idyll, and she hadn't understood how much she needed that until today.

"So," Vince said, after she'd taken a long drink of her

iced tea, "if you could wave your magic wand, how would *you* resolve the issue of the curse?"

Vince watched Edeena closely, not missing her grimace. She'd already given up, he suspected. At barely twenty-seven years old, she'd seen everything she'd decided she needed to see and was going to allow herself to marry some bozo with a pedigree in the vain—and frankly insane—attempt to satisfy the strictures of a made-up curse.

The more he thought about it, the angrier he got, frankly. What kind of father would unload that kind of information on his daughter, then stand back and expect her to upend her life to save the family? It's not like she could make things right with the sweat of her brow or, God forbid, her intelligence and talents. No, she had to marry a guy who came up as bachelor-number-one and then sit back and . . . hope for the best? What kind of plan of action was that?

"Honestly, I think whatever happens will end up being the right thing," Edeena said, and the resolution in her voice made his gut tighten. "I'll go through the most likely partners from the list that Prudence is working through, meet them all, find one of them who's a suitable match, and we'll come to terms. The men of Garronia have a lot to recommend them, and in the end, a marriage is about finding a good partner."

"And what qualifies as good?" Vince worked hard to keep his tone easy, his expression neutral.

Cursed

"Kind, honest, respectful," Edeena ticked off the answers as if she'd already given them a lot of thought. "Financially solvent. I'm blessed enough not to worry about money, but if my husband proves to be addicted to online gambling, that will cause problems I'd rather avoid."

He nodded. "That's all that matters to you?"

"That's what matters *most*," she said, and another twist of annoyance sliced through him. Her answers would have made sense if she was fifty years old, maybe. But she was young, beautiful, and full of life. What in her brief description had anything to do with finding a man who would make her laugh, make her heart race, take her on adventures? She could pick anyone in the world—hell, she had actual *bona fide princes* on her list of possible fiancés—and she was going to net out with "financially solvent?" Clearly she needed an intervention.

Vince put his glass down, reached out a hand and pointed to the back door of the screened in porch. "C'mon," he said. "There's a feature of this coffee house that you gotta see."

She peered from him to the brushy back plot. "That looks like it's completely untended back there."

"It is, but that's on purpose. The owners of this shop are New Age and have a thing for meditation spaces. Let's see if it's still set up."

"Meditation?" She stood, and they stepped out into the afternoon heat. The twisted trees of Pearl Island were built low to the ground, but the brush was thick wherever it could encroach into the landscaping, and that was certainly the case behind the coffee shop. There was a single flagstone-lined path that remained visible through the high grass, and Edeena willingly followed behind him past the thickest section of brush.

"Here you go," he said, "a labyrinth."

"A . . ." Edeena frowned, peering around. "There aren't any hedges."

He pointed to the ground which, though partially obscured by the tall grass, still showed the positioning of stones in a roughly circular pattern. "The goal is to walk along the labyrinth and follow the trail, see where it takes you, while working out your troubles."

"From the looks of things, the owners aren't terribly troubled." Edeena laughed, but she gestured him before her. "You first."

He shook his head. "Nope, we'll go together, and you have to decide which way to turn — right or left."

She frowned. "And if I make the wrong choice?"

He swept his glance over the flat space. "There aren't any walls, Edeena. You can't make the wrong choice. You simply turn around or, worst case, walk off the field."

"Oh." She flushed, then reached for his hand. "Sorry, you're right."

She moved around the first turn and hesitated as the path cut to the right. "How do you choose? I honestly am not 'feeling' whether right or left is the right direction."

"Okay," Vince said. "How about I ask you a question. If your answer is yes, you turn right. If it's no, you turn left. Fair enough?"

She flashed him a delighted smile. "Fair enough."

CURSED

"We'll start with an easy one. Do you love your sisters?"

Edeena grinned and immediately turned right, moving them around the circle. The next opening came in only a few steps, and she looked up at him expectantly.

"Are you enjoying America so far?'

"Oh, very much," she said, turning right again. The path angled to the left without giving them an option, and it took another few moments for them to reach the next choice. By the time they did, Vince was ready.

"Did you enjoy the little stunt we pulled the other night, kissing at the Sea Witch?" he asked, and his voice had dropped a little. Edeena looked up quickly, her cheeks coloring, but she turned resolutely right, pulling him along. The next turn came all too soon, and she hesitated there, not looking at him.

"Would you mind if I kissed you again?" he asked. His words were quiet now, almost a whisper, but he watched the frantic beating of Edeena's pulse in her neck as she turned left into the next passageway. She resolutely didn't look at him again, however, focusing on the ground as she followed the curve of the stones. When the maze opened up again, she paused.

Vince didn't say anything at first, and Edeena glanced up at him, her eyes liquid, her lips parted. Despite the bright sunshine and the fact that they were standing in an open back lot of the coffee shop, the moment felt completely secluded, almost intimate. Almost unbidden, his next words rushed out, low and intent. "Would you like me to do more than just kiss you?"

Edeena's eyes seemed to dilate despite the bright sun, and she drew in her breath with a soft gasp. The blush washed further up her fair skin, but she tugged him along the pathway, definitively to the right.

A moment later, though, she stopped short. "Oh," she murmured, looking around, clearly flustered. "We . . . we've reached the center." She gave a shaky laugh. "I'm not sure if this has managed to clear my mind any, though. I confess I was . . . a little distracted."

"The labyrinth isn't finished yet," Vince murmured, and he pulled her around to face him. Slowly, with exquisite care, he dropped her hands and lifted his palms up, his hands framing her face as his fingertips grazed softly along her cheeks. "Just one more thing."

He lowered his mouth to hers.

They'd already kissed once, even twice before, but it was as if he was touching Edeena's lips for the first time. Excitement bolted through him, thick and surprising in its intensity even though he'd been expecting at least some reaction. Part of it had something to do with how jacked up his body had been since the night at the Cypress Resort . . . and part of it had a lot to do with Edeena's reaction right here, right now.

Her lips parted willingly beneath his, and she swayed forward, as perfect and right as the wind rustling through the breeze, the bright sun in the sky. Her hair smelled like honeysuckle, and the light touch of her hands on his waist sent the entire lower half of his body into rock-hard readiness. He leaned in, deepening the kiss, and something more stirred deep within him, something as sure and true as he felt about his business, his family, everything that ever had been important to him or ever would be.

Edeena Saleri was his.

Maybe not forever, maybe not even for very long, but while he held her in his arms, she was his to protect, his to support, his to give all that he could. Her laughter, her smiles were everything to him, but it was her soft sighs now that were twisting into his heart, tying him to her as readily as if she'd thrown a rope around him and pulled him close. Her hands lifted, soft and firm as she slid up his shirt, and she stood up on her toes to bring them yet closer together.

Finally Vince pulled back, staring down as Edeena's face broke into a wide, wondering smile.

"It worked," she said, breathless. "I feel so much better now."

Chapter Ten

Edeena tried to hold onto her happy place as they crossed over the bridge to mainland South Carolina. She and Vince hadn't been able to linger at the coffee shop for long, since he'd apparently promised to bring her to his family's home for dinner. She'd forgotten she'd asked him about his family, and when she'd tried to dissuade him from taking her to dinner, he'd refused to let her off the hook, muttering darkly about his mother with words like "hell to pay."

Now she was unaccountably nervous as the miles fell away, bringing them into the outskirts of the charming city of Charleston.

"I should have brought something—wine, a gift," she said, brightening with sudden inspiration. "We should stop somewhere so I can pick up—"

"Got it," Vince said, hooking a thumb toward the back seat. Edeena turned to look, and her heart sank. A small grocery bag overflowed with two bottles of wine and a spray of flowers in a wide spill-proof sleeve of water, still fresh. "I planned ahead."

He laughed ruefully at her expression. "You should

relax, seriously." She could hear the dismay in his voice, which made her feel even worse. "I promised this to my mother or I wouldn't put you through it, but she'll be on her best behavior. She and Prudence go way back, is all. She's heard about you your whole life, and feels, I don't know, responsible for you in a way."

That caught Edeena off guard. "Responsible? How in the world can she feel that? She's not even part of the family."

"You'll understand when you meet her," he said, shaking his head. "She's really good at responsibility."

They pulled up to the house a few minutes later, and Edeena's eyes widened as she took in the large white pillars on the modestly framed house, the lions at either side of the driveway, and the profusion of flowers. "How many brothers and sisters do you have again?" The house wasn't very big.

"Two brothers, two sisters, and about fifty-seven cousins and second cousins, neighbors who act like cousins, and strays my mom has picked up over the years. They'll all probably be here, but the upside is, you'll never have to say more than three words without being interrupted."

He said the words wryly, but he was looking down the street at the small house with decided pride. Edeena's heart gave a strange pang and she felt a smile easing across her face despite her nerves. "Tell me about your mother," she said, "so I'm prepared."

"Mom . . . she's something else," Vince chuckled, but his words were more gentle when he spoke again. "She and Dad came over to the U.S. when they were barely kids themselves, determined to live the American dream. We had family here, which made the transition easier for them, but she left a lot behind. You'd never know it by her attitude, though. She's the rock of the family, insistent that we do our best no matter what the challenge—get involved in the community, participate in every pot luck, every church social, every fundraiser. She's loud and emotional and my father worships the ground she walks on, but she gives all that love back and more."

Unaccountably, Edeena felt like crying, and she blinked rapidly, schooling her expression with effort. Vince looked at her, and his expression softened. "Hey, you'll like her. Really. She's truly not an awful person, even if she is forcing you to meet my entire extended family for no good reason."

"No, no it's fine," she said hurriedly. "I'm sure she's lovely, that they're all lovely."

"Well, I wouldn't go that far. And hey, don't get out of the car until I open your door. She's watching."

As Edeena snapped her gaze forward to the silent-seeming house, Vince opened the door of the SUV and slid out, then opened the back to pull out the bag of groceries. By the time he came around to Edeena's side, she'd noticed the faintest swish of a curtain, but nothing further.

Vince opened her door. "She truly was waiting to see if you'd open the door for me?" Edeena asked, but she couldn't keep the smile from her voice. "What about men and women being equal?"

"They're equal in other ways, she would say, but not when it comes to basic politeness," Vince said, returning

CURSED

her smile with a grin of his own. "You take the flowers, I think. It'll give you something to use as a barricade against the throng."

With that they set off, Vince giving her the quick rundown of all his relations, near and far, legitimate and what he called "opportunistic." By the time they reached the front door, Edeena was surprised to realize that she was laughing, the smell of tiger lilies wafting around her and Vince's hand firmly holding on to hers.

Then the door opened, and chaos erupted.

Edeena had taken part in her share of country dinner parties—all with families who were not her own—so she knew she should have expected the sheer volume of sound that billowed out of the Rallis house. But she'd never been the cause of such an outpouring of good cheer.

"Edeena Saleri! You are every bit as beautiful as your cousin said you would be, and Prudence exaggerates all the time, so I had my doubts." A petite woman with fair skin and jet black hair shot through with silver bustled up to her, divesting Edeena of the flowers, then stepping in to embrace her robustly.

"Ah!" she exclaimed again. "Beautiful, just beautiful."

"Mrs. Rallis—"

"Please! Call me Agnes, and I shall call you Edeena, never mind that you are a countess all the way back in Garronia. Here we are all Americans, and we're very glad to have you."

Before Edeena could draw another breath, Agnes turned to Vince and shooed him away with a frown. "Two bottles! Your brothers will finish that before dinner. Go! Go help your aunts in the kitchen while I introduce Edeena to everyone. We are so happy to have you here, my dear. You bring joy to this house."

Agnes continued with her boisterous manner and booming introductions until Edeena's head spun. She was quite sure an entire Greek city had transplanted itself to this tiny Charleston neighborhood, and those who clearly weren't related by blood seemed every bit at home as the tottering elders and racing pre-school children. She met Vince's teenage sisters—both of them more wide-eyed than she would have expected for today's far more sophisticated teens—as well as his younger brothers, his aunts, his cousins, his great aunts, and more neighbors than she could count. All of them were laughing, smiling, and welcoming, but what struck her most was how happy they seemed simply to *be* there. Not for who was there and who saw them present, but because they genuinely wanted to be in the room, sharing, laughing, talking and eventually eating . . .

And oh, the eating.

When Agnes finally summoned them to the meal, it wasn't in the house's tiny dining room, but out in the back yard, where long tables had been set up with white paper covers and blue and white decorations. The meal itself was a feast of epic proportions, from the hummus, pita bread, and spanakopita to the kabobs, lamb stew, and breads. Dessert was an endless array of baklava and honeyed donuts and cheese pie and all of it so delicious that for the first time since she'd set foot in America, Edeena found herself the slightest bit wistful for the cooking of her own country, so similar to this but with less meat and more fruit, in accordance with their terrain and the size of their rangelands.

But that nostalgia was washed away with the very next round of laughter, and Edeena turned to find Vince watching her, a smile on his expressive face, and something approaching relief shining in his eyes.

"You're enjoying yourself," he said, and the return smile she gave him was unfeigned.

"I honestly can't remember enjoying myself quite this much in a long time," she said, staring around as yet another bottle of wine was opened and an appreciative cheer went up. "They're all so . . . happy. Genuinely happy." She looked back to him again. "They can't always be like this, and yet it's gone on too long to simply be good behavior for a guest."

"Good behavior, it is not," barked Vince with a laugh. Still, his own grin rested easily on his face, and his expression was lit with appreciation as he watched his extended family debate loudly the possibility that South Carolina was protected by hurricanes because the Greek gods knew the Rallis family lived here. He shook his head as the argument rose in volume. "They're family, and part of that is being loud and happy to see each other, in good times and in bad."

"Yes . . ." Edeena kept her smile fixed, but her gaze once more roved the room, and that touch of melancholy was back. Family meant something else to her, she supposed. But Vince's definition certainly had much to recommend it.

Vince eased away from Edeena and let his family take over again, the women plying her with after-dinner drinks and asking her everything about Garronia she was willing to share—its people, its traditions, its men. On this last, of course, Edeena was more of an expert than he would have preferred, but the laughter rising up from thei group made everyone in the house happy—men and women, old and young. Even he felt the tensions of the day slipping away.

He realized, with sudden surprise, that he hadn't even checked his cell phone since he'd collected Edeena that morning. That was so unlike him as to make him wonder if he'd caught the flu. He pulled it out now, some sixth sense alerting him in time to shield the move from the watchful eyes of his mother. A quick scan of the phone's display, though, made him realize he'd need to respond to the multiple texts that had come in. He joined a throng of his singing cousins for long enough that his mother turned away, then he slipped to the back of the yard where the fence had been taken down years ago because the magnolia bushes had provided more than enough barrier.

Now he stepped through a break in those bushes with the familiarity of long practice, and paused in the cool shadows. Without bothering to scan through the messages, he struck the few keys needed to reach Marks.

"What's going on?" he said sharply, when the call

connected.

"You didn't read my texts?" Rob replied, but his voice was easy, calm, and Vince relaxed a fraction. If there'd truly been a problem, Marks would have been all business.

"You sent five of them. I figured I'd cut to the chase."

"Just regular updates. Sisters safe in town, sisters returned safely to house, Marguerite delivered to her job at the Cypress Club bar, and—"

"Whoa, whoa. Bar? I thought she worked breakfasts." Vince passed a hand over his brow. At least the club was a normal nightclub in the main part of the resort. Edeena would kill him if she thought they'd allowed Marguerite to moonlight in the shadier section of the resort.

"Cindy confirmed it, shortly after Marguerite arrived for work. She appears to be happy with the change, but we wanted to keep you apprised if it came up with Edeena." Marks paused a beat. "How's Operation Chillout going?"

"Better than I'd hoped," Vince said, smiling as the sound of guitars started streaming through the air. At least his cousins were good musicians. He had a feeling their neighbors would not be so forgiving if they were forced to listen to bad karaoke on the all-too-frequent nights that the family gathered. Normally there were no guitars, but tonight was special, his mother had assured him. Edeena was special.

And on that, she was certainly right.

"You there, Vince?" Rob's voice startled him back into focus and Vince straightened, nodding though there was no one there to see.

"I'm good. Edeena is solid, maybe a little drunk, but solid. I'll be bringing her back by midnight, if you could inform her aunt."

"Well . . ." Rob dragged the word out a little too long, and Vince frowned.

"What?"

"I sort of told dear Cousin Pru that Edeena would be spending the night in the city. At your place."

"At my . . ." Vince didn't even try to hide his shock. "Are you crazy?"

"No sir, I am not. But Prudence was all up in arms over some new boxes that had arrived today while Edeena was out." Marks slipped easily into Prudence's cultured southern drawl. "And bless her heart, but Edeena seemed to know exactly what Prudence was thinking before she even knew it herself, so there was simply no *way* she could hide those boxes from her, and yet how horrible was it going to be when Edeena returned, fresh off her *lovely* day in the country with that *charming* young Prince, and here Prudence had to ruin it all because she could not *possibly* lie to her cousin."

"You've got to be joking me."

"So, of course, since we're in the business not only of assuring peace of body but also of mind, I stepped in with the most chivalrous response I could muster."

"By telling her I was going to be hooking up with her niece at my place."

"By telling her that I would kindly suggest to the charming young Prince that he put up Edeena in one of the several safe residences we'd established in the Charleston area for the evening, assuring her of a safe and restful—and did I mention safe?—evening on the mainland, far away from frightening things like . . . boxes."

"You told her I had a safe house?"

"Several of them, yes. She was ever so grateful for our thoroughness." Once again Rob was talking in Prudence's distinctive southern drawl, and Vince winced. "She's expecting you back after breakfast, and you might want to come up with fresh clothes for the woman and attribute it to a shopping spree." He gave a short laugh. "God knows that's a language the girls speak. Cindy said they flashed enough plastic wipe out a third-world country."

"Noticeably so?"

"She didn't think so, and she knew you would ask," Rob said, chuckling. "Just girls being girls. Girls who maybe didn't get out all that often."

"Yeah," Vince grunted. "That certainly runs in the family."

"So anyway, you've got your free night pass all sewn up, my man," Rob continued. "What you do with it is up to you. Cindy and I are tucking in for the night in the carriage house, to play it safe, and before you think of it later, I did scan the box that arrived today. Inside are documents, papers in folders. No bomb, no electronics of any kind."

"Well, good," Vince said, "and Rob . . . thanks."

"What're friends for?" Rob asked with a grin to his voice. "Just don't do anything crazy. Last time I did, I ended up marrying the girl."

Vince was still laughing when he hung up the phone, but the moment he slid it into his pocket, he froze. He could sense a presence behind him in the shadow of the magnolia trees. He was so busted.

"Hey, mom," he said without turning around.

"Work!" his mother exploded, bustling around to face him properly. "Work. With you it is all about work. You have a beautiful woman on your arm, a countess even, and you sneak off like a thief in the night in order to take your telephone call. How do you know that she doesn't need you? What happens if she is looking for you, searching and cannot find you?"

"Well, it's not like she's going to come to harm in the middle of three generations of Rallises."

"That is not the point!" His mother threw up her hands and advanced on him, bullying him back through the magnolias and into their own back yard. The guitar music and laughter continued streaming out in the warm, humid air, and Vince scanned the space with an automatic efficiency, relaxing when he pinpointed Edeena.

"She doesn't look like she's searching for me," he said dryly as Edeena twirled in some kind of complicated dance step to the delight of multiple women.

"But she could have been. And you would have been on the phone. Wasting a perfectly good summer evening with a perfectly beautiful young woman." His mother eyed him darkly. "Work is not going to be a good partner to you when you are old, Vincent. I should think you would have learned that from your father."

"Dad?" Truly startled by this, Vince glanced over to where his father sat with his cousins and a few best friends that had become permanent fixtures at their house since their wives had passed. "He isn't still worried about work."

"No. No he is not. But he is not because he *decided* not to be long ago, because I told him he had a choice, his work or me—his family. He could not be married to both, and I was not willing to accept half a man. I had to have all of him."

Vince stared at his mother. "But he never quit his job, did he?" All his life Vince had thought of his father as hard working, cheerful, and dedicated. Money had never been an issue for them, exactly, but it was because of his father's work ethic. An ethic Vince had taken as his own.

"He didn't," his mother said triumphantly. "He didn't have to. He learned how to do all that he needed to when his work needed him, so that he could be here for his family when we needed him. And as a result, look at him." His mother's voice softened as she gazed at her husband, his thinning white hair lifting in a sudden puff of breeze, his jowls shaking as he laughed heartily at a joke made by one of his cronies. "Just look at him. He is a healthy man, a happy man. My man."

She turned and poked Vince hard in the arm. "*You* should be someone's man as well. It is well past time."

Chapter Eleven

Edeena swayed a little against Vince as he walked her away from his parents' house beneath a broad canopy of stars, their pinpoints dimmed by the glare from the city. She wasn't drunk—barely tipsy, in fact—but she was happy for any excuse that allowed her to fold herself into Vince's big, warm body, so solid and sure.

"In Garronia, out in the country, you can see so many more stars in the sky than you can in the city," she said, looking upward. She smiled at the memory, and at a newer one. "You can at Heron's Point, too, some nights, when the clouds don't bunch up on the horizon."

"Easy does it, there," Vince murmured as she lost her footing, and she blinked, checking her reaction.

"I'm not drunk," she said, quite certain of that fact. "Really and truly."

"Ah," Vince said evenly. "That's too bad."

They'd reached the SUV and he pulled open the door for her, helping her inside. She climbed in easily enough, but stopped his hand when he moved to shut the door again. "Why too bad?"

His smile was soft and maybe a little bit

mischievous. "If you weren't feeling entirely yourself, I'd suggest you spend the night at my place, versus run the risk of falling ill on our way back to the island."

He pulled away from her and shut the door, leaving Edeena to stare at him as he went around the front of the car. Her heart had begun to hammer recklessly, any residual fatigue from the long day now completely wiped away. She waited until he was seated, then turned to him as casually as she could manage. "Your place?"

"I have a top floor apartment in the historical district with a view of the harbor," he said, putting the SUV into gear. "A good spot to crash, not too far from here." He glanced at her, his expression unreadable. "Very safe, should you ever need it."

She lifted her brows. "And the only way I can finagle an invitation to this very safe location is if I'm sick? Not if, say, I was curious about the residence of this man to whom I've entrusted my welfare and the welfare of my sisters?"

He frowned, seeming to consider that. "It's a good point," he conceded at last. "As my primary current client, you do have a right to know that you can trust me."

"And what better way is there to truly understand a man than to see if he wears pink slippers in his living room?"

Now his glance was a little bolder. "I can assure you, I don't wear pink slippers."

"Satin smoking jacket, then?"

That merited her a laugh. "No satin of any type in my apartment, I'm afraid. Or silk either. I'm much more a cotton kind of guy."

"See, already I'm learning valuable information that could make or break my sense of personal safety." Edeena settled back in her seat as Vince eased the car onto the street, turning toward the lights of the city. "You really must take me there."

"If you insist," he said, and she felt a curl of delicious anticipation whisper through her. She was going to the apartment of a strange man, she realized with almost giddy good humor. It was perhaps the first time she'd done so since she'd been away at college, away from the constant, careful eye of her father. Of course, she'd known she'd been followed at school, but there'd still been something so unreasonably scandalous about being in a student dorm without the usual thirteen layers of security.

She felt the same way now — safe, protected even, yet skirting along the edge of danger.

It only took a few minutes for them to reach the historic downtown area of Charleston, and Edeena's enjoyment was only heightened by her wonder at all the lights and charm of the city center, even at the end of summer. "This place must be beautiful at Christmas," she said, and Vince chuckled.

"Decorating is something we take very seriously in Charleston. Something for you and your sisters to keep in mind, if you plan on staying for the holidays. Any of them."

Edeena winced inwardly, but refused to be put off by Vince's idle words. He had no idea what the future held in store for her, despite all the files he'd seen at

Cursed

Heron's Point. He probably still thought she would find a way to work around her problems. Only, she wouldn't be working around them, exactly. She'd work through them, when the time came. And tonight was not that time.

Vince pulled onto a quaint street running along a park, and whistled as a car pulled out in front of him, affording him parking by the curb. "Definitely my—well," he cut himself off abruptly. Edeena wasn't about to wait for the niceties of him opening the door for her. Instead, she was out of the car almost before it came to a halt, stepping back so she could get an unobstructed view of the line of charming brick homes that marched along the street.

"You live here?"

"Admired it my whole life," Vince said, and she caught the abashed note in his voice. "When I could finally afford it, I almost couldn't believe it."

"You worked hard," she murmured, her gaze dropping to him. "You should receive the benefit of that."

He shrugged. "Worked hard, got lucky. It's all in the mix. Come on, I'll show you."

He took her hand and led her into the building, past the smiling attendant and into a gleaming elevator bay, the modern mechanics at odds with the old-world charm of the building. Vince used a special key to activate the keypad, and Edeena's brows lifted as they sped skyward. "This must be some apartment," she murmured, feeling strangely like the poor relation for the first time in her life.

"I like it," Vince said simply. The doors opened a

moment later onto a gleaming foyer with beautiful hardwood floor and an antique washing stand centered beneath a mirror. A single door rested opposite the elevator, and Vince ushered her toward it.

"You own this?" she said again, and he chuckled.

"The bank owns it, but I'm paying the mortgage. In the spirit of full disclosure, I got a great deal on it." He paused before the door, waving his card in front of the keypad, and then keying in a secondary code. The reassuring click of disengaging locks managed to calm Edeena's nerves. It was an apartment, nothing more. She'd been in plenty of apartments before.

Then Vince opened the door, and she saw straight through the tidy space to the winking harbor beyond.

"Oh!" she said, entering the space. "Please, don't turn on the lights yet."

He laughed softly but the room stayed dark. The effect allowed the floor to ceiling windows to truly reflect the beauty of the harbor—strung with lights, filled with people, the trees along the waterfront swaying gently in the breeze. It was quite possibly the most beautiful thing she'd ever seen.

Almost without realizing it, Edeena moved forward until she stood directly before the window, her eyes unable to go wide enough for her to take in the scene. "You look at this every day," she murmured, "all times of the year."

"When I'm not on assignment, yes," Vince said. She heard him drop his keys and phone on the counter, place the box of food his mother had given him to the side. Then he slowly padded toward her—not quickly enough to startle her, she thought distantly. He knew her well enough after these few weeks to go gently, quietly, to let her be in control.

Only, she didn't want to be in control right now. She wanted to be in his arms.

Blushing against the unexpected thought, Edeena kept her gaze fixed on the astounding view. She barely jumped when Vince came up behind her, his arms going around her as if he'd read her mind. The move was so natural, it felt like he'd been doing it for years. They stood like that for several long moments, her back to his chest, his powerful arms to either side of her shoulders, his hands intertwined with hers as they rested against her chest. "It really is beautiful," she murmured at last, unsure of what else to say that truly captured her wonder.

"Yes," he said, drifting his lips over her hair. "You certainly are."

Vince breathed in the perfume of lilies and honeysuckle that still hung in Edeena's hair and reveled in the moment of having her in his arms. She was warm, her body supple as she leaned against him, and there was nothing in her manner that expressed fear or hesitation of any sort. She wanted this, wanted him.

And he planned on enjoying every last second of it.

First, however, he needed to make doubly sure that his impressions of her actions weren't simply his own wishful thinking.

"Hey," he said, dropping his head further until his mouth was even with her delicate ear. "Before this goes any further, I need to ask. . ."

"Mm?" Edeena turned in his arms until she faced him, her eyes dark and flashing in the reflected light from the street. "You want to know if I want to make love to you tonight, Mr. Rallis?"

He smiled a lopsided grin. "I think under the circumstances, you should call me Vince."

"Would that I could call you Prince," she said, so softly that he wondered if he'd misheard her. Must have, since she smiled with sudden intensity and lifted up on her toes to kiss him firmly on the lips.

"I very much would like to make love to you, Vince Rallis. Here. Tonight. Now."

She didn't have to tell him twice. He drew her away from the windows, but not too far. There would be time later for the large bed that stood next to another wall of windows, despite the blackout curtains he employed to keep the place as dark as possible so he could sleep. Time later for sleep with their legs and arms entwined. At this moment though, he wanted the full display of the city to imprint in Edeena's brain, so that she could never think of Charleston without thinking about him, about this.

He pulled her to the deeply-cushioned couch and she slid easily onto it, half sitting, half reclining as he joined her. He swept his hand up her leg, catching the fabric of her dress and scrunching it up as he went.

"I'll take you to shop tomorrow morning. You can get a new . . . dress, or whatever."

Cursed

Her lips parted in a soft laugh. "Or whatever," she murmured, and the blatant encouragement in her voice had him moving the hem of her dress higher and higher still, until his fingers drew along the silk perfection of her high cut underwear. He followed the line around the toned curve of her hip and realized the panties were thongs.

As if he wasn't hard enough, already.

"I think these are going to have to go," he said, leaning in for a kiss as she turned her face into his.

"I was hoping you'd say that." Without a further word, she pressed her own hand against his, urging him to curl his fingers around the scrap of cloth that served as her underwear, and pushed her hand down. He followed her lead and pulled the thin band free of her hips, sliding it down her legs in one long movement. Though the need to kiss a trail back up her legs was strong, leading him to where she practically pulsed with heat, he wasn't going to do that. Everything about this moment was going to be as perfect as he could make it, even if he was going to be in serious physical pain by the time he was done.

Edeena sighed as he moved back up the couch, half carrying her further back into its plush softness. When the sales rep had sold him the too-deep piece as a third bedding option without the need for a sofa bed, he'd rolled his eyes, knowing he'd never have more guests than his two spare bedrooms could manage. Now he could have kissed the man. Edeena lay before him, her hair spread out on a throw pillow, her gaze on his face curious, almost wondering. A long chenille wrap was draped over the couch, and her fingers swiped at it, curling it against her for warmth or some measure of safety, he wasn't sure which. But she didn't turn away when he dropped his mouth to hers again. She leaned up, meeting his kiss with a pressure and urgency that was undeniable. She didn't know what he was going to do next, but she was giving herself over to his care.

She wouldn't regret it.

With murmured guidance and assurance as she responded with nervous hands, Vince helped her slip out of her dress, then tossed it over the nearest chair. Edeena lay framed by his body and the throw, pressed up against the couch cushions. She was naked except for the silky fabric of her bra, now straining as her full breasts rose and fell in time to her stuttering breathing. Vince lifted a hand to her arm, drifting it over the pebbled skin until he touched the softness of her waist, then the curve of her left breast. She let out a strangled moan as he closed his hand around the weight of it, his own body jacking with desire. Even his calves had gone stiff as a board at this point.

He leaned forward and kissed Edeena, long and sure, massaging her body with his fingers as his mouth explored hers—tasting, touching, savoring. Her breathing evened out and her body seemed to lengthen beneath him as he moved from her mouth, drawing a line of kisses down her neck, nestling his head in the hollow of her throat as he licked his way along her collarbone. She groaned when he moved back up toward her chin, but the heat lifting now from her body told a different tale. She was getting as wound up as he was, and the slow trail down her body was as much the reward as the journey.

Breathing a murmured "beautiful" against her sensitive skin, Vince moved down to her breasts, now able to frame both at once in his hands, lifting them up and capturing the pebbled nipples with his fingers as he raised his gaze to Edeena. There in the reflected light of the Charleston harbor, she was easily the most captivating woman he'd ever seen. She stared at him, her eyes half-lidded, her mouth slightly open, and her expression hazed over with a desire that drove him to focus once more on bringing her pleasure, relief, satisfaction.

He took the tip of one breast in his mouth and sucked gently, reveling in the sharp pleasure that snaked through him as Edeena nearly arched off the couch. She dropped her hand to his shoulder, consciously or unconsciously pushing him down, but he wasn't going to hurry. He lavished attention on her other breast as well, kneading them both, grinning as her startled breaths shifted to deep, whispered moans of pleasure.

By the time he drew his mouth over the soft curve of her belly, Edeena's legs had parted in mute need, her body lifting to meet his questing lips. She shuddered as he pressed his teeth against her hipbone, easing his way into the gentle crease at the top of her thigh. The skin here was smooth and soft, and it trembled beneath his skin, but he hesitated a long moment, his hands brushing her thighs, his breath soft against her rising heat.

"Please, Vince," Edeena managed in a strangled voice. "I can't—"

Whatever she was going to say was lost in a gasp as Vince bent forward, tasting the superheated dampness of her clit as she uttered a broken gasp of pleasure and need. She was already so close, and something deep and primal in him responded to that, not willing to tease and tempt anymore, but driven to give the woman what she wanted, what she needed, everything she desired. He ran his tongue down her center, focusing on the tight bundle of nerves he encountered just as Edeena's breathing fractured, drifting away only long enough for her shudders to subside until he returned again, circling with ever increasing precision.

His hands gripped her hips loosely, and his body lifted with hers as she arched again beneath him. By now, Edeena was muttering incoherently in her own language, and a burst of pure satisfaction shot through Vince as he heard the words. He may not understand them, but there was no mistaking what he should do next.

He slid his tongue up her center folds once more, and flicked once . . . twice.

Edeena came apart in his hands. Her murmurs transformed into a frantic rush of words, she gripped his shoulders hard, whether to move him or hold him steady he wasn't sure, and a moment later her body went absolutely rigid for a long, impossible moment of sheer feminine power, then she jerked with an explosive movement. Her head sank bank in the cushions, her body quaked, and he rode out the tail of her orgasm while showering her legs and her belly with kisses, willingly shifting up in her arms again as she reached for him, holding him tight. "My . . . my God, Vince," she finally muttered shakily.

He lifted his gaze to hers, unable to stop his grin. "Welcome to America."

Chapter Twelve

Edeena allowed Vince to pull her up off the couch, unsurprised her legs were so shaky. "I'm significantly underdressed here."

Heat flared again as he cast a glance back, his eyes dark with intensity. "I applaud that, for the record. Whenever you feel like going naked around me, be my guest."

"Mm." She stopped him as he moved again, her hand on his sleeve. "I'm also feeling a little out of place."

He froze, clearly surprised, but she didn't correct his dismay at first, instead using the opportunity to step close to him. Catching the hem of his shirt, she pulled it up, and he lifted his arms obligingly to allow her to strip it from his upper body.

Vince was radiating nearly as much heat as she was, and Edeena placed both of his hands on his pecs, savoring the hard planks of warmth beneath her palms. "Looks like someone works out," she murmured, drawing her fingers down to his abs, which knotted at her touch.

"All part of the job, ma'am," Vince said tightly, but

he didn't move as she traced a light touch along the edge of his cargo pants. She could see the rim of his boxer briefs, and she dipped a finger behind it tracing it around to his waist.

"Is this part of the job, too?" she asked, dropping her hand farther to grace the stiff line of his erection. Vince hissed as she drew her hand down then up against the sturdy cloth of his pants. Clearly the cloth wasn't so thick that he couldn't feel the pressure, feel it and respond to it with an urgency that made her smile.

It was good to know she wasn't the only one in desperate need here.

She reached out and flicked open the clasp of his pants, then peeled them down and away. Somewhere along the line, Vince had kicked off his shoes and socks, and he stepped out of his pants easily, leaving him only in his boxers. The movement took him a few feet away from her, and she held up a hand to stop him when he would have closed the gap once more.

"Let me look," she said, and she turned him slightly so that the full reflected light of the harbor splashed across his body.

My God, he's built. She'd known about the shoulders, suspected that the chest would be thick and heavily muscled. But she didn't expect the whip-cut abs, the muscles arrowing downward beneath the band of his boxer briefs. Those briefs stretched over narrow hips and then much heavier thighs, corded with muscle. "You don't run, do you?"

He barked a laugh. "No. Too much weight to do that to my knees. I bike, and my cousins run a roofing business where I help out on occasion. Climbing up and down ladders all day will keep you in shape."

"It definitely has." She stepped back into the shadow of his body, savoring his touch as his thick arms came around her again, his hand warm and smooth along her back. He bent her into him and she felt another flare of heat as the obvious evidence of his reaction pressed into her belly.

For another second, she pressed her head against his chest, willing the moment to last well beyond this night, this week, this idyll here in a foreign country. It couldn't, of course, and she sighed against Vince's warm skin, allowing the sound of his steadily beating heart to lull her into her own sense of relaxation.

"Hey," he murmured, tightening his arms around her as he spoke into her hair. "We don't have to do anything else, Edeena. My night's already pretty much perfect."

Edeena smiled against him, hugging him more firmly for the lie. She shifted ever so slightly against his shaft and didn't miss the hitch in Vince's breath, then leaned back to look at him, the arcing movement of her body serving to intensify the intimate touch, not lessen it.

"Don't think for a moment you're not going to finish what you've started here," she said, and a curl of pure feminine delight spread through her at the change in his expression—the hope, the almost desperate need flashing through his eyes. "You have a bedroom, I suppose?"

"You suppose correctly." Vince's voice was strained as he turned, and Edeena let him lead her into the room, realizing as she watched that he was practically trembling in front of her. A new and different sensation washed over her, one she wasn't sure how to handle: power.

She wasn't a stranger to sex, but the men she'd been with up to now had been little more than grown-up kids compared to Vince—college friends and sweethearts, as unused to hard work and the realities of life as she was. Vince wasn't simply a few years older, he'd been working on his own for nearly a decade. He was big and brawny and . . . and he was trembling with desire at the thought of her touch. At the thought of making love to her.

It was like nothing else she'd ever experienced in her life, and she wanted more. A lot more.

"Nice," she murmured as they stepped into the bedroom. Thick curtains hung half-drawn, allowing light to play over the bed, but keeping the rest of the room in heavy shadow. She let Vince advance further, pulling the covers back on the bed, but when he looked back at her questioningly, she gestured him to keep going, only approaching the bed once he'd climbed into it. There was a tense, curious expression on his face, and she chuckled, warming to the possibilities—thrilling to them, really. She'd never felt safer with someone, so certain that she was in good hands.

She'd never felt so wanted, either. Not for her money, her social status, or even for her good attitude and caring demeanor. Vince wanted—her body. Pure and simple. And she wanted to give it to him.

But first, she wanted to play.

"Do you mind if I . . ." she let the question hang as

she leaned over the bed, reaching for the waistband of his boxer briefs. Vince didn't resist as she pulled the briefs down over his powerful legs, didn't object as she clambered up onto the fine cotton sheets, sinking into the plush mattress.

But when she positioned herself between his legs, tilting down, he lifted a hand to her shoulder. "Edeena," he said, and in that word was everything she was sure he couldn't quite bring himself to say—that she didn't need to do this, that he wasn't expecting anything of her, that he should be pleasuring her, not the other way around. The words seemed lodged in his throat, however, and she brushed off his hand.

"Just a taste," she murmured, then smiled as Vince's groan followed her as she leaned forward to the sharp planes of muscle above his thighs.

Vince's sensibilities may have tried to spare her, but his body was definitely on board with the program.

Edeena lifted a cool hand and drew it along the edge of his thick shaft, stroking the soft skin that strained against her touch. Up, then down again; up, then down; her mouth hovering ever closer as Vince's hands flattened on the bed on either side of his hips, clearly requiring a huge effort of control not to grab her.

She liked that she was causing him to twitch so tightly beneath her soft touch, and liked even more the strangled hiss as she circled the base of his shaft with her thumb and forefinger, tightening the pressure as her tongue darted out for that taste she'd warned him about.

Vince bit out a muffled curse.

Taking that as approval, she edged forward another inch, drawing her tongue down the side of his shaft and up again, repeating the movement she'd made with her fingers. When he drew breath to speak — to tell her to stop or to keep going? — she shifted position suddenly and took him into her mouth, plunging over him in a quick, smooth movement.

Vince's words stopped short. She pulled up, then sank down again, learning the rhythm of his body, his garbled sighs and twitching muscles, feeling the pulse of his heartbeat through her fingers. She nipped and licked and tasted, lifting away just long enough to come up with some new variation to try, before sinking back over him again.

She'd never enjoyed this particular act so much, she realized, half mesmerized by the wave of need building inside her as well. She could keep this up all night.

If she didn't knock it off in the next thirty seconds, Vince was going to seriously lose his mind. And his cool. And probably kill the woman with the force of his reaction if she didn't duck and run for cover.

It was bad enough what she was doing to him with her mouth. But the way she was positioned, with her hair falling over his thighs and the curve of her ass silhouetted against the Charleston harbor lights . . . he didn't think he was ever going to get that image out of his mind. Staring at it now was almost enough to throw him over the edge, and the woman had barely gotten started.

"Edeena," he said roughly, and she finally—exquisitely slow and with no real appreciation for how close he was to a heart attack—pulled back to gaze up at him with her dark, liquid eyes. She kept her left hand on his cock, only now, her right slipped down to cradle his balls, and he had to close his eyes for a minute, steeling himself against the new assault. "Jesus, you're killing me here."

"That sounds bad," she murmured. He took advantage of the fact that he could reach her and leaned forward enough to taste her lips, the salt and heat of her mouth tantalizingly close. She slid her hands off him and lifted them to brace herself against his hips, her touch almost tentative, unused to the feel of him.

But it was the soft touch of those long, slender fingers on yet a new part of his anatomy that did it. Though he suspected at a deep level she wanted to control her every move, he couldn't help himself. He snaked his arms around her and pulled her close, his heart surging with renewed energy as she gave a startled laugh, sprawling over his body as dragged her toward him. Her legs naturally fell to either side of his hips, and in another breath, the very hot center of her was pressed up right against his already hair-trigger cock, and the resulting convulsion of said third party made her eyes go wide.

He held her gaze with his, not giving her a chance to look away. "Edeena, you know how we talked about your behavior when you were with me, in the event of a crisis?" he said tightly.

The question completely threw her, but she blinked, nodding quickly. "I . . . I'm to do whatever you say, exactly as you say, and I can yell at you later if you ask me to do something I take issue with."

"Exactly," Vince gritted out. "We . . . are in the middle of a crisis."

Her brows went up, and amusement danced in her eyes as she realized the exact nature of the crisis. Somehow, impossibly, she seemed to grow even hotter, and the warm, damp heat surrounded Vince's cock with what was tantamount to an engraved invitation to come on inside. And he wanted to—God, did he want to—but not like this. Not yet.

"Dressing table, top drawer," he said, and Edeena nodded as gravely as she was able, though a smile tweaked the edge of her lips.

"The table right there?" she asked, shifting her body and sitting more upright, so that her breasts swayed in front of Vince's face. Her beautiful, full, perfect breasts that even now bobbed not an inch in front of his mouth, begging him to kiss, nuzzle . . .

His cock twitched dangerously again, and Edeena chose that minute to wriggle closer, sliding her body an inch higher against him, dangerously close to positioning herself exactly where she shouldn't.

"Sorry," she murmured, now stretching languorously over him. "Brace me?"

Left with no other choice, Vince planted his hands on Edeena's rounded ass, grinding her into him as she reached the top drawer of his nightstand. After what seemed like several years of searching, she dragged something out and rolled back, introducing him to a fresh layer of exquisite torture as she returned to her upright position.

She waved the foil package at him. "I'm not terribly practiced with these," she murmured. "Can I watch?"

His traitorous cock gave the answer for him, and Edeena fell back, returning to her knees between his legs as he ripped the condom package open.

"Just a minute," she murmured and she dipped forward again and once more slid her hot, wet mouth over him, inch by inch, pleasure and need intertwining so much that it was going to be a fucking miracle if he got the condom on himself the first time, the way his hands were shaking.

Then again, the sooner he was done with that, the sooner he could feel Edeena's body surrounding him, the tight heat of her pressing close, the—

Edeena rocked back a moment before he started pleading, and he sheathed himself in one savage thrust, tossing the wrapper away and trying to stabilize his breathing. It was no use, however. No sooner did he brace his hands on the mattress than Edeena was on top of him again, straddling his legs as she pushed his shoulders back into the pillows.

"Edeena, sweetheart, I—"

"Shh," she said, and a moment later she was positioned over him perfectly, sliding down over him in one slick movement.

Vince couldn't help it, he gritted out a half-gasp, half-moan, the tight heat of her so much more intense than he'd expected, the rush of sensation spiraling up within him, demanding its release. Edeena rocked forward and he realized he'd closed his eyes. Snapping them open now, he was greeted once again with her impossibly tantalizing curves, her olive-toned skin soft and supple beneath his rough palms. She sighed with unmistakable pleasure as he closed his hands over her hips, grinding her into him with deep, rhythmic thrusts.

He looked up still further, and he was almost undone by the rapt intensity of Edeena's face. She was staring at him, her own gaze riveted as if she planned to memorize every nuance, every shift of his expression. Framed by the lights of the harbor streaming in through the window, she had to be the most beautiful woman he'd ever seen—and *she was here*, he thought with the ragged edge of his mind. She was his. He couldn't keep her, he would never even try. But for right now, there was nothing to stop him from making her his own.

"What're you thinking," she murmured, leaning down close to him. He sat up more sharply then, taking her mouth with his, his arms snaking around her body to keep them joined as with one quick roll, he reversed their positions, pinning her beneath him with the intimate pressure of their joined bodies. Her hair spilled around her on the pillows and she laughed, the sound one of sheer delight.

"You were thinking you wanted to flip me over?" she asked, and he grinned down at her.

"I'm a big fan of acting on my instincts."

"I'm glad to hear it." Her eyes widened then as he began to move inside her, gently at first, slowly, watching as she stretched beneath him on the bed, her knees bending so she could take him in more deeply.

"Oh . . . yes," she managed and the low, throaty purr

of her words sent his own desire ratcheting up higher again, his pulse beginning to hammer as his gaze swept across her face, her shoulders, the rise and fall of her breasts, the swell of her hips. Her knees bent further and suddenly her legs were rising as well. He caught them in his hands, shifting them so that her calves rested against his shoulders, and she moaned as the position allowed him to sink more deeply into her, pulsing once . . . twice . . .

He could no more stop the flood of pleasure that coursed over him than he could stop a runaway train, and his orgasm caught him almost by surprise. His eyes locked on Edeena's as he convulsed against her, his mind turned inside out. She cried out, too, whether in surprise or shared release he didn't know, couldn't know. All he could hear was the pounding in his own brain, the surge of adrenaline, of need mixing with the utter rightness of having her here with him, perfect and right.

They broke apart and sagged to either side of the bed, Vince up on his feet before the lethargy of his release caught too firm a hold and he lost all will to live, let alone move. He stepped into the bathroom and was back out again within thirty seconds, bearing towels. Edeena curled up on the bed, her beautiful face looking perfectly sated, blissfully content. Exactly as he imagined her, all the way down to her sultry, accented chuckle as she held out her arms.

"I think America should consider you one of its national treasures, Vince Rallis," she murmured as he sank down into her embrace. "I should think it would never let you go."

Chapter Thirteen

Edeena's eyes drifted open as a bright shaft of sunlight lanced across the room, and it was only by squinting that she realized it was coming through a slit in the heavy drape of blackout curtains.

Behind her, his arms still curled around her, Vince groaned. "If I don't shut them exactly right, I pay for it every morning around this time."

"I don't mind," she said. Slipping out of his arms she pushed off the covers and stepped onto the thick rug. In the chair next to the bed, a plush robe rested, and she glanced back to Vince.

"When did this arrive?" she asked.

He rose to one elbow, his eyes glittering as he watched her slip into the soft confection. "You sleep heavily. I had it in one of the guest bathrooms, thought you might want it when you woke up."

"Well, thank you." She kept her words light, but she quickly turned away to focus on the window, annoyed with the ridiculous sensation that she might start crying. What a stupid thing to cry about! It was a robe. Nothing more than a robe.

Cursed

A robe that Vince had thought about putting where she could easily find it, maybe worried that she might feel self-conscious after waking up in the bed of a man she barely knew. A robe that Vince had gone to retrieve silently in the night while she slumbered, taking care not to wake her or disturb her in anyway. A robe she hadn't asked for, hadn't even realized she'd want, yet there it was, just in case.

Edeena thinned her lips as she moved toward the window. She was so going to cry over the stupid robe if she didn't watch it.

She pulled the curtains open with a quick shake, then realized she'd need to walk them all the way back, as if she was raising a curtain on a theatrical production. "These are heavy!" she gasped, laughing.

"Loud, too, or I would have fixed them more completely last night."

She looked back at him. Vince was sitting up in bed now, his face rough with his morning beard. She realized she'd never seen him unshaven, not even one day's worth, and she smiled, smoothing a hand down her robe. "I'll probably need to take you up on that shopping trip before we return to Heron's Point. The girls have no idea what I wore last night, but Cousin Prudence does. I'd feel awkward if she noticed how creased the clothes were."

"Already on it," Vince said. "There's a ladies' shop around the corner that opens at ten, if you don't mind the wait. I figured you could dress in yesterday's clothes and we could walk around the harbor area. There's several fantastic breakfast restaurants, if you're hungry."

Edeena nodded. She was hungry, and a little nervous, too, if she was honest. She didn't know how to think about what had happened between her and Vince. He wasn't a stranger to her, and she did trust him—had trusted him instinctively since the moment she'd met him. And now she'd simply had vindication of that trust. She had the memory of his arms around her, steady and sure, the strength of his body at her command, the knowledge that she had caused him to stare at her wide-eyed with want, with need. It was a heady, almost dangerous memory, and it was hers. Nothing that happened from this point on could take that away from her.

They breakfasted at a sidewalk café and stopped in the first store they found on the walk around the harbor area, Edeena quickly choosing a linen sundress in a bright sea blue, almost the color of the Aegean on a perfect day. She didn't bother trying it on until she got back to Vince's, and he insisted on helping her change into it, which somehow resulted in a long, lingering shower in his unreasonably large bathroom, their hands and bodies intertwined as a pounding waterfall of spray kept the world at bay for another hour . . . then two.

When they finally crossed the bridge back to Sea Haven, Edeena felt almost ridiculously happy, like a teenager giving in to her first vacation crush, savoring it all the more because it wouldn't last, couldn't last. She smiled, looking out the window, imagining what it would have been like if she'd met Vince when she was still a teen and he was some cocky boy on a South Carolina island. They'd have shared stolen kisses and maybe more behind the dunes, staring into each other's eyes and making ridiculous promises that neither one of them believed. They'd have promised to email each other, to visit again, no matter how impossible it was.

"Do I want to know what you're thinking?" Vince rumbled and she glanced over to him. He looked as cool and confident as ever, but he had the same deeply contented look that she suspected she did, and she cocked a brow at him.

"I was thinking that you'd better wipe that smirk off your face before we reach Heron's Point. Cousin Prudence isn't that old, and my sisters aren't idiots."

"Hey, I'm not the one you should be worried about," he said, his words a chiding rumble. "You're the one who looks like you've been pleasured by a master."

Edeena burst into laughter, and they drove like that for the remaining twenty minutes it took to reach the big old house, her chuckles subsiding only as they approached the mansion. Even Vince seemed to be driving more slowly now, lengthening the time that remained for the two of them, together.

"It really is a pretty house," she said, gazing up at Heron's Point. "I'm not sure how we're going to keep from selling it, with father so eager to finalize all of mom's financials now that he's remarried. But I hope, for Prudence's sake, that the market stays soft."

"She's done a fine job with it," Vince said noncommittally, and Edeena felt the first layer of distance build between them. Her selling the house was perhaps the clearest indication she could give that she had no intention of returning to Sea Haven, and that there was certainly no reason to see him again. She wanted to take back the words, to offer reassurances, but what could she say?

Nothing. It was enough that they would have the next few days together.

"Do you . . . do you think we could travel a bit more tomorrow?" she asked almost shyly, aware of Vince's sharp glance. He cruised the SUV to the edge of the parking circle and slowed to a stop. "I was thinking we could go down to Savannah, if you're free?"

She glanced back to him and found him staring her, an expression she'd never seen before in his eyes. "If you don't have time, that's fine. I completely under—"

"No," he said, cutting her off. "I have plenty of time." He worked his face into a smile, but it was still almost too fierce for comfort. "We can definitely go. You should see Savannah. It's one of the most beautiful cities in the South, even if it is in Georgia."

His light words didn't account for the intensity of his gaze, but Edeena nodded quickly.

"We'll bring your sisters, I think," Vince continued.

She was so startled, she couldn't stop her response. "But why?"

Instantly, she regretted her words. Of course they should bring her sisters. They'd love Savannah, love the idea of a road trip, love traveling with Vince. How could she be so selfish as to keep him all to herself?

She realized Vince hadn't responded, however, and she looked up, blinking as she realized his stare had not wavered. "Vince?"

"Don't get me wrong, Edeena. I want nothing more than to travel with you, anywhere, any way. But if I get you back in the car again with the promise of a road trip off this island and it's just the two of us, I can't be responsible for stopping. The next thing you know, you'll look up and we'll be all the way to the Grand Canyon, and I still won't want to let you go."

His words were calm, almost matter of fact, and of course he was joking, but Edeena couldn't stop the blush that flared in her cheeks. Vince saved her from having to respond by easing open his door, and she followed suit, smoothing down her dress as he grabbed her new tote bag and shopping bags out of the SUV.

By the time he reached her, handing her a bag, he was once again smiling and professional, and she found herself wondering if that exchange between them had actually been spoken, or if her fantasies were playing out in her mind.

She didn't have time to consider it any longer, however. The door at the top of the grand staircase burst open and Marguerite came storming out, looking credibly distraught, even for Marguerite.

"Edeena!" she cried, beckoning with her hand. "Thank God, hurry up! Father is on the phone! He seems to think we're all coming back tomorrow!"

Vince stepped into the house with the bags that Edeena had dropped as well as the ones he'd been carrying, his attention drawn to the back porch where he could hear Edeena's voice, loud but calm, speaking in a language that sounded a lot like Greek and yet clearly wasn't. Prudence met him at the door, gesturing him off to the side parlor.

"What happened?" he asked, his mind racing through the possibilities. "Is there a problem with the family?"

Prudence's lips twisted sharply. "Not exactly," she said. "Silas was primarily calling to see if Edeena had had a chance to open the package he'd sent her most recently."

Immediately Vince remembered Rob's text from the day before. "More files," he said.

"More files, yes. Files and a letter demanding Edeena's summary return for her engagement ball."

"Engagement . . ." Vince looked at Prudence in horror, but not surprise. Nothing that happened with these women anymore would surprise him, he decided. "How is that possible?"

"Apparently, there are more edicts set forth about a woman's twenty-seventh birthday in Garronia than we first believed. Edeena doesn't become her father's property to marry off until *after* her birthday, but he's allowed to begin taking steps ten days prior." Prudence made another face. "Spinsterism was very much frowned on in the early days of Garronia. You were by no means expected to produce an heir out of hand, but by God, you were to be in the right position to do so if the need ever fell to you."

"And because we've reached that window of opportunity . . ."

"He's exercising his paternal right to be a horrible, odious man. Never mind that he virtually left Edeena to raise her sisters alone except for when he needed them to execute command performances for the king and queen." She babbled on, fluttering her hands. "The queen is Silas's cousin by marriage, a lovely woman. Treated the children like her blood relations."

"But she can't do anything to stop this?"

"Apparently, no. I'm afraid I've let my knowledge of royal conduct lapse, but I contacted another cousin the moment Silas first called—which was ten a.m., by the way. We told him Edeena was out speaking to the real estate agent, which mollified the cretin, but then he called again at eleven, and just now again."

Vince checked his watch out of habit. "Noon. He would've continued calling every hour, wouldn't he?"

"Most likely. The poor younger sisters are in a state. Neither of them had any idea that the files Edeena was perusing were potential candidates. She always was one to try and hide the truth from them." Prudence's lips tightened. "Her poor, sweet mother felt so badly about escaping as often as she did, but she always assumed she'd be able to make it up to the girls, that she'd be there for them as they grew into young women, ready to launch into the world."

"She didn't worry about the curse?"

Prudence shook her head. "She didn't worry about much of anything, I'm afraid. Marguerite takes that from her. And, truth be told, she was a bit of a force of nature. Who's to say that Ari and Edeena wouldn't have found their way to each other, had her mother still been alive?"

"Ari," Vince said gruffly, tamping down the surge of completely inappropriate jealousy at Prudence's words. "That's the Crown Prince?"

"Yes. Recently engaged to an American, to the shock and consternation of Silas. I think this entire curse business has quite sent him around the bend."

Caroline appeared in the doorway, looking wan. Vince realized that there was no more sound of conversation from the other room. "He's hung up," she said, but she looked miserable.

"And?" Prudence asked, giving voice to Vince's own question. He'd rather not descend on Edeena without knowing the worst.

Caro lifted one shoulder. "She simply kept agreeing to whatever he said—yes, yes, yes. I don't even know what she was agreeing to, but by the end of it he'd stopped shouting." She glanced at Vince, her expression turning grimmer. "She's flying out tomorrow though."

"Tomorrow!" Prudence protested, and she bustled forward past Caroline, her flowing powder blue day dress rustling as she swept into the hall. Caroline gave Vince a small, sad smile.

"She'll do it, too, no matter what Prudence has about to say. I think she'd meant to all this time."

"Do what?" Vince asked. Caro turned, beckoning him to follow, and he fell into step with her.

"Edeena has always had it in her head that one of us would need to beat the curse or all of us would be subject to Silas's madness on the subject for the rest of our lives. She of course took it upon herself to be that person, but though she and Prince Aristotle grew up practically in each other's back pockets, they didn't care for each other that way. Still, whenever she would research the viable princely candidates in the world, she'd simply get depressed. So there was no point in pursuing that until she had to. Then Ari died, and the whole country was plunged into mourning—

"Wait, what?" Vince stopped her. "The Crown Prince died?"

"Well, everyone thought he did. And anyway, Silas stopped badgering us for awhile. It was . . . quite lovely, really. He found someone else to marry, and then his wife turned up pregnant—which has occupied him quite completely." Though Caroline was spilling what had to be the family's most scandalous secrets she seemed unconcerned, her attention fixed on the far end of the house. Edeena would be out on the back porch, Vince suspected. It was her favorite place in the building. "Anyway, that reprieve ended when Ari returned, especially when he had the audacity to have fallen in love with an American." She gave a rueful laugh. "We've had quite an uptick in our American betrothals of late."

"And he turned his focus back on Edeena and the rest of you," Vince finished for her. "According to Prudence, he can legitimately order you back."

"He can, yes," Caroline said. "Whether we accept his order is another thing entirely."

She stepped out onto the back porch and Edeena turned, taking in Caro and then Vince. She started for him almost instinctively, it seemed, then caught herself and turned back toward the panoramic view of trees waving in the afternoon breeze.

"I'm glad you're here, Caroline," she said quietly. "I don't want to have to say this again."

"You shouldn't have to say it at all," snapped Marguerite, angrier than Vince had ever seen her. "This entire curse business is exactly what's wrong with our country! Who lives by these kind of rules anymore? It's ridiculous!"

"Father says he wants us all back, but he doesn't, not really," Edeena said, her words firm and measured. "He wants me, and the two of you only when there's a wedding to attend."

"Well there's only going to be about a half *dozen* of those coming up," Marguerite cut in again. "It's been an American Invasion over the past several weeks. And good thing, too. Americans don't believe in curses."

"They don't have to," Caroline said mildly. "They have politics."

"Enough," Edeena said, lifting her hands. "The important thing is, once I'm there, he'll not badger you. My birthday is in a few days, and after that there will be a host of planning, balls, paperwork—he'll be too busy cackling over his plans coming to fruition to worry about you."

"But what about you?" Marguerite demanded. "You can't seriously believe you'll be happy in some kind of . . . some kind of weird arranged marriage. It was bad enough when Aristotle was still in the picture. He, at least, was hot. But I've seen what Garronia has to offer, and it's gross, Edeena! You know it's gross."

Despite the gravity of the discussion, Vince fought to keep from laughing. Edeena, however, stared at Marguerite, her face scrunching up until she gave up the attempt. Shaking her head, she allowed herself a wry grin. "It is kind of gross," she said. "But I still have to go through with it, play the part that falls to me. I've been half-expecting it for years, so in a way it will be kind of a relief."

The way she said the words grated against Vince's nerves, even as her sisters seemed to be moving toward acceptance.

"But tomorrow, Edeena?" Prudence said, wringing her hands. "Truly? It's so far to travel so quickly, all by yourself."

"Prudence, I—"

Vince had had enough. He stepped forward, and his voice filled the room. "She's not going alone," he said crisply. "I'm going with her. As her security detail."

Chapter Fourteen

Edeena folded and unfolded the linen napkin on her lap for the fifty-seventh time, staring out the window at the gorgeous swath of ocean. The plane banked, bringing them back toward the mainland of Garronia, and the landscape changed to that of the rugged hills she so loved, punctuated by the jewel of the capital city, glinting under the sunlight.

Had she only been gone a couple of weeks? It seemed like it had been a lifetime since she'd herded her sisters on the plane, secretly wondering if they'd be stopped before the aircraft had even left the ground. When they'd successfully lifted off, Edeena's worries hadn't gone away, they'd merely shifted, eventually leading her back to exactly this moment, where she would be hauled back to her father's presence with only the slimmest of plans on how to evade his outrageous decrees.

"You're going to fray that thing into thread," Vince commented beside her, and she stopped mid-fold, dropping the napkin self-consciously to her lap.

"Sorry," she said. "I guess I . . ."

"Thought you'd have more time. I know." Vince said the words without censure, but Edeena still colored at the comment. She'd been repeating a variation on that theme for most of the multiple flights they'd navigated, nearly a full day's worth of flying. When she wasn't fretting, Vince had convinced her to try to sleep. She'd ended up more than a few times nestled against his shoulder, but he'd never once complained, never once disturbed her rest, when she finally dropped off.

Now he looked as cool and crisp as he had the first day she'd seen him in the Charleston airport, and she felt like a frazzled mess.

As if reading her thoughts, Vince shook his head. "You're absolutely lovely, as always," he murmured quietly. He glanced toward the window as the plane began its descent toward Garronia's international airport. "Who will be meeting us, Silas?"

She smiled faintly. He'd taken to calling her father by his first name rather than emphasizing the relationship between them, seeming to realize that it helped stiffen Edeena's spine to think of her father as simply another man standing in her way instead of her flesh and blood relation—a relation who, under Garronois law, still had an unreasonable amount of power over her.

"I don't think so. He abhors anything that takes him away from his cronies at the club or his wife. She should be due to give birth any moment now." Her brows went up. "I wonder if that's why he's pushing this so hard? Maybe he's worried that the coming of the new baby will take up his time, and he won't have time to shepherd me into marriage with some witless noble."

"I see your attitude about the coming social whirl hasn't improved," Vince said drily.

"No, it has not." Edeena collapsed back in her seat as the captain's voice spoke over the loudspeaker again, sharing his instructions first in English, then in Garronois. She smiled to hear her native language spoken so rapidly—something else that had been strange about living in South Carolina. Everyone had talked in a soft, unhurried fashion, as if the words needed time to ripen to their full potential before they could be spoken aloud.

"Either way, we'll likely be met at the bottom of the stairs by a car," Edeena said. "As nominal royalty, it's considered more genteel for me to go through customs in a private venue versus with the rank and file." She managed a grin in his direction. "As my security detail, you'll be temporarily elevated above said rank and file."

"I'm honored," Vince returned, but his smile was easy, and his studied good nature was having the desired effect on her mood. By the time they exited the plane into the warm, welcoming sunshine, she'd almost decided she could endure anything the day threw at her.

Then she saw the limo waiting at the edge of the tarmac.

"Oh, no," she said, stopping for a moment before Vince bumped into her.

"Crowd coming through," he murmured and her feet started again of their own volition, while her attention remained arrested on the vehicle in the distance. They reached the bottom of the stair and Vince set down her carry-on, following her gaze.

"Who are they?"

"Well, I . . ."

A small golf cart puttered up beside them, and a man jumped out from behind the wheel, speaking in rapid Garronois. "Countess Saleri, if you and your guest will come with me?"

Vince looked at her hard when the man reached for her bag, but she nodded, and Vince obediently gave up the tote, watching darkly as she walked around the cart. "Please get in the back, Vince. I'm sorry, I didn't expect this."

Vince's gaze shot from her to the driver, but he didn't ask questions, contenting himself with slinging his big body into the back seat of the cart. The driver whisked them away toward the enormous limo, and Edeena made up her mind. She didn't want Vince to be caught off guard, no matter how high-handed her extended relatives were.

"I'm very honored that we have been sent a car by Queen Catherine," she said, turning to Vince. "Our bags will be picked up and transferred . . ." she glanced at the driver.

"To the castle," he said blithely, and Edeena winced. *The castle!* The queen must be serious about wanting to interrogate her before Silas got his crack at it.

Vince's voice floated forward, deadpan. "The castle," he said mildly, in perhaps a stronger South Carolina drawl than he typically used. "How very nice."

Edeena pursed her lips, but the small burst of laughter billowing up within her went a far distance toward elevating her mood. She and Vince were ushered into the vehicle, and she relaxed further on realizing the queen herself was not sitting in the car, waiting for them. She was known to ambush people right on the tarmac if she felt she needed to.

"Bugged?" Vince asked now, looking around the interior of the limo.

She shrugged. It wasn't as if they wouldn't be monitored the moment they entered the royal residence, but she hadn't been going in and out of the castle since she was a tween without learning anything. There were always pockets where you could secure privacy, if you were careful. "Probably not," she answered truthfully.

"Then what do I need to know about this Queen Catherine? She's related to Silas?"

"Cousins, technically, through marriage, distant enough that there would have been no issue with me marrying Aristotle." Edeena didn't miss the subtle tensing of Vince's jaw, and she rolled her eyes. "That was never going to happen, you should know. Neither one of us wanted it. The idea was way too close to an arranged marriage."

He glanced at her dubiously, and she pushed his shoulder. "What's going on now is different. I need to do this." Even as she said the words the knot of dismay tightened in her stomach. As much as she *did* need to do this, Edeena certainly wasn't looking forward to the whirl of social requirements her father had laid out in his letter. Maybe the queen could help, but she doubted it. The edicts governing the behavior of the nobility predated Queen Catherine by hundreds of years.

They pulled up to the castle a few short minutes later, and Edeena at least got to enjoy seeing the impressive building through a stranger's eyes. Vince whistled low as they entered the outer gate then rolled forward into the lushly manicured courtyard. The primary residence of the royal family was a large stone edifice cut directly into the wall of a cliff, overlooking the whole of the capital city from its perch in the mountain. Though Vince couldn't see the view from here, he certainly got the idea of where the castle was located as evidenced by the clear blue sky surrounding it.

"Nice place," he allowed, and she nodded. Then her eyes narrowed as she saw who was standing on the front stair.

"Brace yourself," she murmured. "The queen has come out to get the first look at the American."

Vince turned to peer through the windows, but there was only so much he could see now that they were nearly upon the stairs. "Do I, um, bow?" he asked, suddenly frowning. "Do you people bow? I didn't really think about brushing up on my royal etiquette. I should have."

"You don't bow," Edeena said, watching as the queen started skipping lightly down the stairs, far too eager for a woman nearly thirty years her senior. "But you may be subjected to some seriously royal hugging."

Vince stepped out of the car in one easy motion, turning immediately to hand out Edeena—in part because it was the polite thing to do, in part to use the poor woman as a shield from the brightly smiling, elegantly regal force of nature who was striding toward them down the long white stone path.

"Edeena Arabelle Catherine Saleri, you are, if possible, even more beautiful today than when I saw you last, and I didn't think nature could possibly improve on its already magnificent work. Welcome home, darling."

Vince realized with a start that the queen was speaking English, which could only be for his benefit. She enfolded Edeena into a hug that appeared truly affectionate, before stepping back and surveying him with a graciously appraising eye.

Edeena cleared her throat. "Queen Catherine, please allow me to introduce Vince Rallis, of Charleston, South Carolina."

"Vince, you say?" the queen asked, her eyes dancing. "From my intelligence, the man's name is Prince."

Edeena looked frozen for a moment, and Vince stepped forward, holding out his hand. The queen it took it with both of hers.

"Prince is a nickname from my childhood, your majesty," he said, using the form of address Google recommended when he looked it up during the flight, Edeena sacked out on his shoulder. "My given name is Vince, and as I'm sure your intelligence provided, no one would ever mistake me for an actual prince."

"I suppose I should ask Edeena that, yes?" the queen asked, swiveling back to Edeena. "He protected you and your sisters during your stay on the island?"

CURSED

She tutted, turning toward the castle and taking Edeena's arm. Vince fell into step behind them, uncomfortable as a phalanx of guards flowed around their trio in a loose oval. "I've never visited the Contos house on Sea Haven island, though of course your mother mentioned it often. I daresay it was one of her most treasured properties. How is Prudence doing?"

The women chatted as if they were old friends, and Vince sensed an unusually intent stare spearing him in the back. Rather than ignoring it the way he probably should, he looked back to see a man who was almost his equal in height and build, peering at him curiously. When Vince lifted his brows, staring back, the man merely smiled but said nothing.

The whole lot of them mounted the stairs and entered a sweeping foyer, far grander than anything Vince had seen in the famed residences of Charleston old money, but with the added resonance of being a space well lived-in. The floor was an endless sea of marble, with a long, thickly-plush carpet runner down the center, and fixtures of gold and silver lined the walls. Paintings hung at regular intervals, and though Vince was no art scholar, he somehow suspected that they all were originals and had been painted by people whose names even he would recognize.

"You must be famished. I recall the flight to America is almost unreasonably long and broken up, and not merely because Garronia is so far east. There simply isn't an easy trajectory, no?"

She directed this last question to Vince and he straightened, peeling his gaze away from the army of staff as they settled a dozen or more trays on an already overstuffed table, before another tuxedoed staff member swept in behind them, offering champagne on a tray.

Vince took one to be polite and immediately began scouting out locations to deposit the glass at his earliest opportunity.

The queen seemed to be one step ahead of him. "Mr. Rallis, while your dedication to your assignment is gratifying, I assure you, Edeena and yourself are now in good hands. We're being attended by members of the Garronia National Security Force. In fact, you remind me . . . Captain Korba, Mr. Rallis here has been kind enough to ally his personal security firm with the interests of Garronia. Would you mind showing him our security protocols — to the extent that you're able — so he can feel assured of Edeena's safety while he's our guest?"

Vince blinked at the barrage of words, meeting the gaze of the man who'd stared at him so disconcertingly on the way into the palace. To his surprise, the man offered him a knowing smile.

"Of course," Captain Korba said, bowing to his queen before turning again to Vince. "If you'll come this way?"

Vince hesitated, and Edeena's soft words cut through his confusion. "I'll be fine, Vince. The queen and I simply need to catch up."

With that he nodded briskly to Korba, and allowed the burly man to lead him from the room.

They hadn't gone more than a few steps when Korba's chuckle finally escaped him. "Don't look so poleaxed, Mr. Rallis. Queen Catherine does this to everyone."

"You're not really going to show me your security systems, are you? That's insane."

"It's a fairly common occurrence, actually," Korba countered. "We bring in diplomats, royals from all over the world, and their security teams want to know what we have in place. We show them enough so they understand the rudiments of our system, so that they feel comfortable. And we are protected, here in Garronia."

Vince quirked him a glance. "Because of your remote location?"

"No," Korba grinned at him. "Because Garronia, she takes care of her own. You'll learn this, if you stay long."

The captain angled down another hallway, then stepped into a room that was nothing at all like a security center. Instead it looked like a shrine to the royal family, with walls of pictures from floor to ceiling, some clearly of the current royals, but far more chronicling what he suspected was several preceding generations of the Andris family.

The room wasn't empty of people, either. As they entered, two men turned to watch them approach, so alike in size and demeanor that they had to be brothers. "Aristotle and Kristos Andris," Korba said, not quite under his breath. "Princes, but don't let that stand in the way of your opinion of them. They are honorable men."

It was clear that the acoustics in the room were excellent, as both men grinned at Korba as he approached with Vince.

"Aristotle Andris," the older of the brothers said,

holding out his hand. "I understand you've had the unenviable task of keeping Edeena safe from herself these past few weeks."

"Vince Rallis," Vince said, shaking the man's hand. "I've made Countess Saleri and her sisters a top priority for my firm."

"You'd have to," said the younger man. Kristos reached out his hand and grasped Vince's warmly. "Kristos Andris. You know why you're here?"

Vince glanced around the room, then noticed a fourth man who'd apparently stepped inside the far door while he'd been going through the introductions. That man, dressed more formally than the brothers in a sharply cut tuxedo, didn't approach them, but stood with his hands behind his back, apparently looking at nothing at all.

Vince brought his attention back to Kristos and Ari, then Korba. "My guess is that whatever is about to happen in Edeena's life is something the Crown would like managed most carefully. The queen has decided, based on what information I don't know, that I'm a suitable inside man to help carry out that management, while presumably keeping Edeena safe from the machinations of her father." He paused, taking in their unmoving expressions. "Am I close?"

"Quite." The voice was from the fourth man, who'd moved silently toward him during Vince's speech. Part of him wondered if they'd have a throw down here in this well-appointed room. The men weren't antagonistic, exactly, but there was the air of a foursome who was always up for a good brawl if the situation presented itself.

The fourth man reached him, held out his hand. His hair was lighter than the others, his skin less olive-toned, and while he appeared fit, he gave the impression of elegance instead of bulk. Vince shook the proffered hand.

"Stefan Mihal, diplomatic ambassador," he said crisply. Vince suspected he was more than that, but let it pass. "The little family drama you've found yourself in has been brewing for a long time, and the queen has decided it has carried on for the last generation. As a Saleri relation, albeit a distant one, she's well versed in the curse and its impact on the Saleri children. She has a particular fondness for Edeena, and would like to see her married to whomever she chooses."

Vince rocked back on his heels. "If she chooses to marry at all."

Stefan shrugged. "That is a matter of less flexibility in most Garronois families, but it's a more complicated matter than we have time for. What matters is this. You'll be assigned as Edeena's security liaison during your stay here, with Crown approval—something Silas cannot balk. We're worried that he might do something stupid."

"Stupid as in . . ."

"Abduction and intimidation. Edeena's lot will be challenging enough in the coming several days, we'd like to ensure she's making her decisions of her own free will."

Vince looked at them, a growing sense of unease developing in his gut. "You're seriously going to make her go through with this."

It was Aristotle who sighed. "Edeena will make herself go through with this, is more the issue. It's going to happen. Edeena will become the figurehead for her family, with the unenviable task of attempting to draw the sprawling group together for her upcoming engagement ball."

"Engagement ball," Vince said flatly. "Except she's not engaged."

The men looked at him with a sense of amusement, interest, and maybe something else in their eyes, an emotion Vince couldn't quite figure out. Either way, as one they answered his exasperated comment with one of their own:

"She will be."

Chapter Fifteen

Edeena tried to keep her smile steady as she stood in the center of three bustling women, all of them fussing with her hair, her gown, her face. By now she should have been used to it. It was her third day in Garronia, she'd not left the royal palace, and she'd not seen her father. But she'd done everything else for her family other than dance on the head of a pin.

The brunch with the foreign diplomats, communicating her value to the press corps, who'd picked up the recent arrival of the Countess Saleri with breathless anticipation. The extended luncheon with the queen's "closest friends," a gaggle of legendary gossips whose necks and ears and wrists and fingers had been practically encrusted with jewels handed down through generations in their families. The women had thrown themselves whole-heartedly into the question of Edeena's marital options, but had come to only one conclusion: none of the foreign princes would be sufficient to address the core requirement of the Saleri curse.

Bringing their highly divided family back together

again.

Edeena grimaced as the queen's head dressmaker gave a particularly brutal tug on her evening gown. It was hard to believe that the Saleris would come together at all if even the father and daughter couldn't see fit to endure each other's company.

Silas had good reason, of course. His wife, being far younger than he, was still in her mid-thirties, and her pregnancy was considered high-risk. God love the man, he truly did seem to care for his bride, and every moment he was able, he stayed by her side. Edeena had yet to see her, had been given to understand that the mother-to-be didn't have the stamina to face a stepdaughter less than a decade younger than she was, and Edeena hadn't pushed it. Lord knew she had enough on her plate with the queen's social schedule.

A movement at the door caught her eye, the palace's staffers standing aside to admit a new man, and for the first time that evening, her heart gave a little flip of joy. "Vince," she said.

She'd intended it to be a mere greeting, but two of the three women fussing with her looked up sharply, and even she heard the note of desperation in her voice. She colored, steadying her next words with a ruthless hand. "We're almost finished here. Have you had a chance to check the ballroom?"

"Security is at the ready. Your father hasn't arrived, but he's not expected for another hour or more." Unlike hers, Vince's was voice was perfectly controlled, his words crisp and cool. He'd been like that since they'd first arrived, a rock of calm in the middle of a building storm. She hadn't seen nearly enough of him as she'd wanted, but every time she was in public or met with any group, inside or out of the palace, he was there, escorting her to and from rooms, buildings, and vehicles with a warm smile, an easy touch, a comforting presence.

But they hadn't been alone for more than two minutes since she'd set foot back in her homeland.

Part of her knew she should feel lucky for what she got. Vince was a foreigner, an interloper many would say, and it was only the queen's approval of his presence that allowed him to be near to her at all. His presence had caused quite a stir among the tittering matrons of the queen's set, especially when the queen had called him Prince in front of the women. There ensued yet another explanation—by Vince himself, with his unfailingly gracious and professional demeanor—yet again why he was known as Prince among his friends. The women had been enraptured, but Edeena couldn't blame them; they didn't get a lot of polite foreigners willing to give them the time of day, despite their vaunted status, whereas Vince seemed comfortable catering to them. All that time he spent with his cousins' families, Edeena suspected, and remembering the boisterous dinner party at Vince's parents' house made her smile.

The expression brought spontaneous applause from her handlers.

"Yes!" said the dressmaker, the bossiest one of the set. "That is the smile that will go best with the way you have been styled this day, Countess Saleri," she said, speaking in rapid Garronois. "This is your official introduction to society, where you will see all the young men vying for your hand. Your engagement ball is in only a few days, and then you may be more sophisticated and arch—but not today, eh?"

Edeena lifted her brows. "This truly is the way it's done?" she asked the woman, for what seemed to be the millionth time. "I go from blushing ingénue to sophisticated socialite in a matter of three days, and people think this is legitimate?"

"It doesn't need to be legitimate, it is pageantry," the woman assured her. She was the queen's own primary dresser, and Edeena had found her to be a font of information—even if it was information Edeena was finding impossible to digest. "There will be no one in that ballroom who doesn't believe you've already found your partner. The game will be to guess who you've chosen."

"But I haven't even met these men," Edeena groaned, suddenly glad to be speaking in Garronois. She hadn't had the privacy to fill Vince in on the more ridiculous elements of this farce, but she got the impression someone had. Even now he watched her impassively, his hands crossed behind his back, waiting for her to be released from her keepers. "Surely they realize how much of a farce this is."

"They would not be here this night unless they were willing to consider the possibility of matrimony, my dear. You are making this far too complicated." She stood back, eyeing her handiwork with a studied eye, then nodding with approval. "In most marriages, you laugh, you dance, then you decide if you will suit. In

Cursed

Garronia, at least for the noble class, it is simply the other way around."

"You decide you will suit, you dance . . . and then you laugh?" Edeena asked.

"With the right man, you will know, eh? And that is who you choose. Come now," she said briskly when Edeena's demeanor clearly didn't convey the appropriate level of enthusiasm. "There is an entire roomful of right men waiting to dance with you beyond that door, each hoping to some degree to make you laugh." The woman tucked a curl of Edeena's hair behind her ear, and gave her a reassuring smile. "There are many women who would wish for this choice, no?"

And that's, of course, what did it. The dressmaker was right—all of them were right. Edeena had been blessed to be born into a family of grace and privilege, and her only requirement was that she found a man with whom she could spend her life in reasonable contentment. For that small sacrifice, her entire family would be strengthened.

She needed to grow up.

She smiled more determinedly now at the dressmaker, and the woman nodded, though her gaze was still assessing. "Not so much focus, my dear. Remember the smile as you were recalling a happy memory. That's what we want. You are not assessing marriage prospects as much as being a young woman, delighted to be at a party that is filled with possibility. You can do that for me, yes? It will make all who have helped you so happy to see their work showcased with your beauty *and* your joy."

Edeena glanced around at the hopeful faces

surrounding her, young women and old giving her shy smiles—some of them dreamy smiles, as if they wondered what they would do in her position, who they would pick, how they would dance.

The whole thing was impossible.

Still as she turned back to the dressmaker, her gaze caught Vince's eyes as he stared at her. Despite his stoic and perfectly professional demeanor, in his gaze was something more than calm assurance—it was dark, intense, and it made her feel admired and adored. Something about this dress, this look was meeting with his approval, and that more than anything fueled the smile she turned on the queen's dressmaker.

"Yes!" the woman exclaimed, clapping her hands together. "Now, you are ready."

Vince walked with Edeena down the wide, gracious hallway, aware of the strange glances he was getting. It'd been like that since he'd arrived at the castle, had only gotten worse after he'd been assigned as Edeena's bodyguard. He suspected it was because he wasn't exactly acting like her bodyguard.

He'd trailed local officials, even mid-range celebrities before, and the routine had always been the same. He was present, he was part of the entourage, but he didn't get too close. He didn't let anyone crowd the client, but he didn't crowd the client either.

With Edeena, however, he *was* the entourage. No other security was conspicuous as they met and dined with various rotations of royal relatives or hangers-on, and he acted less as Edeena's hired help than as her trusted friend. Even here tonight, instead of walking respectfully behind her, she was on his arm—and he was dressed in a freaking tuxedo. Worse, Dimitri Korba, who'd turned out to be a captain of the Garronia National Security Force, hadn't given him permission to carry his weapon inside the castle. Instead, he'd made him go low tech, with a blade for close range strapped to his leg. Vince had trained with knives, but he found he was far more at ease when they traveled outside the castle, and he could holster his own Sig Sauer.

He sensed Edeena slowing and he glanced down at her, catching the tightness of her expression. "You okay?"

Her smile instantly returned to her face, though there still no one to see them. She picked up her pace as well.

"Yes . . . yes, of course. I got distracted."

He nodded. "This is some sort of speed dating kind of thing, right? You go around and talk to all these different guys, the ones you've read those files on, and then . . . what, vote a set of them off the island?"

Edeena burst out a laugh, drawing the attention of some of the staffers hurrying down the corridor with them, including the hatchet-faced woman who'd been chattering at Edeena nonstop when he'd stepped into the dressing room. Which was an actual thing, to his surprise—an entire room given over simply to dress important people in advance of their introduction to the castle guests. He couldn't imagine such a room would be all that necessary, but it'd looked like it was well-used.

"It's rather a bit less dramatic than that," Edeena said, and she squeezed his arm, the move so unconsciously affectionate that he felt like he'd scored a win. When she spoke again, Edeena sounded more relaxed as well. "Essentially, I meet all these charming men who've been kind enough to offer for my hand and subject themselves to the vetting process. Over the next few days, I meet a select few of them in their own homes a second time — though that's optional — and then, at the grand engagement ball at the end of the week, I announce who I'd like to accept a betrothal offer from. It's technically still up to the gentleman in question to go through the motions of claiming my hand, but they are prepared ahead of time, usually. They've never not come through with a suitable proposal."

"That'd probably be a lot to spring on a guy out of the blue, yeah," Vince said. These people were batshit, he decided. Totally and completely.

Edeena continued, oblivious to his thoughts. "It has happened, of course. Silas chose my mother out of the blue, I've been told, and she had to scramble for a response. She'd been so certain he was going to pick another woman."

"Well, your mom would have had to go through this same charade otherwise, then, wouldn't she?"

Edeena shook her head. "She wasn't the eldest child, so no. It's more for a succession planning issue, not to put every one of our young people through the wringer. It's only on occasion that parents use it to truly ruin their children's happiness."

Despite Edeena's light tone, Vince grimaced. He'd not met Silas, but he would tonight, and everyone who mentioned the man's name in the palace did so with the undertone of menace. He couldn't seem to get a straight story on what slight the elder Saleri had made to the royal family, but it had been grave. Only Silas's clear focus on his ailing wife seemed to be cause for anyone to cut him any slack.

Now they slowed in earnest, and Vince glanced ahead, realizing they were queuing up in some sort of reception line. "What's this?"

"You'll be able to take me to the door, but then I walk out solo, the star attraction of the show," Edeena said, her lips twisting in self derision. "It'll be a miracle if I don't fall down or turn into a chicken."

"Tell me that is *not* part of the curse."

"What? No!" Edeena chuckled again, the peal of her soft laughter drawing more glances and smiles this time, as older people he didn't recognize filed through the door. When it came time for him to let Edeena go through, he reluctantly disengaged her from his arm.

"Do I look okay?" she whispered, and she was gazing up at him, not the attendant who was doing something to the back of her dress.

He looked down at her and for a long moment, found he couldn't speak. He'd had the pleasure of seeing Edeena Saleri in a dozen different settings over the past few weeks, from the day she came bustling off the airplane in Charleston to the walk along the labyrinth on Pearl Island to the magical, almost impossible-to-believe night she'd spent in his arms and in his bed. Every time he saw a new side of her, he swore it was by far the most beautiful of all.

But here in Garronia, it was different. This was her home, and as crazy as these people were, they were her people, and she loved them. Dressed up like some sort of fairy tale princess, her eyes shining with a curious mixture of hope and apprehension as she gazed at him, he realized that here, once again, she had outdone herself.

"You are, by far, the most beautiful woman I have ever seen, Countess Edeena Saleri," he said quietly, gathering her limp hands with his and bringing them together to hold in front of his chest. "I've never seen you look more perfect than you do right now."

Edeena's eyes widened in sudden, stunned response, but her face was wreathed in an incandescent smile even as she was nudged by a small, older man in a fastidious tuxedo, speaking something to her in Garronois.

She started to turn, then spun back to him for the barest moment, standing up on her toes to kiss Vince softly on the lips, barely a whisper, not enough to mar her makeup despite the sudden squawk of the women who had followed along in their wake.

"Thank you!" she said urgently, her eyes shining, then she was turning again and sailing through the door.

A loud roll of applause sounded and Vince instantly stood back, aware that he wouldn't be allowed to take up his role until the rest of the muckety-mucks were through the line, but his heart swelled with pride at the response to Edeena's introduction to the crowd. She really was an honor to her family, and her sisters should be proud of her. Her father, too, if he was somewhere in the crowd already. Vince hoped he was. Silas needed to see his daughter through the eyes of others, not through his own myopically warped view of what she could do for him.

"You!" The slap to his arm came so unexpectedly and from such a low trajectory that Vince fell back, his arms lifting in confusion on how to defend himself against the attack. He looked down and instantly recognized the harridan from the dressing room, the one who'd cinched Edeena into her gown and proclaimed her ready, like a perfectly frosted cake.

Now she was standing in front of him with her beetle-dark eyes fixed on him malevolently, her mouth cast into a bitter grimace. "You!" she spat again.

What the hell had he done to upset the old woman?

"Yes, miss—" he attempted, but the woman batted at him again.

"You must go in there and be where she can see you at all times," the woman said imperiously. "Go! You must go."

"I . . . what?" Vince managed, casting around a glance for help. No one else seemed to be concerned that he was being accosted by the tiny dressmaker.

"Today of all days, the young countess must show the people in the crowd—not all of whom are who they seem—that she is a lovely, vibrant young woman who is strong enough to pull off what no Saleri has done in hundreds of years. For that," she poked Vince again, "she needs to smile. She needs to laugh. She needs to be as beautiful and strong as she truly is. And when she looks at you, she is."

With a strength that belied her small figure, she jerked his arm forward, pushing him into line.

"So go!" she commanded.

Chapter Sixteen

Edeena smiled with genuine relief as the applause died away, moving forward as protocol dictated to first greet the king and queen.

King Jasen beamed at her, polite as always, but Queen Catherine looked her over with a shrewd eye. "I'll have to give Magdalene a bonus," she said mildly, and Edeena curtsied, then turned a little to show off the dress's elegant drape.

"If this is what she came up with for the matchmaker's dance, I can't imagine what she has planned for the engagement ball." *Engagement ball.* Even saying those words sounded ridiculous, as if she was talking about someone else. Still, Edeena kept her smile steady as the queen laughed.

"Tonight is all about being the wide-eyed ingénue. The engagement ball is about being a woman with a choice to make. Trust me, you'll like what Magdalene comes up with. She is always astute at what will create the perfect impression." The queen offered her an arm, and Edeena blinked in surprise.

"But the line—?"

"Jasen can handle the meet and greets, can't you dear?" The queen raised a brow to her husband, who looked like he was barely able to restrain himself from rolling his eyes. "You're the guest of honor, Edeena, and the round of the room is considered de rigueur." She frowned, still looking at Jasen. "We haven't had one of these in awhile, have we."

"For good reason," the king responded mildly. "Most sane parents have no need to put their children through this public exhibition. If there's a need for a succession discussion, it can be held behind closed doors, and not with all of this lurid display."

"Lurid," his wife scoffed, though she smiled at him with clear affection. "You simply don't like wearing a suit when there's no one official around to see you in it." She turned again to Edeena and tugged her along. "But come, we've much ground to cover in a short while. Have you already made your selection?"

Edeena's heart sank as she allowed the queen to guide her toward the far wall of the ballroom. It was crowded, but there were nevertheless only about a third as many attendees tonight than what the ball later this week would drag in. Instead there were pools of men, young and old, talking amongst themselves. Every single woman in a five-mile radius of sufficient social status had also been tapped, and they stood in different pools, neither of the two groups allowed to intermingle until Edeena had danced the first dance — with the entire single male population of the room.

The entire thing seemed more ridiculous by the second, and she wondered what Vince must be thinking.

Vince. She lifted her gaze and scanned the ballroom, finding him more easily than she'd feared. He stood near the edge of the female attendees, a few feet distant from the nearest knot of men. Not a part of either group, yet he seemed as blessedly familiar to her as sun on a summer's day. As their gaze met, he gave her a warm smile, and her heart stopped cramping so much.

"Edeena, dear, pay attention," the queen said mildly, and Edeena tore her gaze away from Vince to survey the room. Had Catherine noticed her distraction? Probably not, or she would have already pounced on it. "Your thoughts?"

"Rand Millya," she said, picking out the man in question at the far end of the room. He stood with four other men, and he truly was the best candidate by far. "He's twenty-eight, so arguably more ready to settle down, he comes from a large, gregarious family, their business is profitable, and he's always been polite."

"Not too hard to look at either," the queen observed blithely, and Edeena blinked.

"Well, yes," she allowed, but almost of its own volition, her gaze strayed back to Vince. Even in his beautiful suit, he looked slightly disheveled, his body meant for a level of action the restrictive formalwear simply didn't allow. He wasn't out of place at this proper matchmaker's dance, he was just — too large for it. Much like Dimitri Korba, who also scanned the room with the same studied gaze that Vince had adopted.

Realizing the queen was waiting for some kind of response, Edeena hurried on. "If Rand isn't interested, then the older brother of the Staros family, Pietre, would be next."

The queen wrinkled her nose. "He's a rather fussy sort, don't you think?"

"Is he?" Edeena looked around the room, trying to locate Pietre. She found him at the refreshment table, scowling over the offerings. His plate was empty and as she watched, he moved past three of the dishes, his hand hovering over each before retracting. "Oh."

"Yes, oh," the queen said. "Imagine what he would be like faced with a choice of true magnitude."

"Fair enough," Edeena said. Her heart was dangerously close to heading south again, and she struggled to hold onto her happy place. She'd done seriously thorough vetting of the top candidates in the room, but she was quickly coming to realize that nothing could replace the value of a personal recommendation. "Do you have anyone you think you might be a good match?"

"Oh, of course, darling," the queen smiled, giving her arm a small squeeze. "But I want to give you at least the illusion of not being railroaded by a meddling monarch first. If you choose well, I promise to keep my mouth firmly shut."

The queen turned her dancing eyes back to the milling crowd, her smile broadening as the musicians began to tune their instruments. Then her expression shifted slightly, and Edeena tried not to freeze.

"He's here, isn't he."

"He is. Keep your smile steady, dear, he's currently scanning the room for us, so let's give due attention to young Rico Carras here. He was caught streaking through the Royal Beach by the GNSF guards out on maneuvers only yesterday, so I cannot recommend him to you. But your father is friends with the boy's father, so he'll be mollified if you appear to be paying attention to him."

Edeena nodded, taking on her most appeasing smile as she tilted her head and watched Rico laugh with his friends. At least he had a good smile, quick and easy, his laughter drawing the attention of others in a positive way.

"Excellent, exactly perfect," the queen said. "Now buck up, Silas is heading our way."

"Radiant with joy, subservient daughter, or something in between?" Edeena asked under her breath.

Queen Catherine gave a most un-royal snort. "Screw subservience. Radiance will surprise him more."

With that the queen looked up, her smile wide as if she only now had noticed her cousin. "Silas, oh, thank heavens you're here. How is your sweet Maria faring?"

"Well," Silas said, turning his gaze immediately to Edeena. "Edeena," he said, clipping off the word as if it was a condemnation. "Good of you to finally accept your responsibilities."

Edeena's own broad smile didn't dim as she stepped toward her father and enveloped him in a hug. He was an ass, but there was something about him tonight that seemed to tug at her heartstrings, no matter all the terrible things he'd done in the name of the family — things that would make this polite group of royals and nobles faint if they knew. But seeing him now, he looked . . . well, tired, more than anything else.

He stood back, scowling at her as the queen departed with gracious discretion, and Edeena tried to find the words to mend the fences she'd been diligently trying to destroy between them.

Then he had to go and open his mouth and ruin everything.

"I assume you've made your choice already," he said gruffly, looking around the room. "This is merely a formality. For God's sake, do not pick Millya. He's no better than a pig farmer, I don't care if their production turned to wine this past generation."

Edeena blinked. "Well, I—"

"And Rico, I saw you eyeing him. He's not acceptable. I won't allow it."

Her eyes widened. "But you and his father are friends."

"His father owes me money. You better believe I'll stay his friend until he pays that loan off," Silas sneered. "The quicker you understand how people work, Edeena, the sooner you'll realize that it doesn't pay to become sentimental."

Edeena stiffened. "No one would ever accuse me of being sentimental, Father. Least of all you."

"Sentimental, no. But neither have you paid any attention to tradition. And tradition matters, it has always mattered. The Saleri curse must fall, and it will fall, in this generation. I will be the one to make sure that happens."

"You?" Edeena snapped, irritation flaring despite her best efforts. "You've done nothing but twist everything to your own plans since the moment that

Cursed

Mother died. And for what? Because we're all girls? We're a special generation? Mother didn't care about that—she was simply happy we existed." Edeena threw her hands up in exasperation. "I'm going to break this curse, Father, I know the ancient rules and I am going to bow down before them and do everything I can to satisfy whatever gods still care about what happens to the Saleris. But the moment I do, your power over me, over Marguerite and Caroline is at an end. We'll all be free to build new lives, and they'll be able to find real love and real joy and you and your obsessions, your traditions and your curses will be done. Mark my words, Father, they will be *done*."

Silas's face darkened for a moment, whether in anger or genuine shock at her lengthy outburst, Edeena didn't know—and didn't care. It was more than she'd ever said to her father, but it felt right...it felt true.

The music was starting up in a traditional reel, and she had a job to do.

She whirled away from Silas and headed for the middle of the room.

Vince shrugged off the wall he'd been holding up as the music kicked into some sort of upbeat country reel, not quite a waltz but something far shy of a country swing line dance. Still, it seemed to galvanize the room as if this was what everyone had been waiting for. The men in particular perked up, looking genuinely interested, and Vince hid his grimace. What the hell was wrong with these people?

"You look as if you don't approve, Prince Rallis."

Whoops. Apparently he hadn't done a very good job masking his expression after all. He looked sideways at Queen Catherine, and managed an abashed smile.

"I confess, it's not the way we do things at home, not that we have any particular claim to knowing what we're doing when it comes to relationships back in America."

"And your own parents? They're still living, I hope?"

"Yes, ma'am." He nodded as he watched Edeena twirl around the center of the growing circle of men, all of them engaged in some dance they looked like they'd learned about twenty minutes before entering the room. "Mom and Dad both alive, both still happily married. But they're Greek." He shrugged. "It's a point of pride with them to stay married, give a good example for the younger generation."

"Indeed."

Vince saw his mistake, tried to rectify it before the queen continued talking.

"I know, I know, what Edeena is doing here is also intended to keep up with that idea of good example, but . . ." he winced again as the music changed tempo, and the men broke apart, clapping and stamping their feet as Edeena was squired by the first of their number. The man was an absolute beanpole, tall and cadaverously thin, but he had a wide grin and an affable nature that had Vince liking him despite his awkward appearance. He turned Edeena around the circle a few times, like she was some kind of show pony, then dutifully handed her off to bachelor number two.

Good lord, there had to be at least thirty men in that circle, Vince realized. This was how Edeena was supposed to get to know someone?

As if she was reading his thoughts, the queen spoke again. "And how long did your parents know each other before they realized that they were the right match. Did they ever tell you that story?"

At this point, Vince wasn't particularly listening to the queen. He was too busy watching Edeena. She was laughing, carefree almost, the perfect vision of a debutante being squired around by her partners. The older attending members of this bizarre event were watching and laughing as well, and even the apparently single women in the audience had a strange look. One not quite of envy, but not derision either. Maybe there was something to be said for having a crazy, messed up dance set up for you, where the entire community gave a shit about who you danced with and why.

Almost by muscle memory, he realized the queen had asked him a question. He answered it just as automatically.

"My parents met when they were teenagers, to hear them tell the story. Younger than that, maybe. They were in school, and one day they ran into each other in the hallway—like, literally ran into each other, my father haring off in one direction and my mother barreling along in the other. They crashed and books, pens, papers went flying." He grinned, shaking his head as Edeena bowed graciously to a kid who looked younger than Vince's own brothers, but who proudly stepped up to take her hand. "As the story goes, by the time they had everything picked up, they were already planning how many children they'd have together."

There was no response and Vince tore his gaze away from Edeena to look down at the queen. She was beaming at him with sublime satisfaction, and he scrambled back in his mind over what he'd said, trying to determine what it was that had generated such a strong reaction. Before he could puzzle it out, the queen gestured to the circle. "You must join them, Prince Rallis," she said, and he blinked at her.

"I'm not a prince, nor am I a local. I think she's got her hands full."

"But you aren't committed to another woman? No? Then it's bad form for you not to participate. Remember, we are working here to counteract an old family curse. If any of these old nabobs can find reason to declare we didn't follow the customs exactly, they could use that as a justification for Edeena not doing her job in helping to heal the family. You don't want that, do you?"

It was all Vince could do not to throw his hands up in disgust. "You're seriously not joking here," he said, staring at the queen. "I don't even know that goofy dance step they're doing, and though this probably won't come as a surprise to you, I'm not exactly the type who dances."

"I think you'll do just fine," the queen said. "And I'm afraid it is a royal command, dear. So the sooner you acquiesce, the sooner we can stop this infernal noise."

She gave him a push toward the center of the room, and the men in the circle opened up obligingly, grinning at him as the music picked up tempo yet again. There was a great deal of laughter now, and Vince stared hard at the steps the men were making. He realized that the most complicated part of the dance was staying far enough away from Edeena's twirling skirts that you didn't slow her down. He could do that, he supposed.

As Edeena passed him on the arm of another guy she looked up, her eyes widening in surprise—and, maybe something else? She seemed happy enough that he was there, anyway, and maybe that was the real purpose of the queen pushing him into the circle. Exactly as the dressmaker had said, he helped Edeena relax, to smile, and today above all days, she needed to convey her absolute delight with the insanity that her family was putting her through. He supposed he could go along with that. It was only a country dance, no matter how strange the steps to it were. It meant nothing at all.

Finally, Edeena swirled nearer, and he realized he was the last man in line, although none of the men actually left the circle. If anything, as each finished their turn their shouting and stamping grew more robust.

Then suddenly, Edeena was in front of him, reaching out her hands, and it was the most natural thing in the world to step into the circle of insanity and start twisting her forward and back, keeping time with her turns as he managed to stay out of reach of her skirts.

"Queen Catherine put you up to this, didn't she!" Edeena laughed and he found himself laughing back.

"I asked if I could join in."

Her eyes lit up. "You did not!" she proclaimed, her

outburst loud enough to draw a raucous cheer from the men. Vince noticed a few craning heads, but everyone was smiling, and that was the game.

"I should have," he said. "And you should laugh like this more often, Edeena, you'll make every man in the room fall for you."

"Ha!" Her face blanked for a moment though, and she blinked rapidly, sure signs of a woman about to cry. What the hell had he said?

"You ruin that makeup job, and Hatchet Face is going to eat you for lunch," he warned, and just that quickly the moment passed for Edeena. She whirled away from him then back, her hand tight in his as if she would never let him go.

"I didn't know you could dance!" she gasped as they neared the end of the circuit.

Vince snorted. "This isn't dancing, This is like running alongside a kid riding his bike for the first time."

That merited him another unsophisticatedly hearty laugh from Edeena, and then they were suddenly at the end of their circuit. Vince realized he didn't know exactly how they parted ways. When Edeena came close, their hands together, and toward him as if for a kiss, he felt as if the whole world was watching.

And he couldn't bring himself to give a damn.

He met her kiss with a pressure that had been building up inside him since the last time he'd held her in his arms, six thousand miles and a million layers of sense back in Charleston. For a bare moment, time stopped, and he allowed himself to savor every detail of the beautiful woman in his arms. Her soft mouth, her racing heart, the clutch of her hands in his, the taste of salt and champagne on her lips, the smell of honeysuckle in her hair . . .

Then the moment broke, the music crashed on, and Edeena was stepping back from him. She was radiant, perfect and true . . .

And she was destined for somebody else.

Chapter Seventeen

Edeena leaned close to the window, trying to see beyond the next curve in the road. "You're sure this is the right direction?" she asked in Garronois.

"Yes, ma'am," the driver said, the soul of patience. "We should be there presently.

She sat back with a frown, her mood no better though Vince was right beside her, the way he'd been at her side everywhere since they'd arrived in Garronia. But today, there was something different about him, something solemn and formal, and it added to the misery she sensed was stacking up on all sides.

They drove through a small knot of farm houses, and it was Vince's turn to sit forward. "What's that about?" he asked frowning as a group of men and boys gathered in front of a charming house which set back from the road. It had a tree leaning precariously over its roof.

"Bad storm came through about a week ago, damaged a lot of trees," the driver said, speaking in flawless English. "They're probably—"

"Stop! Stop the car," Vince barked.

CURSED

Before the limo had barely slowed Vince pushed open the door and pounded out of the vehicle, shouting and waving his hands. Of course, he was shouting in English, and the townspeople would have no idea what he was saying. They'd probably think he was a crazy person.

"Vince!" she shouted, but he was already halfway to the crowd before she slammed the door and dashed across the road, grateful for her sensible walking shoes despite the filmy blouse and long skirt she wore. They were already late for her first luncheon, and now this!

"Vince, what're you doing?"

The men were gathered around him looking at him dubiously, and the kids were openly slack jawed. Still, they seemed to view him more as an amusement than a threat, and Edeena's tension eased a bit.

Vince turned toward her. "They don't speak English?" he asked, clearly surprised. "I thought all of you spoke English."

"We all learn it, but not everyone has a need to speak it every day."

"Well, they need to stop what they're doing. Stop right now, and back that truck the hell away from that tree," Vince snapped. "If they keep at it the way they are, the whole damned thing is going to fall straight through that roof."

"What?" Edeena looked from him to the tree. She could see now that the farmers had cut several gashes into the trunk and were looking to lever it away from the house. To her untutored eye, the gashes made sense. The tree should fall well to the right of the building, clearing it completely. "What's wrong with—"

"And these kids! Christ almighty, why are all these kids so close? They should have a perimeter set up and everyone well back. How bad was the storm?"

He asked the question of Edeena, but of course she hadn't been here, she'd been in South Carolina. Still, an older man stepped forward, possessing the gravity of a family elder. Edeena felt the curious urge to curtsey, but she did around everyone who was over the age of sixty. Something her mother had taught her, she supposed.

"I am Guillarmo Aconti," the man said gravely in English, his voice deep and sonorous. "Who are you?"

"Prince—I mean Vince, Vince Rallis, sorry. Old habits, they called me that when I did this work with my cousins." He glanced sheepishly at Edeena who could no more stop the rush of his words than she could stop an oncoming wave. Vince was truly upset, his whole body shaking. "Look, I live in the United States, the coastal state of South Carolina. We get storms all the time, right? Some big, some small, but some of them seem to come in sideways instead of down. That sound familiar to what went through here? And how long ago was that?"

"Seven days." The old man looked first at Vince, then Edeena. "The wind came sideways. It doesn't normally come in so far, but this time," he shrugged, "it did. We have several trees that lost limbs, twisted."

"Yeah, they didn't simply twist. They broke inside. Only you don't know it yet." Vince put his hands to his head. "We need two trucks, not one, and we need ropes, not axes. We need to keep the kids back." He looked hard at the man. "You've got builders, too, here?

Cursed

Someone who built these homes? Because the roofs are going to leak if you don't reinforce them, and then shear clean off during the next perfectly ordinary storm. We run into it all the time in South Carolina. The first storm doesn't seem to cause much damage, but the second one knocks people off their feet."

Edeena stared. She'd never seen Vince so animated, but it made sense, she supposed. He lived in an area under constant threat of storm damage, and he cared — truly cared — about protecting people.

Soon, another man strode forward, then a third, and Vince reached for Edeena. With her as a translator, she was able to explain the problem in simple terms, conveying Vince's sense of urgency that they take a completely different direction to remove the tree than what they were planning. Cell phones came out, and Vince visibly sagged with relief. "Thank God."

Edeena eyed him. "You didn't think we had phones?"

"This place looks like something out of a Disney movie," he snapped back. "I wouldn't be surprised if the chickens started singing."

Someone drove up with a truck a few minutes later, and this man apparently had more construction experience, because he understood what Vince was saying right away — which was good, because Edeena still didn't. Still, to her surprise Vince accepted it when the local men bid him on his way. He shook hands, clapped shoulders, then turned and walked back to the car with her.

She waited until they slid back inside the vehicle to turn to him. "You're okay with them carrying on without further supervision? You're not . . . I don't know . . . worried they'll do the wrong thing?"

"They won't," Vince said, shaking his head. "So much of the time, people simply don't know what they don't know. It's not so much that they're trying to screw up, they're just approaching the problem the way they've approached similar problems in the past. They don't need someone to show them step by step how to do it correctly, they need to know that their way isn't the right way forward. They can figure out the rest on their own." He slanted a glance at her. "Make sense?"

"It makes absolute sense."

She turned forward and realized the driver had been listening in on their conversation, but the man's eyes were on the road, his manner easy, so she supposed there was nothing lost there. It made her feel good to know those strangers were going to save their house, protect their other homes from problems they wouldn't have known about without Vince. It was all the craziest kind of coincidence, but if it helped someone . . .

She reached out, touched Vince's leg. "Thank you," she said quietly.

He looked at her with surprise. "For what?"

She shook her head. She couldn't say more for fear of saying or doing something inappropriate. The driver worked for the queen, but no one's allegiances were fully set. She had to be careful. She contented herself with the briefest response she could summon. "For being you."

Vince reached down and squeezed her hand, below the eyesight of the driver. And he didn't let go.

Cursed

The day's visits were . . . not an unqualified success, Edeena thought hours later, but at least a step in the right direction. She'd met cousins she hadn't seen in years, sharing an invitation with each of them to come to her engagement ball. She'd left extras as well. Some of the families she spoke with no doubt knew about the curse, some didn't, still others didn't realize that Edeena and her sisters were even part of their family tree, or why they should care. Only a few refused to see her, for one reason or another. And every time, Vince asked her why, gently compelling her to explain how fierce the Saleri pride was, and then reassuring her that pride so fierce would eventually prove stronger than any curse the ancients could throw at him.

Now she looked at him, weariness gnawing her bones as they drove back through the countryside. "Probably not what you expected when you agreed to provide security for me on this trip, eh? Countless visits to cousins and aunts?"

"Don't forget uncles, grand matrons and more children than I've seen in my lifetime," Vince laughed. His head rested back against the seat cushion, and his eyes were shut. But once more he grasped her hand with his, as if it was the most natural thing in the world for them to hold hands for no reason. "But they were good people, and their love runs deep. You should be proud of your family, Edeena. Even those who don't know you."

She sighed and glanced out the window. "I only hope I make them proud of me."

Vince felt like he'd run a marathon backwards by the time he and Edeena bid farewell to their driver and turned into the palace. It was quiet and dark, and even the doorman was hushed. A light dinner would be sent to Edeena's sitting room for both of them, they were informed, and the queen would content herself with getting the details of their journey in the morning.

Dinner *was* waiting for them, enough to feed a family of six — dates and fruit and cheese and cold meats and bread, with enough wine and a clear liqueur Edeena called *tsipouro* to wash it all down. It took a moment for Vince to realize what was happening, but as he looked up to meet Edeena's gaze, he understood she was way ahead of him.

She stared from him, to the closed door, back to him.

"We're . . . alone," she said.

He grinned, thoughts of food momentarily forgotten. "You noticed that, huh?"

She pursed her lips, her gaze drifting to the clock on the wall. "I wonder if anyone will notice that you're here . . ."

"Probably," he said, stepping closer to her, "but we do have dinner to consume. And we're both, undoubtedly, extremely hungry. I suspect we have maybe an hour before a staffer will discreetly knock on the door, asking us if, I don't know, we want port or tea or something."

"Port?" she asked, a smile teasing her mouth as he

reached her. She gazed up at him and his arms went around her, cradling her close. "We aren't really much for port in Garronia. We are much more a *tsipouro* drinking country."

"I knew there was a reason I liked you people."

Vince leaned forward and kissed Edeena, feeling the weight of her, solid and sure in his arms, as if she was meant to be there. Two days, three—he didn't know how long he had with her, and in this minute, he couldn't think that far ahead. He could only think the forty or fifty minutes they had separate and safe in this room, away and somewhere else from where everyone expected them to be.

"How hungry are you?"

In response her arms came up around him, her body arching up into his. "Not so hungry that I want to miss a moment of this," she whispered. She pulled away from him, unslinging her bag and rummaging through it for a moment before she plucked free a foil package. Vince's eyes went wide.

"You were carrying around a condom in your *purse*?" he protested, half-laughing as she pulled him deeper into the room, through a door that led to a shadowed chamber. "What exactly were you expecting to happen in the countryside of Garronia?"

"I didn't know." In the darkness, Edeena's voice suddenly sounded small, and Vince moved quickly toward her. She was standing several feet away from her bed, and he realized she was shaking there in the shadows, as if she could maintain all her strength and good cheer for the rest of the world when the lights were on, but once the brightness dimmed, she could only bow under the weight of her own charade.

Vince wrapped his arms around her, her back to his chest, and they stood there for a long moment in the darkness. Then he sighed ponderously, plucking the foil package from her fingers. "Well, it seems as if it would be a crime not to reward your practical preparedness," he said, his words met by Edeena's half laugh, half sob. He tucked the package into his watchband, then drifted a kiss over her hair. "If only you were so resourceful as to also secure us a bed . . . hey, wait a minute."

He stepped back and turned Edeena around to face him, resolutely ignoring the tears shining in her eyes. He didn't want Edeena to have reason to cry. Not today, not ever. But there was only so much he could control.

He could control the next few minutes, however.

He lifted his hands to either side of her face, cradling it with his palms, and leaned forward, kissing her lips softly. "I don't usually make women cry until after I take off my clothes, you know," he whispered, and she coughed a short, hiccupping laugh.

"I guess there's always a first time."

"Not for this," he said. "But let me see if I can recover my dignity." He stepped back from her and pulled his shirt off in one smooth move, his body tightening as her expression changed from one of wistful sadness to distinct desire. Edeena stared as he made short work of the rest of his clothes, until he stood in front of her, fully naked.

"Better?" he rumbled, and a smile tilted her lips as her hands drifted up, her fingers spreading wide on his chest. As always, her touch galvanized him, and his abs knotted under her gentle touch.

"Better," she said. She took another step forward, then lifted up on her toes and kissed him, the pressure whisper soft. "But now I feel out of place."

She moved to unbutton her blouse but Vince caught her hand, moving it gently aside. "Let me," he said, and she blinked in surprise as he smoothly and methodically unbuttoned the silky material, letting it hang free as he focused on her bra. He slid his fingers over the edge, palming her breasts through the thin fabric, and was rewarded as Edeena's eyes drifted half-shut. He quickly slid her shirt off, and she let it fall to the floor, then his hands were at her waistband, peeling back the cool linen skirt, snagging her panties along the way. Edeena had already kicked off her sandals, so it was short work to toss the skirt to the side. As he came up again, he lifted her in his arms, smiling at her startled cry.

"You don't have to—I can walk!"

"I know you can," Vince said, nuzzling his face in her hair. "But this isn't so bad, is it?"

She sighed and relaxed against his chest, and he held her, memorizing the feel of her in his arms. Before she could ask him what he was doing, he stepped forward, carrying her across the wide room to her bed. He laid her in the middle of what had to be a hundred pillows of various sizes, and she collapsed into them, her smile finally broadening as another notch of tension slipped away.

"I confess, I sort of wondered what you'd do with all these pillows," she murmured, as Vince climbed into the bed. He sent a torrent of the smallest pillows over the far side of the mattress, then finally reached Edeena.

"I'm a fan of pillows," he said against her lips, "there are many, many things we can do with the right amount of pillows."

She giggled and he somehow felt that he'd won a victory, then she launched herself at him.

Vince rolled easily, allowing Edeena to straddle him in the center of the ridiculous pile of pillows, and she reached for his watchband, sliding the foil packet free. "As much as I look forward to a circus of the hundred and one pillows, I have something else in mind," she said huskily. "Is that okay?"

"More than okay," he managed as she ripped the foil packet open then sheathed him, smoothing her hands over his cock with a studied care that nearly made his eyes cross. She shifted her body until she was straddling his hips, looking like every Greek goddess he'd ever imagined in the fevered dreams of his youth. But Aphrodite had nothing on Edeena Saleri, and when Edeena slid forward and back in a mesmerizing cadence, his body bucked convulsively. "Where . . . how. . ." he managed, but his own need redoubled as she lifted her body slightly, then guided his cock inside her, sliding home with such a smooth, tight movement that his sight went white for a split second.

When his vision cleared, she was looking down at him again, smiling with radiant pleasure, and Vince knew he would never, ever be the same.

"I like the way you look right now," she murmured softly. "I like it far too much."

She stretched over him again, and he was lost.

Chapter Eighteen

The morning of the most important day in Edeena's life wasn't going according to plan. Less than an hour after she and Vince had arrived in their room the previous evening, a discreet knock had come at the door, and if the waiter had noticed that they both seemed freshly showered, he didn't mention it.

Since then, she hadn't been alone with Vince again, had only been alone herself when she'd slept, the bed offering no sanctuary anymore, as filled as it was with memories of Vince. So finally, after two solid days of lunches, brunches, dinner parties and musicales, she'd convinced the guard at her door . . . then at the front door of the palace . . . and then, finally, at the gate in the wall, that she simply wanted to go for a walk.

Alone. Without Vince, without an armed escort, alone.

And she'd made it all of thirty steps before a marginally familiar and yet completely unexpected voice had hailed her.

"Oh, my God! It's Edeena, right? Edeena Saleri. How cool that you're back. We just pulled in from

France ourselves!"

Edeena turned to see Nicki Clark pounding up the pavement, the athletic all-American girl slowing to a jog as she rounded the corner. Nicki looked appropriately drenched from a run, her compact figure radiating heat despite the coolness of the Garronian morning.

"Are you going for a walk? That's awesome. Mind if I join you for my cooldown?"

Edeena peered at her mistrustfully, but it was impossible to deny Nicki's wide, happy grin. "I'm not moving anywhere nearly as fast as you were," she said, indicating her walking shoes and long linen pants. "I only wanted to get some air."

"That's perfect!" Nicki fell into step with her as Edeena sighed, giving up on the total solitude she'd hoped for in this walk. In truth, though, she didn't mind that much. As one of the four Americans who'd recently captured the hearts and minds of the first family—let alone the attention of half of Garronia and all of its press corps—Nicki was about as different from the rest of the castle's occupants as she could get.

"When did you return?" Edeena asked as Nicki fiddled with her sports watch, logging her workout.

"Late last night—and by late, I mean no o'clock in the morning," Nicki said. "Everyone else is dead to the world, but there was no way, no how Lauren was going to miss your ball tonight. She's been Skyping with designers about dresses since the queen called us about it a few days ago."

Edeena laughed, well imagining Lauren Grant, the most sophisticated of the foursome and the love of

CURSED

Dimitri Korba's life, arranging an armored-truck full of dresses to be delivered for the Americans to try on over the course of the day. "Well, I hope she won't be disappointed. Tonight's ball won't be that big of a deal."

Nicki stared at her. "Are you nuts? It's totally going to be a big deal. First, you pick your husband in a not-too-different way than Kristos was supposed to pick his bride-to-be a few months ago. *Months.* That's like decades in royal gossip years. Then the queen decides to extend an open invitation to Garronois nobility and their friends and neighbors, making it easily the biggest ball of the year. Neither Fran nor Emmaline could miss that."

"Friends and neighbors?" Edeena asked weakly. Setting aside the fact that Francesca was practically betrothed to Prince Aristotle and Emmaline was betrothed to Prince Kristos, it made sense that they would attend such a grand affair . . . but when had her engagement ball transformed into such a circus? "How will they fit them all?"

"They're going to let everyone spill out into the open-air portion of the Visitors Palace, according to Emmaline," Nicki said, practically bouncing on her toes. "I've had enough formal balls to last me for a lifetime, but dancing under the stars? That's going to completely rock. I may even get Stefan to un-kink himself enough to smile." She laughed brightly, and Edeena found herself grinning, too, thinking of the zealously expressionless ambassador. The four Americans had truly brought a breath of fresh air into the castle, and she certainly could understand that—her own Vince had blown into her life like a summer storm.

Her own Vince. Not so much hers, but he'd be there tonight, at least. She wouldn't have to face her future alone. Not quite yet.

She and Nicki chatted all the way down to the center of town and Edeena's favorite coffee shop, then sipped the dark heady brew as they made their way back to the castle. There was something uniquely perfect about Garronois coffee, Edeena had to admit. The country got many things right, and coffee was one of them.

Beside her, Nicki groaned. "I may have to move here simply because of the java," she said, inhaling the rich aroma. Then she quirked Edeena a glance. "But your sisters aren't here. Is that weird? Shouldn't they be?"

"I asked them not to come. It's a long flight, and if things don't go right, I don't want Silas badgering them to marry before they can flee the country again. Besides, they're enjoying their time in America. They should continue to get their bearings there."

Nicki made a face. "I thought my mom was obnoxious. Your dad totally has her beaten. Has he been insane to you this week?"

Edeena smiled ruefully. "He's not been around for most of it, thankfully. His new wife is giving birth anytime now, and she's been having a hard time of it. He's refused to let anyone from his side of the family see her, other than the queen by royal command, but I think she'll be okay. He's been taking it hard, though." She shrugged. "Hard enough that he's only had time to accost me once a day with sharp suggestions about his recommendations on my husband."

"Girl, that is still so weird."

Cursed

Nicki's frank assessment of Edeena's family dynamic made her burst out laughing, and she shook her head. "Weird, it definitely is. But it's law, and no one has seen fit to change it because, well, it generally doesn't get enforced. And in Garronia, we're a little nostalgic about all our old, ridiculous laws."

Nicki snorted. "Which is all well and good until one of them ruins your life."

Edeena didn't have an answer to that. They finished their walk in silence, and when she stepped back inside the courtyard of the castle grounds with Nicki, she didn't miss the American's quick glance around the space.

"You were sent to babysit me, weren't you," Edeena said flatly, and Nicki shot her a quick smile, then shrugged.

"Eh, I was out anyway, and you created a small firestorm with your determined march out of the castle. They care about you, want you to be safe. But they also seem to think you're at your breaking point. I can totally relate to that."

"Well, thank you. I think they worry too much."

To her surprise, Nicki chuckled softly, her expression softening. "I think we all tend to worry too much, only not about the right things. You're more worried than you should be about your family, but not about yourself. This curse or whatever is laid on the Saleris has existed for several hundred years, right? Why does it need to be solved in your lifetime?"

Nicki went on, but her words had the exact opposite of the intended effect, Edeena realized. The curse had gone on as long as it had because no one *had* taken a stand to bring the family together. Because when each generation had a chance to do something about it—and there were several generations that had met the criteria—no one had stepped forth and committed.

But Edeena wasn't going to let this generation pass without at least making the attempt. And that meant she had a party to get ready for.

"Will you be there tonight?" she asked Nicki, who was draining the last of her coffee. "Somewhere I can see you?"

"Oh, honey, despite the dress-up craziness, I wouldn't miss it for the world." She grinned at Edeena and waggled her brows. "It's not every day you get to see a girl give it her all to break a family curse."

Vince barreled into the punching bag for the third and final round of his workout, but he wasn't feeling any better. He didn't know who he wanted to hit harder—himself for caring too much about something that was completely out of his control, or any one of the thirty odd guys that Edeena could pick as her husband-to-be.

"You want to pick on someone your own size?"

Dimitri Korba's voice rolled over the wide, empty room and Vince straightened, turning sharply as the captain of the Garronia National Security Force strode toward him. Like himself, Dimitri was dressed in workout gear and looked like he'd already gone through a punishing regimen, but he had a smile on his face that indicated he'd actually been enjoying himself.

Now he picked up a pair of boxing gloves and slipped them on, gesturing for Vince to come out onto the large square mat. He moved around to Vince's left, his gloves up. "You don't seem to be a very happy man, Prince Rallis," Dimitri said. "That's a shame, for someone who has so captured the interest of the queen."

Vince lifted his brows, and obligingly moved out onto the mat. "The queen? What's she got to do with anything?"

"If you spend any time in Garronia, you'll learn she has everything to do with everything she can possibly pry into. It's her royal right."

Vince jabbed and Dimitri feinted easily, letting him get comfortable as Dimitri kept speaking.

"In your case, she is intrigued by everything you have brought to her attention, such as the Contos home at Heron's Point. The queen is related to the Saleris by marriage, but she's not unaware of the family's holdings. This home in South Carolina interests her a great deal, however. Then there's the curse and Edeena's resolution to resolve it, and your interest in Edeena as well."

Dimitri was watching Vince's face, clearly expecting some kind of reaction to his words, and in so doing left his body open. Vince got in a kidney punch before Dimitri could cover himself, sending the big captain spinning around. Dimitri's face darkened with annoyance, and Vince grinned.

"You're right, this is making me feel better," he said. "Maybe we should focus on the fight and leave the talk for later."

"That's the problem." Dimitri paused to deliver several blows to Vince's head, grunting with satisfaction as Vince blocked him capably, though Vince could tell he wasn't deliberately trying to score a punishing hit, merely spar. "Later, perhaps sooner than you'd like, you're going to be cornered by the queen and she'll demand to know what your intentions are with Edeena. I like you, and you've done your best to protect Edeena, even from herself, so I wanted to warn you."

"Consider me warned, then." After that, the conversation fell away as the two of them sparred in ever more tighter rounds, with Dimitri scoring major hits to Vince's shoulder, torso, and even kidneys, though none to his face. When they finally spun away from each other, both men were sweating hard, and Vince winced ruefully.

"I got to get back into the gym," he muttered, while Dimitri grinned.

"Be glad you will be on display tonight, my friend," he laughed. "Or you'd be sporting a black eye. You stay much longer in Garronia, we will fight again. It helps you to keep your head on straight, no?"

Hours later, Vince was still breathing a little gingerly when he strode down the hall behind a staff member, both of them wearing equally well-cut tuxedos. The man had come for him precisely at seven p.m., but despite Dimitri's warning, the queen hadn't been lying in wait for him anywhere, lurking around corners to spring on him unawares. He hadn't seen Edeena either. Then again, she had a ball to prepare for. Surely that was an hours-long proposition right there.

Cursed

"What is this passageway?" he asked now as they turned deeper into the palace, instead of heading out to the main entryway.

"With the queen's decision to enlarge the ball for more guests, the streets are packed with cars," the man said in heavily accented English. "Though it's a bit of a walk, it's faster to take you the back way, on foot, to the Visitors Palace. We should be there in less than twenty minutes. Most likely you will return this way as well." The man chuckled. "I cannot imagine anyone will be getting away from the castle easily tonight."

Something in the man's words caught Vince up short. It almost made him feel trapped. Then again, they were going to the second formal party in less than a week, and everywhere he looked women were in formal gowns, men were in tuxedos, and even the servers were dressed to the nines.

One thing was for sure, Vince wouldn't miss all the goddamned dancing that seemed to go on in this country.

When they finally climbed the last set of stairs, Vince couldn't deny the ingenuity of the passage. The hallway tee'd off sharply here, one path leading deeper into the complex, the other toward what sounded like a thousand people milling around. The man gave him an engraved card and gestured him on, and Vince was left with no choice but to head toward the madness. In another twenty steps, he emerged into a wide foyer, doors flung wide both to a glassed-in atrium style ballroom and also to the steps leading out to the courtyard. The courtyard was thronged with people, and they were barely contained from spilling into the drive. The driveway itself was now lined with cars that crept forward to disgorge new guests.

"Vince!" At the sound of the familiar voice, Vince turned to see Marguerite and Caroline rushing toward him, Rob and Cindy Marks on their heels.

"Where is Edeena. Does she know? Did you tell her?"

Vince smiled, accepting Marguerite's impulsive hug despite his damaged body, then setting her back. "She doesn't. Your secret is safe." He'd gotten the call from the girls the morning after he'd traveled to the farm country with Edeena. Both sisters had been adamant about attending the engagement ball, and Marks and his wife had been game to come along. Now the Saleri sisters wore evening gowns, and even Rob and Cindy were dressed in a tuxedo and a floor length gown, respectively. Vince couldn't decide which of the two Americans looked more awkward. He figured he was probably a close third.

"Flight go okay?" he asked, smothering his smile.

"I do not even want to know how much that cost," Rob said, shaking his head. He looked around with surprise evident in his face. "And this place . . . I don't know what I was expecting, but this was not it."

Another feminine voice called out, and Caroline turned, her face lighting up in recognition. "Go," Vince ordered and she headed off, Cindy right behind her. He continued then with Rob. "Caroline and Marguerite should be safe here anyway, but make sure none of their own family members leave with them."

Rob grimaced. "You really think there's going to be

Cursed
a problem?"

"I don't know what to think anymore, my man." Vince shook his head. "This entire place has gone nuts."

"Roger that." Rob took off after Marguerite, and Vince finally made it into the ballroom proper. He showed his card to the door attendant, and the woman immediately began threading her way through the crowd, gesturing to him to follow. Though music was playing and people were already dancing, the vibe was very different here than it had been at the gathering earlier in the week. For one thing, there were far more people, and food and alcohol flowed in abundance. It seemed a much looser affair, more like a grand party than a formal rite of passage.

For the other, Edeena was not mingling happily on the floor with all her admirers. She was sitting in the place of honor, her back perfectly straight, her face serene. She seemed to be scanning the crowd and when her glance fell on him, she smiled.

Vince couldn't help the way his heart turned over in his chest. He touched the arm of his guide, and she checked her stride. "Do you know what the agenda is here tonight? He asked. "Is there a set time for the, uh, announcement?"

The woman shook her head. "Ordinarily it would have already happened, but the countess's father has been delayed.

Oh, no. Vince looked hard at the woman. "There's nothing wrong with his wife, is there?" he asked hastily, and she shook her head, her expression wry.

"Nothing that dramatic. Rumor has it she's in perfect health, in fact, and that the old—that the count has merely been using her as an excuse to isolate Edeena with her thoughts and obligations." The woman shrugged. "I guess it's worked. There's an entire betting pool on who the countess is going to choose as her husband, and even the men in question are taking part." She laughed at Vince's shocked expression. "Welcome to Garronia, Mr. Rallis," she said. "We have our own way of doing things, and they're not for the faint of heart."

She cut to the side, taking him away from Edeena, and they stepped into a small open space, something Vince wouldn't have thought was possible in such a packed room. Then he realized that in the center of the space, Queen Catherine was stepping back from a man he didn't recognize, the two of them exchanging formal bows.

Then she turned to him. "Ah! Mr. Rallis, I've been waiting for you," she said, extending her hands to him. "Indulge me with a dance, if you would be so kind?"

Someone moved behind her, and Vince caught Dimitri's rueful grin for a second, then he stepped forward and took the queen's hands.

Chapter Nineteen

Watching Vince and the queen take their turn around the dance floor, Edeena realized that the moment of her decision was nearly upon her. She now understood the reasoning behind the queen's choice to open up the ballroom to a wider audience. Not only would this unquestionably draw some of the straggler Saleris in, if only out of curiosity, but it would also bring an audience. If Edeena's choice succeeded in bringing the family together, then by God, there would be plenty of witnesses.

She smiled a little, her gaze sweeping over the dance floor—then she froze.

"Oh, *no.*" Putting all sense of decorum aside, she rose from her chair and strode forward, hopping off the dais. If anyone noticed that she was entering the dance floor prior to the official swell of ceremonial music, they didn't stop her.

And what she'd just seen simply couldn't be happening.

"Caroline!" Even across the crowded room, her responsible sister's sixth sense for accountability meant

Caro's head lifted as Edeena called her name, swiveling around to see her. But her sister looked entirely unabashed as she squealed, then tugged on Marguerite's arm. Marguerite also had the audacity to appear entirely thrilled to be discovered, and both of them rushed headlong toward Edeena, meeting her in the middle of the floor.

"You came off your pedestal!" Marguerite said triumphantly as she reached Edeena, enveloping her in a warm hug.

"You look absolutely regal," Caro chimed in. Feeling her sisters' arms around her, Edeena didn't realize how much she'd missed them in the few short days they'd been apart. If anything, it gave her a renewed focus on what she needed to accomplish.

"I thought we agreed that you wouldn't come," she protested, pulling back, unable to keep the smile from her face.

"And miss your engagement? To whoever the lucky man is?" Marguerite teased. "I, for one, can't wait to see the results. Do you think Father will turn from beast to real man?"

Edeena laughed in a short, hiccupping outburst and a nearby couple turned to her, clearly recognizing the sound. Her brows lifted. "You brought Rob and Cindy? They could leave their kids?"

"That's apparently what grandmothers are made for," Caroline said fondly. "The two of them have been everywhere with us. We're perfectly safe."

"And they're perfectly *adorable*," Marguerite said, sounding almost wistful, far older than her twenty-five years. "Everything they do, they do together, without really seeming to think that much about it. I wouldn't even know how to begin caring for someone so well."

"You'll get your chance," Edeena said firmly, and once again, her resolve was bolstered. She knew her sisters well enough, however, that it was time to distract them from how that chance would be made possible. "Have you seen the crush of people outside? Do you recognize any of them as Saleris?"

"How could we possibly?" Caroline began, but at that moment the couples closest to them parted in time to the swelling music, and a new couple twirled toward them on the heels of an ending refrain.

"Edeena!" Queen Catherine paused in front of them, laughter sparkling her eyes. "This is most excellent. Mr. Rallis was even now tiring of dancing with me. Perhaps you could allow him to escort you back to the dais? I believe your father has arrived."

Edeena jolted. Of course Silas would arrive the moment she left her appointed post. Even now she saw him at the top of the stairs, talking with King Jasen as his gaze swept the room. She groaned, and Catherine patted her arm.

"Jasen will keep him occupied until you're ready, dear. And Mr. Rallis will keep you safe. I have every faith in him."

With that the queen turned away to exclaim with delight over her sisters, and Edeena found herself once again on Vince's arm. He turned, angling them toward the dais, and she suddenly tightened her grasp on him.

"Could you . . . could you take me outside for a minute instead?" she asked quickly, as he looked down at her in surprise. "I know I have to get back, but it seems like most of the guests are in the courtyard, and I haven't really gotten a chance to see it. I suspect it's wonderful."

"It's a crowd, that's for sure," Vince said. Still he didn't object, his arm moving around her back as he turned toward the thicker part of the congregation of swirling skirts and black suits. They plunged into the crowd, and Edeena sighed as the music swelled up again, seeming to create a layer of anonymity around her and Vince, as if they somehow could slip away without being seen.

A few minutes later they'd reached the great French doors that were flung open to the night sky, and stepped out onto the broad landing.

The place was lit up like a carnival.

A new set of musicians were holding forth out here, their music an echo of the internal reel and yet distinctly different, so that the two rose in perfect harmony no matter whether you were inside or out—or, like she was, caught on the precipice between. Everywhere she looked, however, there were people dancing, laughing, and talking, and the sight of it thrilled her. She didn't know who, if any, among them were Saleris, but surely there had to be some members of her family there. Would they stand up in support of her, of each other? She'd soon find out.

"You're sure you want to do this?"

At Vince's quiet question, she looked up. He stared at her steadily, with an intensity that unnerved her.

"What do you mean?" she almost snapped. "You

know that I have to do . . . to do something, here. All these people are here, Vince. They're here for a reason."

"But what reason?" he pushed. "You have to make a decision, yes. A decision for your future. Do you really think they'll care who you ultimately choose?"

The cold, cutting, aristocratic voice of Silas Saleri somehow managed to drown out the music. "An excellent question, Mr. Rallis," her father said, "and one I'm sure I did not expect you to have the presence of mind to pose."

Edeena had been sparring with her father for too long to show any weakness, and she pivoted now, as calm and poised as she could manage. She had reason to feel confident. Her gown was the stuff of magic, the most sophisticated confection she'd ever seen. Tea length to allow for dancing in the open air on the wide, grassy lawn, it had several layers of jet black skirts and a black bodice, before a striking swath of cream satin emerged at her high waist and flowed upward to a black, ribbon-edged sweetheart neckline. She knew she looked the perfect mix of youth but also sophistication, as appropriate for a woman about to change the trajectory of her future.

Silas, in contrast, looked positively haggard. All of Edeena's carefully prepared phrasing fled as she blinked at him. "Father, what's wrong?" she asked hurriedly.

It was a bad move. Silas drew himself up haughtily, his face turning stony as he scowled at her.

"What's wrong is that, instead of standing where you are supposed to, in the bosom of the nobility who even now awaits breathlessly for you to do your duty at last, you're sneaking around with your American lover and causing whispers wherever you go."

Her *lover*! Edeena stared at her father, aghast, even as Vince bristled.

But Silas wasn't finished. "You didn't land your prince, but you can still do your part, Edeena. Take the first step toward reminding the people of Garronia of who the Saleris are, of all the undeserved misfortune we've experienced. It's long past time that we took our rightful place at the royal family's side, not at their feet."

"I'm not your puppet anymore, Silas," Edeena snapped, her voice shaking with anger. "I'm doing this for my sisters, not you. Even if the extended Saleri family does recognize it as some kind of end of the curse, you won't get what you want."

"You're wrong," Silas retorted, and once again she saw the whisper of anguish in his face, quickly quelled. "This curse has followed me since I was born, the same way it has followed past generations of Saleris since the Andrises usurped our position and rose to power. With its abolition, it will not taint the future."

She stared at him, uncomprehending. "But Marguerite, Caroline and I *are* the future of the Saleris, yet you've done all you can to force us into unhappiness. What part of the future are you so desperate to protect?"

Vince made the realization before Edeena could. Silas no longer had any concern for his older, capable daughters. He was worried only for his unborn daughter. For what the curse might do to her.

"Sir," he said sharply. "I think the important thing here is that it's Edeena's choice how to move forward. If you've finished with us here, I can help her return to the dais.

Silas swung to look at him, his black eyes almost verging on the edge of mania. Vince had never seen anything like it.

"I'll make the announcement," Edeena said quietly, drawing her father's attention once again. "But I'm not going to make it from the dais inside." She pointed to the small dance floor with its tiered sections that had been set up in the middle of the grassy courtyard. "I'll make it there."

Silas spluttered. "Oh for God's—"

"Good," Vince said, his booming voice making both Saleris jump. He held Silas's gaze. "It's the right call. She makes the announcement out here, and it's symbolic of bringing all of the glitter from inside to mix with the general public. Even though there's nothing general about this public. Every one of the families here is linked to the nobility in some way or another, I'm thinking."

Silas drew himself up stiffly. "The Saleri family is one of the proudest traditions in Garronia. Of course every branch of it is linked to the nobility."

"Well, her making her announcement in front of God, the world, and everybody is going to make that statement carry even more weight, then," Vince said brusquely. "It's a show, but it's a show you guys have been waiting to put on for a long time. Might as well do it right."

He wheeled Edeena away and she took a few steps, enough for him to turn back to Silas and speak to him in relative quiet.

"If you touch her or her sisters ever again, I will personally take you apart," he said, watching as Silas's perpetually morose expression was replaced by something else—indignation, and even the start of outrage. Good. "And I have the backing of the queen to make that happen."

It wasn't an empty threat, and Silas seemed to know it. Queen Catherine had not been idle during her turn around the ballroom with Vince. She'd spoken quickly and assuredly, and he had no doubt she'd meant what she'd said. Vince was hereby no longer to be paid by the Saleri family to ensure the security of Marguerite and Caroline back in South Carolina. He would be paid by the Crown. As such, he had the authority of the Crown to take whatever measures were necessary to ensure the safety of the two women.

He'd agreed, of course, but he couldn't help being annoyed at the same time. The queen had seemed to assume that Edeena's new husband, whoever he may be, would be enough to assure her security. That he'd have the money and social standing to oppose anything Silas might try. Vince wasn't so sure about that, but there'd only been so much time for him to process and respond to the queen's commands.

Still, Silas appeared unbowed. "There are four daughters in the generation," he said, curling his lip. "The first three are damaged. Failures. I can do no more with them. Instead, I will lift up the fourth to restore the family to our rightful glory."

Vince stared at him. "Failures?" He positively spat the word. "Seems to me Edeena's doing everything you wanted."

"Not the way I wanted it, not the way it should and must be done." Silas held up an imperious hand. "The Saleris are a proud and ancient family, and we will prevail--eventually. But I'll take no more part in this charade. It is finished."

The older man pivoted on his heel and moved away, saving Vince the need to deck him. Edeena was going to prove her father wrong, of course. She'd save the family, no matter the cost to herself.

Vince moved beside Edeena protectively, shouldering them both through the crowd as she kept her attention on the gazebo. As they moved through successive pools of people, he noticed the attention of the crowd fixing them with increasing intensity. Edeena was certainly the woman of the hour, and the ball was well underway. They'd be expecting her to make her announcement soon, and her presence out here simply fanned those expectations.

The closer they got to the gazebo though, the slower Edeena seemed to move. Her hand gripped his arm tightly, and he realized she was trembling. Something shifted hard in Vince's chest. Despite his dedication to helping her to be strong, he found his own courage was flagging. Not because he didn't think Edeena couldn't make the best of her situation, though. If anything, it was because he knew she would.

Just then a small space opened up between them and the gazebo. He hissed a sigh of relief. Almost there.

"Prince Rallis!"

Both Edeena and Vince froze as a voice boomed across the clearing, then they turned as one. How had he ever allowed that stupid nickname to take hold in a country where being a prince actually meant something? Back in the states, his name had been a benevolent joke, here it was rapidly becoming a liability.

Still, it had the effect of getting his attention, and he recognized the speaker at the same time Edeena did.

"Guillarmo," Vince said, nodding quickly. He half shielded Edeena with his body as he stepped forward to shake the man's hand. "I didn't know I'd see you again so soon, but I'm glad of it. With so many strangers in this courtyard, it's good to see a familiar face."

"Agreed." The man turned to Edeena and bowed to her, speaking in rapid and effusive Garronois. The words startled, but seemed to delight Edeena, and she relaxed a little bit, to Vince's intense relief.

Guillarmo turned to Vince again. "I told her she was good to have found you, that it spoke well of her character that she made such well-considered choices in her friends."

Vince grinned. "You managed to get the rest of the trees cleared without incident?"

"Trees cleared and roofs reinforced. If the seas wish to vent their rage again anytime soon, we'll be prepared."

"I'm glad to hear it," Vince said. Guillarmo clapped his hand on his back and half-turned, raising his hands to his mouth to strengthen his cry.

"Tsipouro!"

"Oh, well . . ." Edeena's startled glance met Vince's and she frowned, but there seemed to be nothing for it. Guillarmo waved off their worry.

"Indulge an old man, eh?" he asked with a wink. "There will be time enough for doing your duty, Countess Saleri. Life is also meant to be enjoyed."

"Of course," Edeena said, recovering gracefully. She smiled gamely as more of the townspeople worked their way through the crowd, two or three of them waving bottles of the clear, fragrant spirits. Glasses appeared and quick work was made of pouring out the libations, all of them raising their glasses at once.

"To celebration and good fortune," Guillarmo said, repeating the words in Garronois and waiting until they were announced back to him before he tossed back the fiery drink. Vince touched his glass to Edeena's, then brought his glass to his lips, stopping only when he realized her gaze was transfixed on him.

"What is it?" he lowered the glass and took a step closer, and she shook her head.

"Nothing! Nothing," she said. She lifted her glass to him, then she also drank, Vince following her lead.

The spell that had been dragging her down appeared to be broken, however, and as he finished his drink Edeena was once more smiling.

"You ready now?" he asked and she nodded. There were too many other people around for her to say much more, and they moved the short distance up the walk until they finally reached the gazebo.

Edeena mounted the steps quickly. Vince moved with her. The small platform was packed with people as well, but he suspected it would clear quickly enough when the time came. For now, he and Edeena were safe, cocooned against the outside world. And the look on her face indicated she knew it.

"It's funny, isn't it?" she asked, gazing out over the crowd. "In some ways, I've been waiting for this moment my entire life. Waiting for the test to happen, the judgment to be made. I'll announce who I'd like to wed and . . . what? The ground will open beneath us? The sea will rise up out of its bed?" She shook her head ruefully. "I have a sneaking suspicion no one will even notice. Father's already left, like he's already given up on me."

Vince grimaced, hating the pain in her voice. So, she *had* noticed Silas's departure—of course she had.

"I'll notice," he said, staunchly. "Your sisters will. The king and queen will, too. Somewhere in this throng of people there have to be Saleris as well. They'll notice, Edeena, they will. It may not be enough for them to stand together, but it will be a start. And that's more than anyone else has given them up to now—in longer than anyone can remember, I suspect."

She smiled at him, and he knew he'd said the right thing. Then his heart sank as she straightened her shoulders.

"I'm ready now," she said. "Please, somehow, get me a microphone."

Vince signaled and the order was relayed as his phone crackled. He drew it out of his coat pocket, scanning the screen quickly.

Then he froze.

The text was from Rob, but what he'd typed couldn't

possibly be true.

Problem. Drunk suitor just blabbed. Says Silas has rigged tonight's outcome. Wants new baby daughter to break curse. Anyone Edeena chooses will reject her. Curse will stand til he breaks it on his terms.

Silas's own words returned to taunt Vince. *I'll take no more part in this charade. It is finished.* Shock and anger seared through him, but as he looked up, he saw the truth of it. The men who'd been in the line with him and Edeena at the dance a few nights ago had a different air about them now. Some were nervous, some were smug. Some simply looked resigned.

None of them looked like the way they should, like men about to be given the greatest gift anyone could ask for, the loyalty of a woman as remarkable and beautiful and strong as Edeena Saleri. They expected to make a fool of her.

Not on my watch.

Chapter Twenty

Edeena had entered a strange and surreal place. Distantly, she watched Vince fish his phone from his pocket, unsurprised that he'd already worked out the logistics of her announcement no matter where she made it. A few moments later, a castle staffer hurried through the crowd and approached the gazebo, mounting the few steps and stopping in front of her with a lavalier microphone. He pinned it to the bodice of her dress with quick efficiency, rattling off instructions.

The crowd was swelling now, and she smiled automatically, looking out over it. She could see several of her supposed suitors in the throng—good men, capable men. Then she looked at Vince. He was standing not three feet away, solid, sure, and capable, the way he'd been solid, sure and capable since she'd first strode off that airplane in Charleston. He'd taken her and his sisters into his careful hands from the very first moment, and had stood by through every adventure, big and small, never once making her feel silly, stupid or small.

"Are you ready, Countess?" the staffer asked.

She nodded, but Vince strode forward, causing the staffer to shift to the side. "Is this on?" he asked gruffly.

"No sir, not yet."

"Good. Give us a minute."

In the newly-cleared space of the gazebo, Vince fairly dragged Edeena to the side, his hands warm on her, his manner tense. From the look on his face she could tell he was thinking furiously, selecting and rejecting things to say in rapid succession.

"What?" she demanded, steadying herself against him. "What's wrong?"

Something in his face put her instantly on edge. It was a flash of — what? Pity? Anger? Outrage? But not for himself, she realized quickly. It was outrage for her.

Now it was her turn to race through the possibilities. He'd escorted her all the way here, supporting her at every turn, and now he was having cold feet? That wasn't possible. He wouldn't do that to her, not as her security detail, not as her friend.

Which meant he was still protecting her. But from what?

"Edeena," Vince said, and his voice was gravelly. "I . . . I can't let you go through with this."

She frowned. "Why not?"

She didn't think it would be for the reason she wanted. She didn't think it was because he was about to prostrate himself in front of her, and declare his undying love.

Right?

Even the possibility sent her heart rate soaring, but Vince was too grim for a wide-eyed declaration of love.

Too serious.

"What's going on, Vince?" she managed. Her carefully prepared bubble of happiness was quickly losing its ebullience, wavering under the hard glare of the lights. "What's happening?"

He blew out a long breath. "Look. I'm not going to lie to you Edeena. That's not the way I've ever worked, not the way I want to be, even with you—especially with you. So I'm going to give this to you straight." He tightened his lips. "You're about to be set up."

Of all the things he could have said, she hadn't expected that. "What?"

"Set up, made a fool of," Vince snapped, as if that was the part she was having difficulty understanding. He explained the rest of it quickly enough, however. "Your father apparently didn't like the way you were handling things after you spoke at the matchmaking dance the other night, so he took matters into his own hands. The man you pick—whoever you pick—is going to reject you."

She stared at him. "What do you mean, reject me? Tonight? In front of all these people?"

"Tonight," Vince nodded. "The moment you choose, most likely. He'll lose some face, or maybe he won't. I'm not sure what the protocols are here. These men aren't under any obligation, right?"

"No, but . . ." Edeena could only stare at him, her voice dropping to a whisper. "No one's ever done that before. The family . . . I mean, the curse is going to stand, then. All this time, all this effort, and Silas would rather keep the curse going than let it fall, because I stood up to him? And then, by law, he can choose my husband. He *will* choose my husband, too—simply out of spite." She drew breath to say something more, then faltered. "How can he hate me so much?"

"Oh, sweetheart." Edeena blinked, shocked at the endearment in a public place, but Vince continued as if it was the most natural thing in the world for him to say. "He doesn't hate you, he doesn't. Not specifically. But he's one of those people who has built up so much fear and anger in his world, so much of a sense of entitlement, of being wronged, that he sees defeat at every turn. I don't know why he became the man he did. Maybe he has every reason to be bitter. Maybe he feels, even now, that life is doing him a disservice, and that you are the one standing in his way, that you're the one who symbolizes everything that's held him back his whole life."

"But I . . . I would never . . ."

"Shhh," Vince said, dipping his head forward so that their foreheads touched. It wasn't an intimate move, not really. It was perfectly respectable gesture. Yet when Vince did it, it was as if he was wrapping her in a warm hug. "It doesn't matter what your intentions are, Edeena. Your father isn't lashing out at you, he's lashing out at the world. He wants control more than he wants happiness. I suspect he's been that way his whole life."

"Yes, but . . ." Edeena pulled back from him, schooling her face into an expression of bright joy, all the more jarring for how false it was. "What am I going to say to all these *people*? They're expecting me to announce a betrothal, and they all know why I must.

This . . . this whole thing has become a joke, Vince. A joke. And my sisters are going to have to live with the embarrassment of this night for the rest of their lives. They're going to feel like they need to make it up to me somehow, when the whole point of everything was for me to be able to cut *them* a break, for me to make *their* way easier."

She glanced quickly to the crowd but couldn't see her sisters in the mix. She knew they would be there though. They'd be standing in solidarity, the stalwart Caroline and impetuous Marguerite, their hands clasped, their eyes shining, and they'd be waiting for her to name some young man in the crowd.

And then that man . . . that man would stand forward and make a laughingstock of her.

She closed her eyes. "You're sure?" she asked. Vince's sigh told her everything she needed to know before he spoke.

"The texts keep coming in. I thought something wasn't making sense about the setup of this thing, the energy. But I didn't expect it to go down like this, I truly didn't."

"I'm going to have to say something though." Edeena tightened her lips. "What am I going to say?"

Vince made to speak again, his face fierce with fury and protection, and she stepped back, suddenly resolute.

"No," she said. "This is my problem. I'll handle it."

"You don't have to do everything yourself," Vince said, but she shook her head.

"Who else will do it with me, Vince? You said it

yourself. Every man who participated in that event has been reached by my father. Whether he coerced them, flattered them, intimidated them, it doesn't matter. They've thrown in their lots with him and left the Saleri family, the future of our family, to be solved by some future generation, some future woman. And I *wanted* to solve it. I wanted to protect my family, to keep them safe. Was that so wrong?" She glanced at him, only to find that he'd gone a bit blurry with the tears building in her eyes. "Would you have done anything differently?"

"I wouldn't have," Vince finally said, heaving a sigh. "I would have wanted to save them, too." He gave her a lopsided grin. "It's what we do."

"It's what we do," she repeated, and she drew in a shaky breath, blinking several times. "Okay, then." She swallowed. "How do I look?"

"Like a woman capable of breaking a family curse," he said staunchly, and she laughed despite herself.

"One day my prince will come, right?" she said, shaking her head. "Well, it looks like he's got about five minutes.

Vince watched Edeena square her shoulders, then approach the front steps of the gazebo. If anything, the intervening few minutes while they'd conversed in the shadows had given more people time to flow out of the main ballroom and into the courtyard. The entire place had the feel of a carnival now, raucous and festive, exactly what the queen had had in mind when she'd invited such a large crowd to attend.

His sharp gaze didn't miss the media either, lurking at the edge of the throng. The royal family wouldn't have invited them, Vince knew. That had to be Silas's doing, as well. Silas, who was so frightened or miserable that he'd sacrifice everything to recover the illusion of control.

He glanced again to Edeena. She wanted that control, too, craved it, but she had her limits. She would never sacrifice her family's happiness to achieve it. She wouldn't sacrifice anything, really, except herself. Her own happiness was always a suitable bargaining chip.

Vince blew out a deep breath. He'd be there for Edeena when this was through, that was a given. But he wished like hell she didn't have to go through it. Wished like hell she could flip the script, be confronted with something so entirely different that it took all the attention off the men who were about to embarrass her, about to make her feel she wasn't wanted, wasn't special.

She'd survive, of course. Edeena knew all about surviving. But for once, he wished she didn't have to. For once . . .

To hell with this.

Edeena held out her arms and spoke a few words in Garronois, obviously welcoming the crowd or something like that. Vince didn't care. Now that he'd made his decision, he was single minded in his pursuit of action.

His beautiful, strong, responsible Countess was

about to have a problem on her hands. Only it wasn't at all the problem she expected to have.

The crowd was still applauding something else Edeena said when Vince reached her. Mindful of the microphone attached to her neckline, he reached out for her hands, pulling her close.

"Countess Saleri, you must hear me out first, before you make any decisions," he said in his loudest, most urgent voice. It boomed out over the courtyard and suddenly, everything fell silent. Hundreds of people seemed to freeze in their places, no one more than Edeena.

"Vince?" she finally managed, the word coming out half strangled.

But now that he was here, Vince realized that it was the most natural thing in the world to gaze down into Edeena's beautiful face and imagine himself making this declaration to her anywhere, whether it was on the beach back in his beloved South Carolina in front of his entire family, or on a gazebo platform in front of two hundred strangers, none of whom even knew his name.

"Edeena Arabelle Catherine Saleri, I have loved you since the moment I first laid eyes on you in America, when you traveled to my country with your sisters, hoping to help them start a new life, in a new place, with new experiences and opportunities, like any older sister hopes for her family. But you were more than their older sister," he declared, and it was if everyone in the courtyard had stopped breathing, so silent had it become. "You were the person in their lives who, more than anyone else, was responsible for their care. Though you were barely a few years older, you had shouldered that responsibility for them since your mother died. By the time I met you, you were so used to taking care of everyone that you'd forgotten how to take care of yourself."

"Vince, stop," Edeena mouthed, but she couldn't quite speak the word aloud, couldn't quite seem to do anything but tremble in his grasp, her eyes brimming over with tears.

"You came to my home excited about anything and everything—until you heard me called a prince. Do you remember that?"

Edeena's eyes flared in confusion, but Vince pushed on. "A prince was the last thing that you needed all the way in America, the last thing you wanted to think about. Because a prince was required for you to break the curse your family had labored beneath for hundreds of years, and though you wanted nothing more than to break that curse, you knew in a flash I was no true prince. No, for me the word was just a nickname, a harmless prank first made when I was barely more than a kid myself. The fact that the name stuck . . . well, it was a cross I could easily bear. No one much cared about princes in America."

He smiled, looking down at Edeena with so much intensity, he could feel his own hands shake. "Little did I know that there would come a time when all I wanted in the world was to truly *be* a prince, to be the one person that this incredible woman had a need for. I met you, Countess Saleri, when your guard was down. You were this beautiful, rare creature whose heart was filled to the breaking point with love for your sisters, whose dedication to them was evident in your every word and action."

He gripped her hands more tightly. "But it wasn't only responsibility for your sisters that was important to you. It was responsibility for your family as well. The family you knew, the family you didn't know. To break this curse, you needed to marry a prince. Or, failing that, a nobleman of your country who had the comportment and strength of a prince. Then, and only then, would your family feel safe in coming back together again, standing together as a single unit, strength building on strength. Then, and only then, would you feel like your sisters could move on with their own lives, finding loves of their own, raising families outside this curse that has hung over the Saleris for far too long. Am I right?"

At the question, Edeena seemed to come back to herself, blinking quickly. "You're right," she managed, and her words were strong now, resolute. "Bringing my family together, ensuring their safety, is all I really wanted to do."

Vince nodded encouragingly, his heart swelling as Edeena's words echoed across the courtyard, everyone in the crowd of two hundred Garronois leaning forward now.

"And here I am, not a prince," he said, "not even a nobleman of your own country. But I'd be a fool not to pledge myself to you, Countess. I'd be a fool not to offer myself to be your husband, your partner, your friend. To help you mend the fences broken by generations of misunderstanding and pain, pain that, maybe, no one even knows the reasons for anymore. I can't offer you anything but the strength of my hands, the sharpness of my mind, and the stubbornness of an American who doesn't know his place among such things as counts and princes and born nobility. But if you will have me, Edeena Saleri . . . if you'll have me, I will be forever yours."

"Vince, I can't ask you to do that for me."

The statement was so calm, so measured, that it took Vince a moment to realize it was coming from Edeena. But though gratitude and something approaching joy shown in her face, she was shaking her head. "It's too much—too much of a sacrifice for you, too much of a change. You are to be commended even for offering, but the people of Garronia, they take care of their own. I will find a way to break the curse the way it was intended."

"The way it was intended?" Vince squeezed her hands, knowing that she was trying to find some way, any way, to let him off the hook, to close this drama out without any permanent damage. As it was, the pageantry of the evening was assured, and no one would expect her to name some other suitor in the wake of his bid.

But Vince didn't want to be let off the hook. With each word, he realized that none of this was merely a Hail Mary attempt to save Edeena from the machinations of her father. He did love her. He did want her. And he did wish for nothing more than to be a part of her future, of her family's future. More than anything he'd ever wanted in his life . . . he wanted her.

And so, he did what generations of Rallises had done, no matter that they weren't princes or noblemen or rich. He did what his own father had done all those years ago, the very first moment that he met his mother, and knew she was the one.

He dropped down to one knee, and then the other. "Edeena Arabelle Catherine Saleri," he rumbled, "would you marry me?"

Chapter Twenty-One

The crowd erupted into a cacophony of cheers, but Edeena couldn't concentrate on that, couldn't concentrate on anything except for Vince kneeling in front of her.

"What are you doing?" she mouthed, as soundlessly as she could, fiercely aware of the microphone at her neck.

"Say yes," Vince mouthed back with a grin, equally aware but somehow still maintaining the presence of mind to keep up the act.

Only . . . was it an act? If it was, it was one of genius. And yet the way he was staring at her, his entire face flushed with intensity, his eyes boring into hers as if they could see into her soul . . . surely he was merely trying to help her, trying to save her from being embarrassed.

Right?

He squeezed her hands, hard, and Edeena said the only thing she could think of, the only thing that made sense in that moment.

"Yes!" she blurted, the sense of surrealism crashing

over her again. "Yes, Vincent Rallis, I'll marry you. If you will have me in return, you will be the next . . ." she swallowed, suddenly aware of the weight of silence that had once more fallen on the world around them. "You will be the next Count Saleri."

To her surprise, there was no more cheering in the crowd. In fact, the entire place had fallen dead silent.

All the blood drained out of her head, and even Vince was looking a little green. At her gentle tug, he rose to his feet, but he didn't step away from her. Instead he turned with her, one hand stealing behind her back, the other gripping her hand. He wasn't about to let her face any of this alone, she realized, and for once, she was okay with that.

In fact, if what she'd agreed to was true — was real — she'd be okay with it for the rest of her life.

Her gaze swept the crowd, and she finally spotted Marguerite and Caroline, both of them looking like they were ready to jump out of their skin. Instead, they were being restrained, not by Rob and Cindy Marks, but by the very real, august presence of the King and Queen of Garronia, who now stood on either side of them. Also flanked between them was Silas Saleri.

For once, Silas wasn't seething with malevolence either. He looked . . . more shocked than anything.

Edeena could understand how he felt.

The urge to say something — anything — grew intolerable, and Edeena took a deep breath. As Vince squeezed her hand, silently giving her the courage to step forward again, however, there was a new movement in the crowd.

Casually, with surpassing dignity, Guillarmo Aconti

strode out into the space between the gazebo and throng of people. He bowed deeply to Edeena and Vince, then turned to face the gathering.

"I am Count Guillarmo Aconti Saleri, son of Lisbet Saleri, oldest daughter of Marcus Saleri, son of Antonio Saleri, son of Isabella Saleri," he boomed. "I bless this union and cast my lot with Countess Edeena Saleri and her new husband."

Edeena stiffened. Guillarmo Aconti *Saleri*?

Another man strode forward, and she recognized him as their driver from the day in the country. "I am Count Martin Saleri," he said proudly, holding out his arms wide as he shouted out a similarly complicated lineage, this one even longer than Guillarmo's. "It has been one hundred years since my family has laid claim to the Saleri name. I lay claim to it today. I am honored to count myself a member of this family, and I bless this union and the strength of the Saleri name."

Then a woman bustled forth, and Edeena blinked hard, unable to stop the sudden, irrational surge of tears that came to her eyes. It wasn't one of the polished nobles she'd met over the course of the endless brunches and breakfasts, dinners and tea parties — it was someone she would have never imagined.

The ancient, sharp-eyed dressmaker bustled into the space opening up in the crowd, her dress a vision in black silk with a cream collar, subtly continuing Edeena's own elaborate tea dress colors but in a style far more suited to her petite frame and mature years. "I am Magdalene Anastasia Rigotto Martine *Saleri*," she said triumphantly. "My family cast its lot with the Andrises

CURSED

of Garronia, and it continues to be my pleasure to serve them. But I, too, bless this union. On this day above all others, I am proud to call myself a Saleri."

After that, there was a rush of people to the front of the crowd, all of them claiming solidarity with the Saleri name as Edeena and Vince stood, their hands gripping so tightly, Edeena thought she'd go numb. Within the next five minutes, a new movement started, and the crowd parted to let the king, queen, and her father and sisters make their way to the gazebo.

Marguerite and Caro were radiant with joy, Silas still looked faintly shocked, but it was Catherine and Jasen who looked the happiest, and—Edeena was surprised to realize—clearly relieved.

Jasen took a proffered microphone. "It is with great pleasure that I also endorse the engagement of Countess Edeena Arabelle Catherine Saleri and Mr. Vincent Rallis, and heartily applaud the remarkable solidarity of the Saleri family. Apart, you have been a credit to your country. Together, you will be the pride of all Garronia."

Another cheer went up, and the music surged forth once more, sending the party into a fever pitch as their small group lay trapped on the gazebo stairs for another moment more.

Marguerite and Caroline converged on Vince, pulling him away from her, which left Edeena staring face to face with her father.

In the privacy of the gazebo, he no longer looked shell-shocked. He looked nearly manic.

Hesitantly, Edeena reached out to touch him on the arm. "Father—"

"It's not going to work," he snapped, his gaze

connecting with hers. "It's close, it's very close. But it's not perfect. The engagement won't hold."

She blinked at him, her outrage all the greater because it spoke to her own insecurities. She couldn't really expect Vince to marry her—they'd known each other all of three weeks! It was preposterous! But to have her father throw his disdain so boldly at her stiffened her spine.

"It will hold, father. The curse will stay broken, and if there's any way for us to stamp it out forevermore, we will. You should be happy. Now you won't have to subject your youngest child to such a ridiculous quest. Now that beautiful new baby can be born into a new dawn of the Saleri family."

The mention of the child seemed to recall Silas to himself, and Edeena's heart twisted in her chest at the change that came over her father. He suddenly looked like he was going to cry and she stiffened.

"What is it?" she asked, horror beginning to well up inside her. "Is there anything wrong? Please tell me nothing is wrong with Maria or the baby."

"Nothing . . . nothing's wrong," he said, but his words were almost anguished. He stared down at his hands, then up at Edeena. The words he spoke next seemed to be pulled out of the center of his being with pliers.

"Your mother was a good woman, Edeena. She tried, but she never believed in the reality of the curse on the Saleris, that we were to be doomed to eternal strife unless we married into royalty. She never believed it—and when she was alive, I almost didn't believe it either. But then . . . then she died, and everything fell apart."

Despite her long-stoked anger toward her father, Edeena couldn't help her hand beginning to tremble as a sob wracked his body. "For a long time, I thought I could make things right by connecting you with Aristotle, but it . . . it wasn't working, it never seemed to work, and it should have! You were beautiful, gracious, strong, and he was an idiot not to see it."

"We were friends," she said gently, and Silas laughed — a laugh which at one time would have been bitter, but was now simply sad.

"Friends, yes. I know. But I was so sure . . . I met Maria, you and Ari were practically engaged, I . . ." he sighed. "I proposed to her. Then Aristotle disappeared, she became pregnant and instead of believing that I could finally have a new beginning, I was caught up in the horror that the Saleri curse would continue and I would be destined to lose anyone I loved."

His voice cracked, but he soldiered on. "And I do love her, Edeena. Her and the precious child she carries. At the last minute, I decided we would have a better chance if that child carried on the fight — not you. I'm not proud of what I tried to do, to induce all these men to stand down. In truth, I suspected it wouldn't work. But I had no other choice! You defied me at every turn, you didn't seem to understand how difficult the curse would be to break. But everything was in place and there was no time to call off the ball. You certainly weren't interested in listening to reason."

"Reason . . ." Edeena echoed.

"So I did what I could to control the outcome, to

control you." He smiled ruefully, the first genuine smile she'd seen on his face in years. "I should have known it was no longer possible."

"Silas."

Vince turned away from Marguerite and Caro as he heard the queen's strong, quiet, but above all, compassionate voice, and realized the queen was folding the tall, lean man into her embrace. Silas was crying, and Edeena looked stricken.

Vince moved toward her instinctively, but her sisters got there first, not realizing the scene they'd just missed as the king and queen quickly and covertly escorted Silas off the gazebo and into a phalanx of guards. To anyone else, he would seem overcome with joy at his family's good fortune, but Edeena's face had told a different story.

Still, as he half listened to Caroline's and Marguerite's joyful reunion with their sister, Vince watched the trio make their way through the crowd. Despite the net of security, they stopped for one man, then another, and at each new contact Silas stood a little straighter. One man shook his hand, another clapped him on the back. No less than three old women hugged him. A young couple approached, and then another, and the king and queen stood at his side in silent affirmation of his status with the royal family, as he slowly, and then with greater speed, welcomed the distant relations of the Saleris, come to pay their respects.

Vince didn't know what would happen once the shock wore off for the man, but for the moment, he was away from Edeena, and that was all that mattered.

"Vince." Edeena turned to him now, and the slightly dazed sound to her voice matched his own reaction. It was almost impossible to believe that he'd proposed to the woman, she'd accepted, and what seemed like half the country had applauded the move. He wasn't at all sure how she would feel about it in the morning.

Then again, that wasn't very fair of him. He knew how *he'd* feel, after all.

But still . . .

Edeena reached out to him when he didn't respond, her expression now shaded with worry. "We'll have to run the gauntlet at some point," she said, motioning to the teeming throng surrounding the gazebo. "Are you ready?"

Her voice was as hesitant as her gaze, but he quickly stepped forward, letting her pull him down the gazebo stairs. They made their way back through the crowd much the same way Silas had—with rounds of back clapping, hand shaking, hugs and smiles from people he'd never seen before but who now were addressing him as if they were old friends. Marguerite and Caro got into the act, too, meeting relations they didn't know they even had—as well as some they clearly did—each reunion more boisterous than the last.

By the time they re-entered the more formal internal ballroom, Vince knew that if he never saw another crowd as tightly-packed as this one, it would be too soon. Still, the interior of the Visitors Palace atrium wa like an oasis of calm after the rowdier open-air party. He grinned as he watched Caro and Marguerite give one look to the more staid couples dancing in a formal waltz, then disappear back through the open doors.

That left him alone with Edeena—his favorite place to be.

Liberating two champagne glasses from a passing waiter, he offered a flute to Edeena. She took it, but there was no missing the sudden nerves that sparked in her expressive eyes.

"Countess Saleri," Vince said, touching his glass to hers. "I'd ask you what you were thinking, but I think I already know."

"Vince . . ." Edeena blew out a quick breath, pursed her lips. "I . . . all of that happened so quickly, I don't know what to say."

He nodded. His heart had suddenly stopped beating correctly in his chest, but there was no better time than now for them to have this conversation. It would have to happen sooner or later. Better to know whether he should be working on contingency plans or, well . . . on moving plans.

The unexpected weight of that thought must have shown on his face, because Edeena drained her champagne flute, then eyed him over the rim. "You don't have to go through with this, Vince."

"Edeena."

"No, let me talk. I've been preparing for an arranged marriage of one type or another since I was ten years old when my father first told me about the curse. He'd told me his generation didn't fit the criteria to solve it, but mine did, and when the time came, that would be that." She released a long sigh. "So while I could never have predicted the events of today, I . . . well, I was ready for them, in a way. You weren't. All of that happened so quickly, there's no way I will hold you to a mar — an engagement to me."

She smiled bravely, then went on, already solving the problem aloud. "We'll wait a day, let everyone get back to their routines — maybe two days. Maybe a week. Then we'll announce a long engagement. You'll go back to South Carolina, and my sisters will as well, if they want, and I'll . . . well I'll . . ."

Edeena's manner was fraying along with her words and her smile started to wobble around the edges. As much as Vince wanted her to have her say, he found he couldn't take it anymore.

"Edeena," he said again, setting his own flute on the table next to them, then taking her hands in his. "If you're telling me that you don't want to marry me after all, then of course I'll respect that decision." He waited a beat, watching her eyes flare in dismay. "Is that what you want?"

"I don't want you to feel trapped, Vince."

Her words were so soft it was a miracle he even heard them, but he squeezed her hands, drawing her closer.

"You didn't trap me tonight. You didn't force me to say the things I said out there, to offer to spend the rest of my life with you, loving you, supporting you, helping you to achieve whatever dreams you set your heart on."

"Stop," Edeena practically groaned, her eyes once more bright with tears. "You don't have to talk like that anymore. No one is listening."

"No one is listening," he agreed. "Apparently, you least of all." He laughed as she blinked hard, a single tear trailing down her cheek. "If I need to pledge my love to you every morning and remind you again every night, Edeena, I will. If I have to wake up next to you with reassurances for the first year of our marriage, and kiss you to sleep every evening when we're both white-haired and frail, I will. I'm aware we only met three weeks ago. I realize it's sudden. But the Rallises, we have a long-standing tradition of knowing the woman who will change our lives the moment we meet her, and well, you changed my life the day you stepped off that plane. I fully expect you to keep changing my life every day forward." He peered at her, trying to read the expression in her eyes. "Does that help?"

"But you don't even know me," she whispered, her gaze searching his, as if she needed to somehow warn him away from her.

"I don't," he agreed, making her blink with surprise. "Not all the details. I definitely don't know all of your newfound cousins and distant relatives. I don't know where you live, I don't know your favorite book or vacation spot. But there are some things I do know already, Edeena. I know you love your sisters and would do anything for them. I know you feel responsible for everyone else's happiness, but aren't so good about your own. I know you miss your mother terribly, and it's driven you to try to be everyone else's caretaker."

He drew her yet closer. "And I know you make my

heart pound every time you walk into the room, that your smile lights up every dark place in the world. I know that I would be lucky to call you mine, and that my family will spend the rest of their lives wondering what I did to deserve someone as beautiful and gracious as you."

"Your family!" she gave a little gasp. "Your mother has no idea."

Vince smiled, thinking of the last conversation he had with his mother — had it really been less than a week ago? "I think she has some idea," he said wryly, "and trust me, when we do finally make our way back to Charleston, I'm pretty sure she'll let everyone know she knew it the moment she met you." He smiled, brushing away another tear as it softly tracked its way down Edeena's face. "She's got a knack for things like that."

Chapter Twenty-Two

"Isn't it funny how I'm overlooking one of the most beautiful oceans in the world, and all I can think about is a totally different beach?"

Edeena glanced over to Caroline, who was sitting under a large umbrella, staring out at the Aegean. They'd all gathered on one of the palace's tiered decks, sipping mimosas and eating from great platters of fruit. Edeena hadn't realized how much she'd missed the fruit of Garronia, how much she'd missed its sunlight and beautiful views. Strange that Caro was taking the exact opposite approach. "I'm not sure most of our neighbors here would even classify that little sandy inlet a proper beach."

"I know!" Caro gestured to the rolling blue-green waters that were as much a part of the Garronois life as the mountains and the blue sky, and shook her head. "South Carolina is so much... softer, in a way. All those trees hanging with moss, the silence of the water, the nature preserve on the other side of the waterway from Heron's Point. It's like it has all these secrets to hide, and it won't give any of them up easily."

"Well, I'm only interested in the secrets its people give up," Marguerite commented from Edeena's other side. She adjusted her position on the teak bench, tucking a pillow underneath one arm. "You would not believe how people act like you're not there at all when you're refilling their coffee cups. And the best time of day to get the best dirt is in the morning."

"The morning?" Edeena frowned. "I would have assumed at night, when there's alcohol flowing."

"I totally thought that, too, before I started working at the Cypress. But I was wrong. It's breakfast or brunch — sometimes lunch, but the secrets that usually get dropped there are work related. Totally boring." She wrinkled her nose.

Edeena considered her sister from under the brim of her wide hat. "You'll go back, though? With Caro?"

"Well, duh," Marguerite swatted her calf. "I've already missed days of gossip. I may never catch up."

"Gossip about anyone in particular?"

"Well, if you must know, yes," Marguerite said, pitching her voice in the signature slow drawl of a South Carolina matriarch. "I do hope that Wyndham Masters is finally done sowin' his wild oats. He is a *disgrace* to his mother." She pitched her voice in another falsetto, as Caroline giggled. "You don't say. Tell me he hasn't done anything else to blacken the family name." And back to the first. "Why, I can tell you no such thing, Penneh, because it simply would not be true."

"Stop!" Edeena cried, staring at her younger sister. If she didn't know better, she would have thought her Prudence's own daughter, her drawl was so exactly right. "They didn't actually say those kind of things."

"Oh, honey, that was only the beginning," Marguerite grinned. "I've decided that after Caro finalizes the house sale, I'm going to write a book set on an unnamed fictional island, and I'm going to title it something insane, like *The Wicked Ways of Wyndham*. And then I'll send him an email about it from a cloaked account when it goes on sale."

"You'd better hope you're hiding out on an island halfway around the world when you do," Caro said, though her tone was more indulgent than serious. "Wyndham Masters's family owns half of the Eastern Seaboard, according to the shopkeepers I've chatted with. And what they don't own, they recently sold."

"Ooooh, I'm totally using that line." Marguerite sat back in her chair and grinned out at the gorgeous late summer day. "But enough about me, Caro. When are you going to tell Edeena what you've been doing up late at night since we've returned to the fair shores of Garronia?"

"Oh?" Edeena swiveled her head in time to see Caro's eyes flash wide in dismay. "What is it, Caroline? Have you found your own Wyndham?"

"What? No!" Caroline shook her head vigorously. "I simply thought, well, depending on how long it takes us to sell Heron's Point and get Prudence resettled, maybe I could look into taking some classes. I'd be allowed to do that, right? Take classes as an overseas student?"

Edeena considered it. All of them had attended college at the National University in Garronia, of course, but Edeena's classes had been business, and business only, under Silas's strict rule. It'd been worthwhile, since she now had her mother's fortune to manage, but Edeena couldn't get out of college quickly enough. Marguerite hadn't even made the attempt to study anything outside her core courses, but Caro had legitimately enjoyed learning and had taken the widest variety of classes. If she wanted to continue her education with a course or two in South Carolina, why shouldn't she? Perhaps she'd finally let herself relax and meet someone.

That settled it. "Absolutely," Edeena said. "Wherever you want to go, as long as they accept international students, say the word. We've got more than enough money in the trust, and masters courses would be an excellent way to use it. That goes for you, too," she said, turning back to Marguerite. "Once you can tear yourself away from the adventures of Wyndham the Wicked, if college is appealing to you . . ."

"Ugh, no thanks," Marguerite lifted a hand. Still, her face had taken on a pensive aspect. "I'll need to figure out a focus, though," she mused. "With you and Vince checking off the marriage box and Caro going all Brainiac, I suppose I should have a game plan."

"You could become a spy," offered Caroline from the shade of her umbrella. "I'm sure Garronia needs another secret agent."

Marguerite barked a laugh. "Excellent. And that's probably easier than a life of crime."

"Better accommodations for sure," Edeena said drily, but she studied her sister closely. She knew Marguerite better than to encourage her too much toward a particular path — her sister would go the other way simply out of contrariness. But she'd continue to watch both of them carefully over the next few weeks while she plowed her way through the Saleri family records. Apparently, if her marriage to Vince was going to stick, she was the new head of household for the Saleris. Silas had stepped down to focus entirely on his own new family, and from the sound of their lawyers and accountants, he'd paid no attention to their various holdings since he'd taken on his new bride.

She smiled, shaking her head. A month ago she would have scoffed that anything could draw her attention away from her obligations so completely. Now . . .

As if in answer to her thoughts, a door opened behind her, and a rich, rolling South Carolina drawl flowed out to surround them all with warm amusement.

"Now, how did I know that this would be where I'd find you fine ladies," the soon-to-be Count Vincent Rallis Saleri asked.

Dragging Edeena away from her sisters was easier than Vince feared it would be, and for that, he was grateful. Because if he had to spend another minute facing the gauntlet of family advisors, lawyers, concierges and — God forbid — tailors by himself, he was seriously going to lose it.

"What are you doing?" Edeena giggled as he hustled her back down the long corridor to the suite of rooms that had been given over to the Saleris in the wake of the unprecedented success of the engagement ball. Apparently, the Saleri mansion was being staked out by the press, waiting for the Countess and her Count-in-waiting to nest there, and wiser minds had advised that they all remain safely locked away in the royal castle until some other news story had taken hold.

Now, Vince pushed Edeena into the conference room where he'd been closeted away with a half-dozen Saleri functionaries for most of the morning. He'd finally sent them away for an early lunch—never mind that it was barely past eleven—but they'd taken pity on him and told him they'd be back after three. By three, he and Edeena surely could make some sense of the mounds of paperwork in front of him. Even though much of it had been translated into English, it was still far too much for him to take in at once.

"Did you know you have family holdings in thirty different countries?" he said to her as she looked from the stacks to him. "Thirty!"

She smiled. "Yes, Vince, I'm aware of that, though I've inherited management responsibilities only. Silas remains the signatory on most of those parcels."

"Of course," he grimaced. He wasn't worried about the real estate holdings, though they had given him pause. But he wanted to work up to what he was worried about slowly. Edeena had already been through a lot, and he didn't want her to worry. About anything.

Especially something so strange as what he'd discovered in the real estate account logs of Heron's Point.

"And the charitable foundation. You know your

father hasn't made one appearance at any of those events since you fled the country."

"We didn't flee the country," Edeena protested, but Vince raised a hand.

"You absolutely fled the country, Countess Saleri, for which I'll forever be grateful." Her face softened with the flattery, and his heart gave another tug. Maybe he could put off telling her the bad news for another few minutes, anyway.

He stepped closer, even as Edeena cast a glance down to the nearest ledger book, a smile playing over her face as she drew her fingers along its top. "I can't believe there's so much history we didn't even know about," she said. "With the curse so entrenched in Silas's mind, he refused to look at these old books. He didn't have any idea how far the family had spread, or where our distant cousins had landed when they'd stopped including the Saleri name in their family trees." She shook her head. "I didn't either."

"But the disaffected Saleris themselves did, even if they didn't claim the name any longer," Vince said. He'd moved closer to her, and when she looked up, he was only a step away. Her eyes, always so beautiful, now warmed in genuine affection as she took him in. He could spend the rest of his life staring into those eyes, he knew, and never grow tired of that soft look.

"They did," she said. "They kept the rolls and marked the books, and they knew the curse as well as anyone — better, really. It was the queen's dressmaker who reminded her that the Saleri curse wasn't capable of being overturned merely by princes, and the queen, of course, told Silas, worried about him marrying me off indiscriminately."

"And Silas, in turn, called you home, where we seemed to find more Saleris around every corner, even though we had no idea who they were."

"Exactly," she laughed. "They knew me, the curse, and your potential place in it . . . and we didn't have a clue."

"Yeah . . . about that clue," Vince began, and Edeena's head tilted as his arms went around her. Somehow, holding her so close made what he had to say a tiny bit easier.

"What is it?" she asked, but her smile remained on her face, the worry about her family somehow banished to a manageable level now, no matter what life threw at them.

"Well, you know those jewels we found on Pearl Island? The ones the Saleris left behind in a box eighty years ago?"

"Yes . . ." she said, though her tone was teasing. "Don't tell me you care about getting those back. They really aren't worth—"

"They're apparently part of the curse."

That stopped her, and her hands tightened on his arms. "What do you mean, part of the curse?"

He disentangled one hand and pushed a book aside, pulling another one forward. Still standing close to Edeena, he opened the book. It was a ledger from the late 1800s through mid 1950s, with notations about moving residences.

"I got curious about the history of Heron's Point, thinking it might help with the sale, if you all decide to go through with that, and one of the pencil pushers remembered that the original purchase details of the house were kept in this ledger, along with all the esteemed guests from Garronia over the years."

"That's outstanding," Edeena said, momentarily distracted. "We should have that in the house for when people come through."

"My thoughts exactly, up until I got to the part about the things those esteemed guests brought to the house. It was written in English so the local caretakers could double check their records and . . . well, here."

He opened the book to the correct page, and pointed. Edeena leaned over the musty tome, reading quickly. When she got to the relevant line, she froze — just as he had frozen, not an hour earlier.

Edeena looked up at Vince, unwilling to believe her eyes. "The Pride of the Saleris?" she gasped. "What does it mean?"

"No clue. Not even the history geeks understood it, but when I told them about the jewels matching the description listed here sitting in some island house in a glass case, they about stroked out. Apparently, they'd thought the jewels long gone, spirited away by a particularly bitter branch. If we bring those jewels back, however, the rest of the Saleri clan will fall in line as well — because, um, apparently the jewels are charmed." He shook his head at the continuing superstition of the Saleri family. "You guys don't give up on your curses easily, do you?"

Edeena's lips twisted. "It's a gift."

"But according to your people, there's no way in hell you'll be allowed out of the country for the next six months," he said. "Apparently, your upcoming wedding to the indisputably handsome Count Saleri is going to take up all of your time."

"Well, it is going to be a grand occasion, I'm told." Edeena replaced the book on the table and turned back to him. But still, she couldn't stop the dread building in her stomach. "This is bad, though," she said. "I want this curse to be over and done with."

"Then we'll get the jewels back," he said firmly. "I'll take care of it, Edeena. Let me help."

She blinked up at him, ready to argue . . . then something unraveled inside her. Yes, she decided. Yes. She would let him take care of it, take care of her, in this way. But she would take care of things, too.

"I will let you," she said, putting her arms around him and leaning back, the smile once more in her eyes. "But here's a suggestion. My sisters want nothing more than to embrace adventure, and it's time I let them do that. Caroline would love that old Pinnacle House with all its treasures, especially if Mr. Blake's grandparents are present with stories to share." She smiled. "If you could spare a security guard or two, maybe we could send her there with a replacement set of jewelry as a peace offering. Then, everything will be okay." She said the words like a benediction, but it had the ring of truth.

Vince lifted his brows. "I hadn't thought of that," he said, a smile playing about his lips. "Does everything work out the way you want it to, in the end?"

Edeena gave a soft, quiet laugh. "No," she said, looking back at him with her heart in her throat. "Sometimes I just say the right thing at the right time, and the universe responds."

She lifted up on her toes, her lips a bare inch from his. "Like this one time, I closed my eyes and whispered an old Disney princess lyric about a prince I'd been waiting for all my life . . . then I opened my eyes, and you were there."

She smiled, Vince's face sliding softly out of focus as the tears built behind her eyes. "Someday," she barely managed, singing in a terrible falsetto, "my prince will come . . ."

Vince tipped up her chin, dropping the softest of kiss on her lips, but when he spoke, it wasn't in falsetto, but in his beautiful, rich South Carolina drawl.

"And he and that beautiful Countess of his?" he asked, holding her close. "Why, they most assuredly lived Happily Ever After."

~~~

Charmed

With the curse of the Saleri family all but vanquished, Caroline Saleri returns to the picturesque idyll of Sea Haven Island, South Carolina. There she plans to lose herself for a few months in low country bliss--helping to prepare her family's vacation home for sale, attending local lectures...and trying to forget the aggravating, enigmatic professor who's mocked her family's superstitions on a public stage.

Unfortunately, one detail remains to ensure the family curse is never invoked again. Caroline is tasked to recover a collection of supposedly charmed old jewelry from a local private museum--a simple afternoon adventure. Then she recognizes the museum's proprietor, and her life turns upside down.

Determinedly misanthropic Professor Simon Blake has long since kept the world at arm's length. The one chink in his armor? His beloved grandparents and their eccentric collection of friends. But when an angry attendee of one of his lectures turns out to be the woman his grandparents and their cronies have been talking about for more than eighty years—a real-life fairytale countess, intent on breaking an ancient curse—he doesn't know whether to throw her out, welcome her in, or call the cops.

One thing's for sure...he's in no mood to be *Charmed*.

Available Now!

About Jennifer Chance

Jennifer Chance is the award-winning author of the New Adult/contemporary romance Rule Breakers and Gowns & Crowns series. A lover of books, romance, and happily-ever-afters, she lives and writes in Ohio. She's also urban fantasy author Jenn Stark, whose Immortal Vegas and Demon Enforcers series are now available; and YA author Jennifer McGowan, whose Elizabethan spy series, Maids of Honor, is also available. She really, truly, loves to write.

When she's not at work on her newest book, you can find her online at jenniferchance.com, on Facebook at facebook.com/authorJenniferChance and on Twitter at @Jenn_Chance.

Made in the USA
Coppell, TX
17 March 2021